Secondary Impact

A Doctor Danny Tilson Novel

Secondary Impact

by Barbara Ebel, M.D.

A Doctor Danny Tilson Novel

Book One: Operation Neurosurgeon
Book Two: Silent Fear: *a Medical Mystery*
Book Three: Collateral Circulation: *a Medical Mystery*
Book Four: Secondary Impact

Paperback ISBN-13: 978-0-9911589-7-3
eBook ISBN-13: 978-0-9911589-8-0

This book is a work of fiction. Names, characters, places and events are the product of the author's imagination or are used fictitiously. Any resemblance to actual events, persons, or locations is coincidental.

In memory of my mom and dad

Chapter 1

The home-court spectators cheered as their Alabama opponents missed an easy basketball shot. Danny Tilson gave his ex-wife Sara a thumbs up while his daughter Annabel sat back down with a sigh of relief. Playing skillfully and competitively, the Nashville college's team yearned for a solid ranking and their possible inclusion into the March Madness frenzy.

The white-uniformed home team regained the ball. Advancing toward their basket, they passed it between players. The Tilsons keenly watched Annabel's quick-moving boyfriend, David, whose six-foot-three height was average amongst his teammates. He caught the ball, dribbled, and broke short of an opponent. With fingers spread and the ball at his fingertips, he sailed up with a shot that dropped the ball dead center through the basket.

Bolting up, Danny hollered. Annabel waved her arm in a power fist, proud of David as well as her school; and Sara beamed a smile, as happy for her ex-husband and daughter's enthusiasm as she was for their hometown score. As they settled down in their chairs and watched the scoreboard, they tried not to let the next point from Alabama upset them. Nashville was still ahead by one point.

Excitement was high - muscles tensing, sweat accumulating, eyes sharply focused - as the home team again ran, dribbled and passed the basketball back and forth, the net drawing nearer and nearer. A lanky opponent almost intercepted the ball but the point guard dodged and turned, sending the ball flying to David.

The roar echoed in the arena as fans cried out. With his four teammates skillfully positioned and helping him, David found Alabama's weak spot. He zigzagged, eluded opponents, and prepared for a jump shot with a natural rhythm like an eagle in flight. He soared and, while in midair, released the ball over the head of a defender.

However, Alabama's Number 9 shadowed David's movements and simultaneously touched the ball on its downward trajectory to the basket; he snapped his elbow out, smashing David on the side of the head.

While a referee was already signaling the violations and an outcry was heard from the crowd, David went down with a thud, his head whacking the floor.

Danny's eyes narrowed and he gritted his teeth as he stood up in an attempt to closely watch the scene on the court. He could feel Sara and Annabel brush against him on either side as they, too, were locked into the scenario unfolding below.

"I'm going down," Danny said.

Although he knew his daughter's college sports' games always had a team doctor present - an orthopedic surgeon named Roberts – he wanted to offer his services as a neurosurgeon. He excused himself and passed in front of other people in the row. Sara and Annabel followed behind him as spectators groaned for blocking their view.

As Danny made it to the stairs, he stole a glance at the offensive zone. To his surprise, David had gotten up; the coach was next to him and players were closing in. When Danny got to ground level, he lost sight of the situation. He weaved through crowds and onto the court as play was still suspended while Sara and Annabel stopped and waited several feet behind the backboard.

Getting inside the group of towering players was fairly easy as Danny's six-foot-two height helped him fit in like he belonged. When he got close to David, the two surgeons made eye contact.

"He's standing," Dr. Roberts said. "Glad to see you, Danny."

Danny nodded; David stood quiet, his eyes set in a squint while he rubbed the back of his head.

"How about we walk you off the court?" Roberts asked.

David glanced at both doctors and followed them on his own accord.

Danny walked with David and the team's doctor into the locker room where they were greeted with a smell of dirty athletic uniforms. Sara and Annabel stayed in the hallway, respectful that it was a male changing room.

Both doctors signaled for the young man to sit down on a bench and David's perfect square shoulders seemed to slope as he took his hand off the back of his head. He looked imploringly at Danny as if realizing his body needed medical care.

Dr. Roberts took a step back. "Danny, I couldn't have a better expert here for a fall like that. I don't mind if you take over."

"Sure. I'd be happy to. Anything for the team. And for David and my daughter," he added. He winked at David, who responded with a small smile.

David had been dating Annabel for six months, since the beginning of their fall term. His mild manner and the dimple in his chin had attracted Annabel from the first night they met at a party. They shared a biology lab class together and had even been caught red-handed at the family's log cabin retreat after a 'sleep over.' As Danny thought about David's relationship in the family, he glanced towards the hallway. Annabel stood watching, her hands wringing in front of her blue jeans.

He then focused on David as he squatted in front of the bench. "I lost sight of the field as I walked down to the court after you hit the floor," Danny said. "Did you lose consciousness?"

With a subtle shake of his head, David said, "Not that I know of."

Danny looked up at Roberts. "No, he didn't Danny, but he sure looked stunned."

"Yeah, stunned isn't the word," David added. "And really lightheaded when I got up although somebody gave me their hand and helped me to my feet. And I have a little headache." His long arm reached behind his head and massaged into his ample brown hair.

"Are you seeing any bright lights, hearing any ringing in your ears, having any blurred vision?" Danny asked.

"No."

"Good. In particular, because I saw that nasty fall, we're going to play it safe. I'd like to take you to the emergency room right now where I can get a better look at you. Not to worry, okay?"

David glanced towards the door and his eyes narrowed as he saw Annabel's concern. "Sure, Dr. Tilson."

"I'm going to ask Annabel and Sara to come in here. Tell them where your duffel bag is with your clothes and we'll bring it along."

Danny nodded at Roberts and they both stepped into the hall while the team's coach, Lester Newman, hurried their way.

"We're at half-time," the man said, catching his breath. "How's he doing?"

"Not bad as far as I can tell," Danny said, "but I'm taking him to the ER where I can examine him. You gentlemen may know there is no universal agreement on the definition and grading of concussions but my guess is that he has a very mild one."

"Are you sure you need to take him?" Lester asked.

"I'm as concerned about a skull fracture which would require at least a CT scan. As Roberts probably knows, specific guidelines for when to perform brain imaging on a head-injured athlete also don't exist. Let me take him and we'll all rest more comfortably about it tonight."

Lester rubbed his chin. "Okay, doc, thanks. I'll talk with him for one second to tell him we're all concerned about him and then I have to get back on the court." He turned toward the doorway.

"Just one thing," Danny said. "When's your next game?"

"In six days. Not home court, so we'll be traveling."

"I don't want him in that next competitive game no matter what. I'm being extra cautious with the only information I have now and if I find anything more deleterious with his condition once we get to the hospital, I'll let you know. However, I'll issue him my own medical clearance when I deem it appropriate as well as in compliance with the school's return-to-play policy."

Lester flinched with disapproval. "We sure need him on the team."

"Better to have him out for a short time than the whole season."

"I understand. I'll talk to him real quick and also tell him what you just said, doc. Thanks for your help."

"One more thing … can you get word to his parents?"

"They're in one of the front rows. I'll make sure they know he's doing okay and to meet you all at the hospital."

"Thanks. I prefer to take him with us so I can keep my eye on him."

The ER doctor did an initial screening of David knowing that he was passing his care along to Danny. After he left, Annabel walked in and, for the first time, David and her were alone. She took his hand and with her brown-auburn eyes softening, she squeezed.

"Don't worry about me," David said. "I don't think I'm good enough to make the NBA so my career isn't in jeopardy."

"You're good and you know it. You're just too modest to say so." She leaned in and they kissed briefly, then touched their foreheads together.

A short knock sounded at the partially-closed door and Danny entered.

"Should I leave?" Annabel asked.

"I think that would be better," Danny replied.

Annabel nodded. "I'll be in the waiting room with my mom. I'll see you in a bit." She left but still glanced backwards at him from the door.

Knowing he had to focus on the possible signs and symptoms of a concussion, Danny asked David to stand up.

"Are you feeling dizzy?" Danny asked.

"No."

"Why don't you walk back and forth to the counter? Turn quickly, too."

David did as he was asked, came back and stood still. It appeared as if he had no difficulty with balance or coordination and looked extra tall in the small room, still dressed in his team uniform.

"What day is it?" Danny asked.

David frowned.

"Just checking," Danny said.

"Friday."

"What did you eat for lunch?"

"The team and I had lousy sandwiches in the back room of our school cafeteria hours ago."

"Do you have any nausea and is your headache still there?"

"Don't feel sick and my head hurts a little back here," he said, pointing. "It's only natural. I cracked it pretty hard, Dr. Tilson."

"Yes, you did." Danny smiled as he took a penlight from the counter. Besides giving favorable answers to his questions, David didn't answer slowly or inaccurately so he was feeling relieved that the young man would be fine.

After Danny finished his assessment, he leaned against the counter. "To dispel any doubt about a significant brain injury or skull fracture, I'm going to send you for a CT scan. It's probably overkill, but it's a rapid and superb diagnostic test appropriate for this situation."

David looked worried about how long he'd have to wait to play again and Danny patted his knee.

"It also serves as a baseline head image. Trust me, okay?"

David nodded and cracked a smile.

Danny waited on purpose. The last thing he wanted was to talk to his daughter, his ex-wife - who he was as good as married to - or to David's parents and give them encouraging information only to find out that the young man's CT bore bad news.

He slipped into the small ER break room, poured coffee, then went to the CT suite. He sat in the technician's room watching as the table moved David into the large-domed machine.

Light poured temporarily through the door as Casey - Danny's best friend and brother-in-law - stepped in.

"I heard what happened. Is he alright?"

"I think so," Danny replied, "but I have to check if he has a slight subdural hematoma or skull fracture."

"I hope you don't find anything. He's a good kid."

Danny laughed. "It's funny that I'm fifty and you're forty-nine and we now refer to college-aged students as kids. They're not really, you know."

"But just think of everything that's happened to us in the last thirty years. In that respect, we were kids."

Danny smiled as he realized the truth behind Casey's point, especially to think he had lost a teenaged daughter during those years. That was enough experience for a lifetime.

"Good point. Men and women that age *are* grown and possibly mature. However, their wisdom will accumulate."

Casey's hand ran over his crew cut, his biceps flexing in his short-sleeved paramedic uniform. He regularly worked out, with or without Danny, though he had made strides with helping his friend get more fit and toned than he was a year ago.

"By the way," Danny said. "I agreed to do Matthew's morning rounds on Sunday because he signed up for a mini-marathon. I can't drive Julia over to Rachel's place for visitation so she agreed to stop by the house. Can one of you make sure all goes well?"

"I have off Sunday. No problem."

The Tilsons had a unique family situation, mostly attributed to their parents leaving their large house to their daughter, Mary.

Casey and Mary lived there as a married couple but Danny and Sara lived there as well because they had converted the downstairs to a separate residence. Annabel lived at college most of the time but their next daughter – Nancy – was still in high school and also lived with them. In addition, Danny's young daughter by an extra-marital affair, Julia, resided with them, too.

Since the family situation had recently grown into a more thought-provoking one, Danny liked to think that with modern times come modern family situations and living arrangements; this was particularly true since he and his ex-wife were expecting a baby. He loved Sara dearly and they now lived together although she did not want to marry him a second time.

He grinned thinking about Casey's response to his request as well as his own relationship with his children. He was the father of two living children by his previous wife and, with a baby-on-the-way, he would have one child with her not as husband and wife. And Julia's mother, Rachel - the 'other woman' - was a source of never-ending trouble. He often wondered what was the more complicated part of his life … being a neurosurgeon or a family man.

Chapter 2

"I'll see you at the house later," Casey said to Danny. "Mark is getting information at the ER desk and we're off to pick up a patient." He placed his hand on his friend's shoulder for a second, trying to alleviate Danny's concern over David.

Danny glanced up. "When is Mark quitting before starting medical school?"

"Definitely in a month, if not sooner … if I get a decent paramedic partner. Spending time in an ambulance with someone else requires solid teamwork and compatibility. I have my fingers crossed."

"I bet," Danny acknowledged. "It's almost like a marriage."

Casey left and Danny resumed sipping on his coffee. The CT table backed out making loud bleeping noises and then stopped; David was escorted back to the ER and the technician processed the films. Before putting them in the radiologist's stack to be read, the tech handed them to Danny.

With a deep breath, Danny felt better looking at the results on the X-ray viewer. He pitched his empty cup and went to talk to David and his parents as well as Annabel and Sara.

Without expecting it, Danny found all of them with David who sat sideways on the table, legs practically touching the floor and absent-mindedly rubbing his head.

Aware that he wasn't wearing his white lab coat and knowing he had never met Mr. and Mrs. Bell before, Danny realized he was meeting them under both professional and social circumstances.

"Mom and Dad, this is Dr. Tilson, Annabel's dad," David said as soon as Danny entered the room.

Mrs. Bell gave a warm smile. "I'm Tara and this is Floyd," she said waving to her husband on the other side of the table. "We're happy to meet you. We've heard ... good things about you and Sara from our son."

Tara had an intermittent stutter especially after she briefly closed her eyes in thought. Danny figured she was younger than Sara's age of forty-eight although she had striking silver-blonde hair.

Danny extended his hand to Floyd. "Nice to meet you both, although I'm not happy it's under these circumstances. I helped with your son's care as I was readily available and deal with head injuries."

"And we're grateful you did," Floyd said.

Danny smiled. "We wanted to check David out as soon as possible after the dreadful spill he took on the court. I can fill you all in but perhaps Sara and Annabel can leave as there are rules for confidentiality of a patient's information." He tilted his head in a pleading manner while exchanging glances with the both of them.

"If it's okay with my mom and dad, I'd like them to stay," David said.

"Please, yes," Tara said to Danny.

"I'd like to interject, too," Floyd said. "First, do we have to worry about the CT results? And I hear about head injuries or concussions occurring in sports quite often so I'd like to know about David's fall in simplistic terms but also in more detail than that ... as much as I can understand from a neurosurgeon's perspective."

"I can explain," Danny said, "but if you want me to stop, just say so. First, I ordered the CT scan because it can reveal any of the four types of intracranial hemorrhages or bleeding in the brain, swelling in the brain, or to detect a skull fracture. It's quick, cheap and easier than getting an MRI. The good news is that David appears to be clear of those problems. Otherwise, he could be in surgery right now to fix, for instance, a subdural hematoma."

"Having said that, what we are also concerned about is a concussion. They are sneaky because they are injuries we may not see and they don't show up on CT scans or most MRIs." Danny shifted his weight and leaned against the table near David's leg.

"So there's no surgical dilemma here," Tara echoed, "but David could have a concussion, which is *what* exactly?"

"I'm not being facetious, Mom," David said while frowning, "but I think it's more than a bump on the head." He looked at Danny. "Our coach told us almost half of all sport-related concussions happen in high school football so I didn't think basketball was that bad. Is it?"

"Coach Newman is correct about football which ranks the highest. Even soccer, lacrosse and wrestling come out ahead of basketball. Statistics are even worse for girl's basketball than boy's. And what I really hate to see are head injuries from bike riding," Danny lamented, "because so many times a kid wasn't wearing a helmet."

"My parents always made me wear a helmet," David said, smiling at his mom.

"We were the same way with our girls," Sara chimed in, lowering herself into a chair.

"We should be grateful when our kids make it to twenty-one," Floyd remarked.

Danny nodded, knowing the truth about that. "Anyway, to answer your question. A concussion is a brain injury; it's caused by the movement of the brain inside the skull and that sudden movement causes the brain to swell. Many people think it's only from getting a hit to the head or hitting the ground but you can get it by a sudden acceleration or deceleration force. Like a motor vehicle accident when you're rammed from behind and your head lurches forward and backward."

David inched himself further on the thin paper draping the table, extending his arms behind him and leaned back. Danny gave him a reassuring look.

"In David's case, it appears he has a low-grade concussion with few complaints. We can all monitor him for the possible physical, mental, and emotional symptoms like headaches, nausea, balance issues, dizziness, light sensitivity; trouble remembering or concentrating. Let us know if you feel unusually sad, nervous or irritable and if your sleep patterns change, like getting too tired during the day."

Danny stopped and then chuckled. "Now you're not going to be happy with me at all. I'm going to prescribe that you have no physical or mental exertion for a week. No raising your heart rate, no studying or school work, and no partying on campus. For your brain to recover, it needs to rest. I'll give you a cheat sheet with the do's and don'ts and an office appointment in five days to see if I can give you clearance by the week's end."

David scowled and rubbed his hands together. "And I thought we were friends, Dr. Tilson. You're going to cause me to have the symptoms of a concussion. How can I not feel irritable by doing nothing for the next week?"

"David, Dr. Tilson is looking after your well-being," Floyd said.

"That's okay," Danny said, "I understand. But most people's concussions get better in seven to fourteen days. When your brain is normal at rest, I'll give you medical clearance. If it's in one week, I hope you can be on track with your studies again and slowly get back to basketball."

After a few more questions, Danny waited a minute for David's parents and Sara to leave the room. Annabel sprang up to get David's things from the counter so he could change back into street clothes. "And just one more thing to be clear," Danny added as he started to walk out the door without looking at them, "no sex allowed either!"

Clad in only long pajama bottoms, Danny emerged from the bathroom and sat on the edge of the bed where Sara sat against the headboard, covers up to her waist, book in hand. The door squeaked open and Dakota pranced in; he put his muzzle on the comforter and then turned sideways to give Danny his rear end to pet while giving Sara his face.

Danny laughed as Sara put her paperback aside and Dakota swiped her hand with his tongue. "Thanks a lot, Dakota," Danny said, "for giving me your butt."

"But you've got his happy end," Sara said, rustling his head.

"So true." Danny dug his fingers into the dog's haunches and massaged. Dakota extended his head with pleasure, almost as if he were eating treats from the air.

"The basketball game tonight was full of surprises," Danny said.

"I hope David is going to be all right. He was lucky you were there and able to help out."

"His coach, his parents, and you and Annabel were important, too."

"In all these years," Sara said, "from med school until today, that was a first."

"What was?"

"To see you working in your professional role. Well, I didn't see you performing surgery or anything like that and, although we know David quite well, I nevertheless watched you interact with a patient and his family as a neurosurgeon. For me, that's never happened before."

Danny leaned in closer and gazed into her eyes. "That's interesting … I never realized that. So how did I do?"

"I don't want your head to swell or you may need one of your colleagues to do a bur hole."

Danny laughed. "You *have* learned the lingo after all these years. Will you tell me anyway?"

"Your bedside manner is artful. You had empathy, the perfect tone of voice, and explained the overall situation as well as David's personal circumstances excellently. You made sure they understood the gravity of his head injury as well as the optimism for him getting better."

"Wow. I'm speechless. I appreciate that."

"No wonder you are now the doctor in charge of your neurosurgical group. Things often happen for a reason."

"I wish someday I could see you on the job, too."

"You've been in my classroom before. Maybe not that much but as much as practical."

"What I've seen is that you are one heck of a teacher and the high school kids adore you."

Sara blushed. Her teaching meant a lot to her.

"As far as David and his parents go," Danny said, "I stopped short of giving them more sport's related information as they had enough to deal with."

She looked at him quizzically while bending one leg under the covers.

"Like the fact that concussions due to sports have doubled in the last ten years and the fact that ninety percent of them don't involve a loss of consciousness. I consider David to have a Grade I concussion without a loss of consciousness but, as athletes accumulate them, about forty-percent will be catastrophic, leading to a permanent neurological disability."

Sara shuddered. "Makes me glad I don't have to worry about the girls since they aren't really involved with contact sports. And if David rests on campus this week instead of going home, maybe Annabel can be influential in keeping him inactive."

"I hope so." Danny gave the Chesapeake one more animated massage. "Okay, that's it, time to settle into your dog bed." Dakota let out a loud breath as if disappointed and plopped down right next to Danny.

"I know we haven't talked about it too much," Danny said looking back at Sara, "but which day next week is your obstetrician's appointment?"

Sara pulled down the covers and rubbed her abdomen. "On Monday."

Danny put his hand down next to hers; Sara's pregnancy was too early so he barely felt a bump.

"Even though it's your second routine appointment, it's going to be exciting because of the first ultrasound and baby pictures. But you know she'll ask again if you want to schedule an amniocentesis."

After a big sigh, Sara pulled the bedspread up to her chest. "Too bad I'm forty-eight. Otherwise, she probably wouldn't have mentioned it."

"It's only because the baby's risk for a genetic disorder rises with age. Your doc is making sure we're given the option to diagnose a chromosomal abnormality."

"I know," Sara said. "Especially for Down's syndrome which is why you and I are shying away from talking about it. But it's an invasive procedure putting a needle straight into my womb and she said it carries a risk for a miscarriage. But I guess it's just another way of helping a woman's decision to abort a baby that she finds out isn't as perfect as society would like." Sara frowned.

Danny kept silent, then he took her hand. "Either way, I'll stand by your decision."

"What do you think?"

"I don't know what I would have thought before getting more religious after last fall's trauma in that tornado but, now, I'd prefer us not to have the amniocentesis. This surprise baby was conceived in love and deserves a right to life just like all living things."

Dakota popped his head up, his brown eyes looking searchingly at Danny. Sara glanced at the dog and then Danny.

"Well, then, I guess we all feel the same way. No amniocentesis. And when I come home on Monday with our baby's first ultrasound pictures, we'll know if it's a boy or a girl. We'll all celebrate. And you and I, Casey and Mary, and Annabel and Nancy can make suggestions on naming her!"

It wasn't long before Sara was fast asleep. Danny quietly slipped out of the room and into the next bedroom. He knelt on the floor and studied Julia, her eyes closed, her small hand tucked beside her cheek. "Sleep tight, love. You're going to be a big half-sister to a new baby girl or boy within a year. But Sara thinks she's having a girl."

Chapter 3

The night before, Casey had worked extra late, having transported a patient over the border to Kentucky at the end of their shift. He still wasn't rested on Sunday morning as he headed downstairs with a big yawn. Mary sat at the counter with a mug of coffee and the weekend newspaper.

"Morning," he said, giving her a rub on her shoulder.

He looked across the room where Nancy worked quietly on homework. In the latter half of her junior year in high school, her work load was substantial, especially since she was fanatical about grades; she had high hopes to be as smart as or more successful than her older sister.

"Yo, Nancy," Casey said. "How about going to get Julia? Her mother is picking her up soon for the day."

His niece closed a notebook. "I was just finishing. Do you mean that witch is coming over *here*?!"

Casey glanced at his wife who shrugged her shoulders. "Julia didn't hear that," Mary said, "so I can't blame her for calling a spade a spade."

Nancy quickly got up and disappeared down the steps while Casey opened the yard door. Dakota had been waiting to come in, his eyes glued on the door frame, his body quivering because he had yet to give Casey a hello.

"There you go, boy," Casey said, rustling Dakota's body in a double-handed greeting. "Your favorite little girl is on her way up so I better enjoy you before you leave me flat."

The basement door opened up, Julia ran in and headed straight for the dog.

"Da-Ka!" she squealed and Dakota play-bowed as she plopped on the floor in front of him.

"Sara had her all ready," Nancy said coming into the room, "and had packed a few things for her. She's had breakfast, too." She placed the small duffel bag on the counter.

As Casey poured his wife more coffee, the phone rang. "I'll get it," he said.

"It's me," Rachel said. "I just pulled into your driveway. If you could bring my daughter out, I'd appreciate it."

"I can do that. Sit tight," he said and hung up. He squatted to face Julia. "Okey dokey. Your mom's outside so say good-bye to Dakota. You'll see him again later today."

Mary went to the bag and pulled out Julia's outerwear. Looking into Julia's eyes, she tucked the little girl's fine dark-blonde hair into a woolen hat, helped her with her jacket, and gave her a kiss.

Casey took Julia's hand and led her down the hallway. "Bye, Julia. See you later," Nancy yelled.

"You stay here, boy," Casey said to Dakota as he opened the front door. In the double driveway to the left stood Rachel, leaning against her Miata.

Julia let go of Casey's hand and skipped over. "Hi, my love," Rachel said. She stooped down, hugged her, then walked to the passenger seat where she strapped her in. Casey followed and stood there with the bag.

"We love you, Julia," Casey said before Rachel closed the door.

Rachel spun around and stared at him. No one would have known about her previous facial trauma, Casey thought, as the surgeon did a great job. He waited for her to speak again as it still amazed him that such a seductive voice - which could probably narrate every romance novel to be a best-selling audio book – could belong to someone that Nancy had labeled a 'witch.'

"You just said 'We love you,'" Rachel said to him, "but no one loves her like her mother." She took the bag from Casey's grip and marched in front of the car to the driver's side. She wore a butternut-colored pullover with a matching cap and, below her velvet pants, low western-style boots which clicked against the asphalt.

As Rachel got into the car, Casey stooped low and waved to Julia.

"I'll be back promptly at five o'clock to drop her off," Rachel said through the open window. "I have to be somewhere after that. I'll be in a hurry then … like I am now."

"We look forward to it." Casey smiled. He turned and walked briskly to the door.

Rachel turned the ignition key but, to her surprise, the car didn't respond; she turned the key forward again and her Miata just growled. "Damn thing," she mumbled. "Crappy timing." She tried again but the car wouldn't spring to life.

Casey glanced back the second time she cranked the motor. With displeasure registering on his face, he wondered if the sporty little car ever had regular maintenance.

Rachel opened the door halfway, put one leg on the ground, and leaned over the open window. "Do you think you could be a gentleman and help us out?" she asked with a more appealing tone than a minute ago.

Casey shoved his hands into his pockets and walked back to the car.

"I really have to get home," she said with urgency.

"Okay, open the hood."

The front end popped open. Casey propped it up and leaned to the side. "Don't start the engine," he shouted.

Scanning under the hood, the battery and parts looked clean and intact so nothing struck him as being amiss. He leaned in a bit closer; he especially took a closer look at the belts, what he thought of as the workhorses of a car.

As he arched further in, he moved his left hand onto the alternator belt. To his astonishment, he heard the engine crank on which made him jump with surprise. But his reaction was too late.

With a snap, his middle finger was amputated from the second knuckle.

"Crap," Casey said, his left finger gushing blood like a severed artery. When he took a fast step backwards, he yelled loudly. "I told you not to start the engine!"

Rachel turned off the switch. "What happened?"

"This is what happened," he said, holding up his left hand. "I've lost most of my finger."

"I have to get going."

Casey heard her comment as he stepped back to look for his chopped-off finger in the bowels of the engine. Spotting it, he let go of the open wound, retrieved it and stuck it into his right palm, pressing it there with his three end fingers; he then used a pincer grip to tourniquet the blood flow on the other hand. As the pain intensified, he hurried into the house leaving Rachel with a frustrated look on her face and Julia sitting clueless in her car seat.

Danny finished making morning rounds for his colleague, Matthew, hoping he would place in the top few runners of his mini-marathon.

He draped his white coat over a chair in the doctor's lounge, grabbed a juice and a pastry, and sat down with a section of the newspaper. He finished reading the local news when his iPhone dinged with a text message from Mary.

If you're still in the hospital, don't leave. Meet Casey and I in the ER.

His heart thumped and he frowned; the message brought back memories of his daughter Melissa in the ER when she'd make emergency visits with Sara for asthmatic attacks. Glad that the text didn't say anything about his other girls, he pushed back from the table and headed down the stairs to the ER. What could be the problem and was it Mary or Casey who needed help?

Passing the patients' board over the desk, Danny immediately spotted Casey Hamilton's name and he swallowed his worry as he rounded the corner into Room 2.

The emergency room doctor's referral for Casey to see a hand surgeon had already been made. Standing over his stretcher, she held Casey's left hand while placing another thick, blood soaked bandage to the side. Mary stood back, looking pale and on the verge of tears as her husband's gaze shot to Danny. Casey titled his head and gave his best friend a slight shrug of his shoulders.

"I'm putting you on the OR schedule," the female surgeon said, "but it may take a few hours as our service has a case on the table and two to follow. I'm glad you brought in the severed last joint but it may be too shattered to reattach. Plus, sometimes patient's don't want it put back on. Your finger may not end up functioning as well with it as without it and sensation may feel odd if not bothersome."

The hand surgeon wrapped clean gauze over the top and continued. "We'll talk about it more before we start. Either we'll clean up what's left of that finger and make a decent closure or see about putting the end back on if you'd like us to." Following Casey's gaze, she looked at Danny.

"Hi," Danny said. "I'm Dr. Tilson. I don't think we've met."

"Dr. Parsons."

"What happened?" Danny's mouth turned down as he looked at all three of them.

"Rachel started her car when …," Mary began to explain.

Casey gently interrupted. "I had an accident. Rachel was leaving with Julia and she had some car trouble. My hand was in the wrong place at the wrong time. That's all."

"It's more than 'that's all,'" Danny said. "What exactly did happen to your finger?"

Casey glanced at Dr. Parsons. "He's lost the distal phalange of the left long finger," she said. "He's lucky it wasn't more."

"I'm grateful it wasn't my thumb or index finger," Casey said," which could have impacted what I do as a paramedic."

The surgeon nodded. "If there are no more questions at this time, I'll get my notes written and I'll see you probably this evening in the pre-op holding area."

"Thanks," Casey said.

"From all of us," Danny agreed. "And, by the way, he's probably not going to be a good patient so please also give post-op instructions to his wife or me."

While staff transported Casey to a hospital room where he'd wait until his surgery, Danny took Mary into the doctor's lounge. They sat in the back corner as sunshine filtered through the window. It did little, however, to brighten Mary's mood.

"I'll stay with him until after surgery tonight," Mary said. "But you better go home. Sara and Nancy stayed there because Rachel will be coming back with Julia."

"And what happened with her car?"

"As we left, she was calling a tow truck. I don't know what the outcome was."

Mary twisted her hands in her lap. "I've never seen that much blood. I thought he was going to bleed to death."

Danny pushed back his sister's long red hair. "He'll be okay. He has you."

"And you, too," she said. "But sometimes all of us cause him the biggest troubles or worries. And he never asks for anything. He's the best."

"You're right." Danny said. "And his childhood - what happened - shaped him though he never, ever talks about it. We were already friends when his younger sibling died but, after that, I became like his brother. We've been his family for a long time."

Mary nodded, finally letting a tear stream down her face. "And if it hadn't been for you being his best friend, I would have never been able to sometimes tag along, get to know him, and then fall in love when I moved back from Alaska. Although I probably loved him going back a lot longer than that." She dabbed her eyes with a tissue. "You know, he didn't even tell you back there."

"What?"

"I half-scolded him about why he put his hand in the hood of the car with the engine running. That's when he said the engine wasn't supposed to be on."

Danny cocked his head with a puzzled expression.

"He looked under the hood of Rachel's car to see why it wouldn't start. He told her not to start it but she did and that's why he lost his finger."

Danny scowled and took a deep breath, pushing his fist into the leather cushion.

"I am so sorry, sis. It's my fault. I regret every day that I ever met that woman."

Mary took Danny's hand. "She met you on purpose, Danny, and it was one of her great plans. Just like what happened with your patient and his bankrupt soft drink business last year. But don't think that way because you have to forgive yourself. And don't forget, you wouldn't have Julia if it weren't for Rachel and she was meant to be in your life."

Despite the morning's circuitous events, Rachel made up for lost time. All she had to do was shorten a few activities and hurry like mad. A tow truck took her vehicle in to an open local car shop which was lucky for her since the Mazda dealer was closed on Sunday. With a little extra attention to the mechanic, he changed the snapped-off belt in no time.

Next, she took Julia to a park beside her apartment complex where she made sure her daughter played and used the children's equipment for over an hour until her energy level ran out of steam.

Back at the apartment, Rachel made them both a late lunch and then nestled the sleepy little girl in her lap in front of several lit candles on the coffee table. The flames flickered and even warmed the small area around them.

"Didn't you have a swell time with your mother at the park today?" Rachel whispered in Julia's ear.

"Mmm hmm."

"You and I must stay together always," Rachel said, stroking her daughter's hair. "It's the best way because Mommy loves you the most. I miss you way too much because you don't live with me. And I cry, too, when you're not here."

Julia tilted her head up. "Don't cry, Mommy."

Rachel let out a sigh and held her daughter even closer. "I can't help it when you are with Danny and those people."

"It's okay, Mommy."

"It would only be okay if you only lived with me. You could still visit that other house once in a while."

A long silence ensued. Rachel continued stroking her.

"But Mommy, Da-Ka is my favorite."

"I know, sweetheart, and I'm sorry Danny took Dakota away from me. I know what!" Rachel exclaimed. "I'll give you the biggest present ever. I will buy you a puppy that will be your very own dog!"

A smile erupted on Julia's face and she clapped her hands. "Mommy, can I name her?"

Chapter 4

Since Mary stayed with Casey while waiting for him to go to surgery, she insisted that Danny go home.

"Otherwise," she said, "you'll be here until late at night and Julia will be back at the house at five."

Casey nodded from the bed; a morphine shot had eased the throbbing, intense pain from his hand and had also made him groggy.

"You stayed with me when I was hospitalized last fall," Danny said. "You didn't move from my bedside. What makes you think I wouldn't do the same?"

"Because, you dumbass," Casey said softly, "the 'one and only' is bringing Julia back to the house."

"I'm sorry," Mary said to her brother. "It's the medication that's talking."

"No, it's not," Casey said while staring at Danny. "And if you don't know what a dumbass is you're really a stupid dumbass."

"Casey!" Mary exclaimed.

"It's alright. He's angry at Rachel and he's too much of a gentleman to say so, so he's taking it out on me. At least I'm good for something."

Danny leaned over and kissed his sister on the cheek. "Keep me posted. I will go home for Julia. That will also assure me that Sara won't have to deal with Rachel either." He looked up at the ceiling as if praying. "God forbid if Sara is the next one in line to render Rachel some kind of assistance."

"Good plan," Mary said.

"And one more thing." He took a step closer to Casey. "I can't tell you how sorry I am. If I could give you one of my whole fingers, I would." He turned and left with a heavy heart.

"You told him what happened?" Casey asked his wife.

"Think of it this way. You wouldn't like it if I kept quiet about something happening to Danny. Would you?"

Casey crossed his arms. As usual, Mary was correct. He finally let his lids close and rested … almost comfortably.

The garage door was open as Danny sprayed cleaner on a back window of his car and wiped off Dakota's nose smudges. The dog was behind him following his steps as he thought about Casey. He said a small prayer for him; he'd be going to surgery soon and, whatever the outcome, he hoped his friend would not have future limited abilities at his job.

The sporty car pulled into the driveway and came to a stop. Dakota trotted over with his tail wagging and Rachel said, "Hi, my boy," while getting out.

"Julia ate a late lunch and had a little nap afterwards," she added as Danny approached; she opened Julia's door as Dakota nudged in to greet the youngster.

"Hi, pumpkin," Danny said, helping his daughter to the ground.

After Julia gave Danny and Dakota a slight acknowledgement, she skipped through the garage, tippy-toed to the door handle and went inside. Danny picked up her bag as Rachel went back to the driver's seat.

He stood next to the open window but before he could say anything, Rachel spoke first. "By the way, I had my car fixed immediately and hurried to get Julia back to you on time."

As she didn't even ask about Casey, Danny's anger boiled up. "Well, aren't you the saint?"

"Thank you." She lowered her sunglasses. "Now if you don't mind, please step back. Casey already got himself hurt in this driveway today. I know you two are close but you don't have to follow his stupidity."

With disbelief, Danny moved backwards. His mouth agape as she pulled away, he realized she was right. He had been ready to ask her why she had earlier turned on the car engine. Had it been a total accident because she didn't hear Casey's wish to not turn on the ignition?

He had been ready to tell her the status of his brother-in-law at the hospital but it would have been on deaf ears.

Danny finished his first surgery on Monday morning and bounded up the staircase two steps at a time hoping to see Casey before his discharge.

"Good morning, you two," he said on entering the room.

Mary sat on the end of Casey's bed with an open newspaper. She'd been reading to him from the Sunday's sport's section, a short article about Friday night's basketball game.

Danny sat down and leaned forward. "How did it go? And what did they do?" He eyed the bulky bandage wrapped around Casey's left middle finger.

"They cleaned it up and made a perfect closure. The hand surgeon thought the reattachment wouldn't work and the severed piece was worse than she thought. Otherwise, it went smoothly. The anesthesiologist that you know gave me an axillary block with sedation and the finger was still numb for most of the night."

"But now he's hurting," Mary said, "even though they gave him a pain med this morning."

Danny rubbed his hands together, looked up and frowned.

"What," Casey said.

"I hope you don't get phantom limb pain."

"What's that?" Mary asked.

"That's where an amputated limb or appendage is left with unusual feelings. It happens to patients over half the time. It feels as if the missing part is still attached to the body and the nerves that would have innervated the missing part cause pain."

Mary grimaced and glanced at her husband.

"It can be agonizing," Danny said. "Some patient's report it as a burning or shooting pain and others experience tingling, itching or other sensations. It can't be pleasant."

Mary buried her face in her hands, her red hair fell free alongside her face, and Casey reached out with his right hand to comfort her.

"I've been thinking about it," she said. "We're not going to let this go."

"Mary wants me to sue Rachel," Casey said, "but I'm not exactly the litigating type."

Danny raised his eyebrows. "You can make an exception, you know. It's not uncommon for greedy litigators and lawyers to sue for pain and suffering."

"I can't do that." He looked at his hand, now resting on the white sheet. "Although I wonder what my medical bills are going to be after all this is said and done. Why don't I sue her for all my out-of-pocket bills?"

"You're a gentleman, Casey Hamilton," Mary said, "if you don't sue her for more."

"That's one reason you married him," Danny said. "But possibly recouping your medical bills is better than nothing. Plus, it will be a thorn in her side although a cactus couldn't penetrate her. Why don't you use my attorney, Mark Cunningham?"

"Sure thing," Casey nodded. "I suppose he knows how to deal with Rachel, too."

"I'll give him a call to start the ball rolling," Danny said.

Danny patted Mary's shoulder. "I must get back downstairs for my next surgery. But do you know that today's the big day? We'll all be smiling later when Sara gets home." He shook his head with amusement. "After work, she's going for her obstetrician's appointment and we get our first baby pictures. I can't believe I'm going to be a father again."

After Danny left, Casey and Mary grinned at each other.

"I haven't seen him this happy about anything since our wedding day," she said.

Annabel strolled back to her dorm after her last morning class; during the lecture, she'd received a text message from David. He had been off campus for the weekend, his parents insisting he'd get more rest and fewer distractions at home. The previous night, his father had driven him back to his dorm where he was to skip classes until his doctor's appointment with Danny on Thursday.

Annabel piled the load of books she'd been carrying on her desk and looked again at David's message: *Grab a bite later? Meet you in the cafeteria?*

She couldn't wait to see him. This had been the first weekend since they had met that they hadn't spent time together. It had been a miserable two days, she missed him so much. He dominated her thoughts and it was difficult to get any studying done. Her two thumbs wiggled across the keypad and she typed back to him: *For sure.*

In the small mirror Annabel had hung near the door, she ran her fingers through her hair to enhance its natural curl and looked at her teeth. After having braces for years, she was proud of her straight, white smile and still flossed her teeth regularly like before.

She went back out and resumed thinking about David. At least they were sharing another biology lab class together this semester but, unless she saw him between classes this week, she wondered if she would see him at all.

Annabel realized since they had been going together and having sex, her hormones seemed to ramp up as time went on instead of feeling like she was being fulfilled. Just looking at his dimpled chin and perfect shoulders made her yearn to be in his arms. And above all that, he had a fun personality, treated her terrific, and they hadn't had a disagreement or misunderstanding yet. He was a source of strength and companionship for her and she began to realize that he may be in her life for a long, long time.

Dressed in faded blue jeans and a long college sweatshirt, she walked over to the cafeteria and bounded up the steps to the balcony lounge where they occasionally met between classes or before lunch. Convinced that she didn't see him on either of the two couches or chairs in front of the coffee shop, she stepped over to two of their classmates.

"Hi, guys," she said. "Have either of you seen David?"

A short teen with a Caribbean accent answered, "He was with us for a while. Left a few minutes ago with some basketball buddies."

"Do you know where they went?"

"The guys were going to the gym," the other one said, "to play ball for a few minutes. They were laughing that they rarely play outside of team practice anymore when Coach Newman can't be so hard on them."

The corners of Annabel's mouth turned down.

"Don't worry, Annabel," the first teen said. "David said he was going to watch."

The second teen tapped his friend's forearm. "But they were giving him grief to shoot balls with them." He looked at Annabel. "They said David was grounded from playing and from team practice, but what was the harm if he was their fifth player just fooling around on the court."

"Okay, thanks." She turned and ran down the stairs, biting the inside of her lip. Maybe it would be best if she convinced him to come back to the cafeteria with her and not watch them. Since he loved basketball, watching his teammates may be like purgatory since he wasn't allowed to join in.

She crossed the street south from the cafeteria and went into the large athletic center. After passing the Olympic-sized pool on the right, she went into the basketball court. A group of students were playing on her side and a shot to the backboard startled her as she passed by, not seeing David.

As she continued to the other side of the gym behind the first row of benches, she finally made out the next group of students playing ball. Five of the school's male basketball players were there, David included.

Knowing she couldn't get their attention until they took a break, Annabel sat on the bench. She thought about her father's instructions; as far as she knew, there weren't any exceptions he had listed to allow David to play sports. She had to admit he looked handsome in dark sweatpants and a logo tee-shirt but, damn it, he shouldn't be out there. Grimacing, her heart rate sped up with anticipation. He better just be watching them and not get sucked up into playing.

Always impressed with David's style – which the coach said he was still perfecting – she sadly saw him line up for a free throw. To his advantage, he'd learned to use flexibility to create greater energy. With ball in hands, he took a wide stance. Annabel wanted to shout at him to stop. But with his shoulder forward and relaxed, he made his release point high and made the shot.

All five players then grabbed for the ball and in the scramble, David lost his balance. As he began falling to the floor, he was struck in the head by a knee.

Chapter 5

Having moved to Nashville, the only downside Rachel could think of was that she was a two-hour drive from Phil Beckett, her continuously-retained lawyer who she had used for many services. Although she sometimes gave him grief, she trusted him because of their shared history and because he usually procured the outcomes she desired.

Pretty much anyway. Perhaps he'd met his match with a grand jury that had convened due to charges the prosecuting attorney had brought against her. Kirk Thompson had successfully brought a manslaughter rap against a former boyfriend but, in the interim, she had gotten tangled up in the mess.

Rachel had not been proactive against stopping that boyfriend – Leo - from abusing Julia, who was an infant during the time they had lived with him; in addition, she had blackmailed him in exchange for keeping quiet about it. So Kirk Thompson made an example of her. Besides the blackmail charges, he wanted to come down against people who don't ensure the safety of minors.

She had received her own attorney's phone call last week. With an exterior as thick as a T. Rex, Rachel had experienced or provoked more calamities than most people had in their lifetime but Phil had told her the scariest news she had ever received.

"The grand jury made their decision," he'd said. "They believe the charges and evidence against you warrant a trial."

After she had hung up the phone, she gasped for air and the only physical sense she felt was a tight squeezing in her chest. Even the remaining numbness around her upper lip from a previous facial trauma was exaggerated as she couldn't feel parts of her face.

She had finally restored her breathing and normal heart rhythm. Hell, she'd thought, what could be the sentence if I was found guilty?

Surely, I can't go to jail if I didn't even hurt someone. Not like the dirt bags who shoot, torture or harm other people. It's ludicrous that the legal system is making a big deal about this. In essence, she continued thinking, she'd been a more lucrative weasel in matters other than this.

Phil Beckett had gone to work immediately by calling Kirk Thompson and trying to hand over some reconciliation on Rachel's behalf instead of preparing to go to trial. After a tense few days of back and forth bartering, both attorneys and Rachel agreed to appear before a judge at 8:00 a.m. on Monday morning.

The pressing court appearance in Knoxville had been the reason Rachel was in a hurry on Sunday afternoon. She'd finally put Julia down for her nap and scrambled to pack a small suitcase After dropping off Julia back at Danny's, she had to drive to Knoxville. It would be much better to stay overnight in a hotel there than take a chance of being late Monday morning coming all the way from Nashville.

Of course, what she hadn't banked on was Casey's dim-wittedness in getting his finger lopped off in her engine. That man had been a pain in her side ever since she'd first met him a few years ago. That was when she'd taken a precious historical book owned by Danny and placed it in the resale market.

She had to admit, however, that Danny had one special friend in Casey. She should be so lucky to have a friend like that. Maybe the next man she meets will be as dog-trained as him and won't go off to some sick-person hospital like a previous boyfriend, Varg … or go to jail like Leo … or leave her flat like her policeman, Evan, had.

At 7:00 a.m. on Monday morning, Rachel and Phil Beckett met one street over from the Knoxville courthouse in a busy coffee shop. It was a routine stop for lawyers throughout the day. Rachel heard them tactfully talk to each other about cases; she even heard one making disparaging remarks about his own client as she stood in line waiting for a cappuccino.

She took the hot mocha over to Phil who she had spotted when she first walked in; the almost middle-aged man hunched over his iPhone so that his thinning, combed-over hair practically glistened with a thickening product.

"Good morning," she said, placing the paper cup on the table. She took off a jacket that matched her skirt and pulled out a chair.

Phil nodded. "Excellent attire and I didn't even tell you how to dress."

"I'm not stupid," she mumbled. She'd worn a light rose blouse with a soft white scarf tied in front as well as short heels with the skirt. Her skin glowed like she'd healed after a chemical peel. As she sat down, the man at the adjoining table did a double-take.

"What is this judge's name?" Rachel asked.

"Patton." Phil leaned closer. "We're lucky to have gotten this far. I didn't think Kirk Thompson was even amenable to discuss some kind of compromise. He loves winning trials. However, I think he was just given another high-profile case, so he may be wanting to clear his plate of the small stuff."

A spark shone in Rachel's eyes as she hoped Thompson's greediness for notoriety would make her case seem less important to him. Even do-gooders have ulterior motives, she thought. Yes, she sensed victory down the road; all of a sudden she could feel it.

"There's probably nothing more we need to discuss about this then before going into the courtroom," she said.

"Except that you better be amenable to their suggestions for your punishment."

"Punishment? If you don't wheedle it down to as little as possible, then I will."

"Whatever you say. It's your head on the block."

"Yes, and you get paid regardless." She took a sip and looked sharply at him. "Now, we have a few moments to talk about something else – my daughter's present custody situation with Danny Tilson."

"What's on your mind? Your daughter's father has been quite cooperative with you and you're seeing her without those visitation restrictions that were in place."

"Please. Don't make out like he's some hero. We have two steps to take. First, we are going to litigate for me to primarily have Julia full time with the small visitation to Tilson … the way it was initially when I had her as an infant in Knoxville."

"At the moment," Phil said, "I don't see that happening. But, if it does somehow swing your way, I don't want to hear later that she gets abused by one of your boyfriends."

She swiped her hand in the air. "I can't believe you're pretending to care. But, no, that won't happen again. It obviously caused a repercussion of events and not just for her. I'll shoot any guy square between the eyes who tries to do that to her again."

"And I take it, you'll want a child support change?"

"Obviously. And a lot more than that."

"Like what?"

"You'll see."

In the courtroom, Rachel and Phil waited for the judge to enter. She glanced towards the table to the right. She had met the prosecuting attorney before when he had questioned her as a witness in Leo's manslaughter case and, in one way, she had respect for him because he had brought her old boyfriend down.

Knowing that Kirk's legal focus was now on her, she smiled across the aisle and leaned to the side. "Mr. Thompson, everyone is so grateful that justice was done after the mayor's daughter died so tragically and unnecessarily. Thank you so much for putting Leo Ramsey in jail where he belongs."

As Rachel's comments took Kirk by surprise, he considered his response as the judge walked across the front of the room and was announced.

Now she focused on the judge. Bingo, she thought, liking his gender and age range; better than she had hoped for. Due to the circumstances of her case, she felt a male judge would be to her advantage and, if he was around middle-aged or slightly younger, he'd have fresh experience with small children. He may be in the throes of juggling a young family himself whereas an older judge would be forgetful of the daily difficulties of having that task.

Silence swept the courtroom while the judge took thirty seconds to review the paperwork before him. Then he looked over the frames of his glasses. "Mr. Beckett, it appears your client is trying to dodge a trial that Mr. Thompson now has the tools to make happen."

"I believe we can come to an arrangement and spare this court's time."

Thompson heard a sniffling and peered to his left. A tear welled up in Rachel's eye and started rolling down her cheek.

The judge glanced and pointed towards Kirk. "Mr. Thompson, is the State willing to accept some modification of these possible sentences that you have outlined?"

"I believe so, Your Honor."

"Hmm." He focused on Rachel while swiping the black wave of hair bridging his forehead. "Miss Hendersen?" he snapped.

Rachel stood with grace and walked slowly from behind the table to the aisle. "Yes, Judge Patton, Your Honor, sir." Her voice was butter-soft as she dabbed her eye with a tissue.

"What would you like to tell this court? There are two serious allegations here," he said, his tone mellowing a tad as he neared the end.

Rachel dropped one arm to her side and kept the one with the tissue poised over her heart. "I totally regret having had my daughter anywhere near the abusive man I was dating. I need to have better judgment in men, Your Honor. I was sucked in with his lies and deception and my daughter's safety was put at risk. As I believe in a supreme being, I hope he helps me to never fall for men like that again. I am so sorry. I love my daughter more than anything and I'll stand in the way of any man that ever appears to want to harm her again."

Rachel sobbed and swiped the tissue across her cheek.

Judge Patton cleared his throat. The tone in his voice softened yet again. "But, Ms. Hendersen, you took a great deal of money from him in the end as well, a payoff for your silence."

"Judge Patton, the abuse had already occurred. I am a single mom struggling to raise my daughter all by myself. I had to then get far away from Leo Ramsey and the money helped me get free of him. Otherwise, Julia and I would have ended up in some state center for abused women and children, leeching off of the taxpayer's dollar."

Patton's eyes softened. Phil Beckett didn't want to add a thing so kept quiet. Thompson rolled his eyes.

"Ms. Hendersen," the judge said, "in all sincerity, you could have been the woman who Leo Ramsey fed lethal doses of drugs to. Please be more careful in the future. Men are not always who they seem to be."

"Yes, Your Honor. Thank you, Judge Patton." She sidestepped to the left and lowered herself back into the stiff chair.

"This is what we are going to do," he said, looking at each attorney in turn. "Hendersen will give back the ten-thousand dollars she pocketed from Mr. Ramsey. It will go to The Center for Abused Children here in Knoxville."

Although Rachel's pulse quickened as she became irritated, she realized he did not tack on an additional monetary penalty. She could live with this so far.

"And what to do about your failure to acknowledge the abuse your daughter suffered? To not take her out of harm's way, report it, or get medical treatment?" He gave her a soulful stare.

"Your Honor," Thompson said, "we put some possibilities before the court."

"Yes, I see," he said, reading over the list. "These may be a little harsh and we don't want Ms. Hendersen not being gainfully employed and able to take care of her daughter appropriately. Eight hours of community service per week for three months should be sufficient. She can volunteer at a children's hospital. You two can see to the details."

The two attorneys glanced over at each other and nodded.

"Miss Hendersen," the judge said after clearing his throat. "Again, watch yourself. You're too pretty to be mixed up with bad men."

"Yes, thank you, Your Honor … thank you so much."

Kirk Thompson stepped forward first as Phil picked up his briefcase and nudged Rachel to leave.

"Glad to wrap it up," Kirk said quickly in his northeast accent.

With a quick gesture, Rachel pocketed the tissue she'd been using and stood before Kirk in the aisle. "Now that I will be sure to follow the judge's advice, I hope we meet again under less stressful conditions, Mr. Thompson. Perhaps a situation that's more social," she purred.

Kirk wasn't one to skip a beat but he paused to consider what she'd said.

"Ms. Hendersen, consider me unavailable to do 'social.' If you are something between an angel and a witch, I think you lean towards the latter."

Before Rachel had time to respond, he exited the courtroom while Phil prodded her again to leave. When they entered the outside hallway, Phil said, "That was quite a performance in there."

"Had I been devoid of that skill," she said, "I would have taken acting lessons before coming here today."

Chapter 6

At the basketball court, Annabel gasped as she watched David get hit in the head by a player's knee. She rose from the bench and clasped her hands in front of her face. David scrambled, assumed an upright posture, and didn't fall any further. As she sighed a breath of relief, one teammate held the ball and another patted her boyfriend, checking to see if he was okay. The shortest one of them glanced at his watch and then all of them exchanged words. It appeared they decided to quit playing and get back to afternoon classes as they began walking off the court.

After Annabel stepped over the front row bench onto the gym floor, she waved while approaching them. She focused on David who was between his buddies in body but not in mind. Walking along, he seemed dazed and looked past Annabel like she wasn't even there.

When she was within five feet of him, a dread gripped her as she held back speaking to him as she was afraid he wouldn't answer her back.

Annabel's suspicions proved her correct and, in a few seconds, David abruptly fell to the ground, his tall frame hitting the wood floor with a thud. Like a gathering of giraffes, the long arms of the other players swooped down all around him and Annabel wiggled between them.

"David!" she exclaimed. She hovered over his face; his eyes didn't move and yet his pupils were getting bigger and bigger.

"Oh my God," she said as she crouched down. "Somebody, call 911. Right now."

Danny was closing a lumbar laminectomy case with an assistant and small talk filled the OR. For the second time in a minute, Danny's iPhone wiggled on the table; it was set on the vibrator mode, adjacent to his pager.

"Dr. Tilson," the circulator said, "somebody's persistent in trying to get you. Do you want me to check the number or answer your phone?"

"What number is showing up?"

She rattled off what she saw.

"That's my daughter," Danny said. "She occasionally texts me or rings the office. It's rare for her to call my cell phone during the day. Please, answer it."

Danny glanced over, pausing a suture needle above the patient's back.

The nurse grew concerned as she listened to the voicemail which had already been left and then stared at Danny. "Your daughter said something happened to David. He's in an ambulance on the way to the hospital right now and she's in her car headed this way, too. She said you must see him."

The surgical assistant nodded at Danny. "I'm good here. Go ahead."

Danny looked at the anesthesiologist. "Patient's fine. Don't see any problem waking him up and getting him extubated."

After backing away from the table, Danny stripped off his gloves and picked up his tech gadgets. "Thanks, everyone," he said.

"Hope everything is okay," the anesthesiologist said as Danny went through the door.

Danny practically ran through the ER as the unit secretary looked up. "I was just calling you," she said.

"Don't have to," he replied. "I already see the back door opening and the ambulance outside."

Within minutes, the ER doctor and Danny both followed the two paramedics and stretcher into the trauma room. David was unconscious on the stretcher as the doctors wondered what had happened; no one said a word as they attached new monitors. The respiratory therapist arrived and began squeezing the Ambu bag a medic had passed to her.

"We intubated him at the scene," the medic said, looking at Danny. "Your daughter had already started giving him mouth-to-mouth respiration as he wasn't breathing."

Startled by that news, Danny raised his hand over his eyes but then went to work by pure instinct. David's pupils were dilated and he had no eye movement. As he continued the physical exam and then gave orders for him to go to the CT scanner, he realized Annabel had come through the ER back door and the staff were trying to restrain her from coming into the room.

Through the commotion, Danny and Annabel's eyes met. How was he going to tell her that David was in a coma?

After wrapping his arm around his daughter's shoulder, Danny walked her to an empty room designated for family conferences. Annabel had lost her rosy complexion and her facial muscles were taut. She held back tears as they sat on the couch but he nevertheless handed her a tissue from a nearby box.

"Tell me.," Danny said. "What happened?"

"I went to meet him for lunch but he wasn't there. He had already left with some friends who were going to shoot some basketball," she sputtered. "I mean, didn't you tell him? He wasn't even supposed to practice? Right?"

Danny clenched his jaw. "He wasn't supposed to have any mental strain or physical activity until I was to see him in three more days."

"He didn't feel too bad. He must have caved into peer pressure, Dad. It sounded like the guys egged him on."

"Did he fall and hit his head?"

"Not really. He got hit in the head with a knee first. He was dazed but otherwise fine. Then he suddenly went down."

Danny nodded with understanding as a knock came on the door. He opened the door a few inches. "Dr. Tilson, David's parents are here," an ER employee said. "Do you want to talk to them?"

"Send them in. Thanks."

"I can leave in a minute," Annabel said.

When David's parents came in, Annabel was still clutching her knees with her hands. "I'll leave so you can all talk," she said.

"If it's okay with your father, we don't mind if you stay," Mrs. Floyd said. "Do you know what happened?"

After Danny and Mr. Bell positioned themselves on two chairs, letting the women sit on the sofa, Annabel told them what had occurred. After she finished, Tara closed her eyes for a prolonged pause.

"Dr. Tilson," she said, "the ER doctor explained some things to us but wanted us to talk to you. Please tell us what's happened to our son. First of all, I can't believe he's in a coma if all he did was get smacked by a knee. This can't be right."

"I don't understand any of it," Floyd chimed in. "Is there some kind of precedence in what's happened?"

Another knock came at the door and Danny stepped out.

"Dr. Tilson, CT results are back on David Bell," the X-ray technician said.

Danny poked his head back in. "I'll be back in a few minutes," he said. "This is the most comfortable place to wait."

It took more time than a few minutes but Danny caught up with David's condition and called the OR for them to hold up his next case for the time being. In the interim, he'd grabbed a cup of coffee. He needed the hot caffeine to give him a boost on this terrible morning.

He walked slowly back to the small room. When he stepped in, Tara, Floyd and Annabel looked at him with anticipation, as if they'd held their breath since he had left. At least it appeared that Annabel had stopped crying.

"Your son is the same," Danny said, unbuttoning his lab coat. "He's being transferred to the ICU. You'll be able to see him there later. In the meantime, I can tell you my theory, my diagnosis, of what's happened. After our previous discussion about concussions, I think you'll be able to follow what I'm saying."

"Please … do," Tara stuttered.

"If this were nineteen-eighty, I would not be able to give you such clear information. After that, we gained insight into David's type of condition. It began with the death of two football players who received seemingly minor blows to the head after they both received previous first blows. And now our specialty has reported around two dozen cases like those – mostly male adolescents or young adults – who were involved with boxing, football and ice hockey accidents."

"But basketball?" Floyd questioned, shrugging his shoulders more than usual.

"The pathophysiology is the same," Danny said. "Just like with a concussion. What happened was that David had a blow to the head before recovery from a previous blow to the head. The athlete's second blow can be minor but it can jerk his or her head and indirectly impart accelerative forces to the brain."

"This second-impact syndrome is an uncontrollable increase in intracranial pressure due to diffuse brain swelling," Danny sadly added.

Tara's eyes looked blank as the Bell's couldn't ignore Danny's dire words.

"The physiology of intracranial pressure is simple, Mrs. Bell," Danny continued. "Think of the skull as a closed space containing three things: brain tissue, blood in blood vessels, and cerebrospinal fluid. Since it is a closed space, if one component increases too much, it puts pressure on the other components. If the tissues swell, it will compromise the blood flow coming to the brain which in turn can't give the brain enough oxygen. All three components need to exist with a healthy balance."

"It's making more sense," Tara said.

"And in more difficult terms, there is something called autoregulation of the brain's blood supply. In this secondary impact scenario, it is lost, causing vascular engorgement in the cranium. The increased intracranial pressure is difficult, if not impossible, to control."

Danny scanned each of their faces. "This potential condition should be a main concern for coaches and doctors who must make return-to-play decisions in players after a head injury. It's why I was going to see David this week for re-evaluation."

"Dad, what did you call it again?"

"A secondary impact," Danny said.

"You can't operate?" Annabel asked.

"No, I would do that if it were something like the hematomas we discussed a few days ago. Surgical evacuation in those scenarios would relieve the pressure and be therapeutic."

"You can't do anything?" Tara asked.

"There are measures we can take. They are being implemented as we speak."

"I don't know if I should ask," Floyd said. "I don't know if I want to hear the answer. What are David's chances of getting better?"

Danny flinched. "Not good."

"Tell us," Tara said. "We are parents who can handle the blunt truth. We would rather hear it and expect the true possibilities than be given scenarios meant to camouflage what will most likely occur."

"Morbidity is nearly one-hundred percent and mortality under the circumstances is a fifty-percent chance."

Danny glanced at his watch as he walked down the hallway. The OR had sent for his next patient but it would take a while before he could see him in the pre-op area so he still had a few minutes. Pausing his hand on the doctor's lounge doorknob, he knew he had to grab lunch. But perhaps what he needed more was sustenance of a different kind.

He turned around and went far down the hallway past the nurse's lounge, waiting rooms, and offices to the room at the very end. Staring at the brass sign for 'Chapel' on the wall, he realized he had never gone in. Interestingly enough, he thought, the door was a lighter wood color than any he'd seen in the hospital. Was it meant to be a subtlety? As if for enlightenment upon opening the door?

It may be a stupid thought, he realized, but that was okay. If this partitioned part of the entire hospital building renders comfort and strength, then they can color it in sunshine.

Inside, the space was no bigger than a patient's room. The ten rows had an aisle in the middle to a step-up with a podium and a clothed, elongated table. He slid into the front row and knelt down. The isolated, sparse chapel was a far cry from his regular church where he brought Julia … or any church for that matter. What a treasure.

Yesterday and today, he thought, have been harsh on Casey and David; Annabel as well. He couldn't think of a reason why they deserved what happened to them. But bad things don't need a reason, he knew. It's how to deal with life's blows that is important.

He prayed: God, please allow Casey to heal and make use of his hands like always. They are needed to heal others. And David … his fate is in your hands and my medical care. Please don't allow him to die. The young man and I can't see to his recovery all alone. We need your help. I'd be indebted.

Danny sat on the pew, rested his forehead on his fingers, and closed his eyes. He sighed to think that bad luck comes in waves. What was it about airplane crashes? They come in threes as well as many other disasters. He shuddered.

The Tilsons had just had two nasty events. That's all, he prayed again … please let no more bad events strike this family.

Chapter 7

Ever since Sara learned about her pregnancy, she'd been more cautious about eating a nutritious diet and avoiding over-the-counter drugs that could be harmful to her baby. She also took a long walk with Dakota every day after arriving home from work. Getting lots of fresh air and vitamin D from sunlight was good for her and her unborn child, she thought, and this pregnancy was not like the three she'd had years ago. Being wiser in her ways, and more appreciative of this surprise child, she was doing everything possible to deliver a normal and healthy baby.

Dakota waited in anticipation for Sara to get home every afternoon and, after hearing her car pull in, he'd tug his leash off the door handle to present it to her. He knew this was a tethered walk versus a free run in the Tilson's large yard.

However, Sara always used the bathroom first because the urge to pee had increased, just like the morning sickness had reared its ugly head and given her queasy hours in the classroom before noon. She also had to be careful about certain smells. The coffee in the teacher's lounge had an overwhelming aroma that she now despised but had found wonderful before. Despite the inconveniences of the pregnancy, she walked around most times with a big grin as if she knew the ultimate answer to the fountain of youth.

But this Monday proved to be different from the others. Dakota would have to wait until after her obstetrician's appointment. Her last student left the classroom, she packed up her things, and started for the door.

"Good luck," one of the other teachers said.

"Thanks," she said, beaming.

"Are you going to let us know tomorrow if it's a boy or a girl?"

Sara stopped. "I sure will. But it doesn't matter at all. I have lots of experience with girls but a boy would be nice. I'll have a new learning curve," she said.

Sara glanced around the waiting room in the obstetrician's office after she filled out more paperwork than during her last visit. The lounge was full of working women further along in their pregnancies than she was. One of them moaned to get past her belly trying to tie a shoe and another sprawled on a two-seater couch; Sara had not seen this many pregnant women in years.

Finally the door to the back opened. "Mrs. Tilson?"

Sara got up and followed the nurse.

"You can undress and slip into this gown," the assistant said once they stepped into an exam room.

Sara changed and soon the doctor rapped on the door and entered. Dr. Carr was a big brunette with a small smile. "How are you feeling, Mrs. Tilson?"

"I'm feeling like I'm pregnant," Sara replied. "Actually, I've probably had less nausea in the last two days than the previous week."

The doctor skimmed her chart. "Well, I see you decided against having an amniocentesis. We won't have to set that up then. But let's go ahead today and get your first ultrasound. You are over six weeks so your baby's vital organs are in place and will continue to develop, and he or she already has a four-chambered heart."

Sara smiled. "My husband said the heart rate of an infant is very fast. Not like ours."

"That's true. About 160 beats a minute. Ask your husband all about the difference between an adult heart and an infant's heart. The anatomy and physiology of it is fascinating." She grabbed her stethoscope and listened to Sara's lungs and heart, then asked more questions.

"Okay," the doctor said when she was satisfied. "I'm sending you across the hallway to our ultrasound tech. She'll do your scan. Off you go."

Sara scooted off the table, held her gown tight and went to the other room.

"Ma'am, come on over and lie down," the tech said. "I'm Susan and I'll be doing your ultrasound."

Sara stepped over and, with extra pillows, got comfortable on the hard table. The tech adjusted the machine, dimmed the lights and then squeezed ultrasound gel on her lower abdomen. Sara flinched.

"Sorry," said the tech. "I know it's a bit cold but we do need a conductive medium."

"It's worth it. Will I see arms and legs and eyes yet?"

"Appendages won't be fully formed, just small. But you'll love seeing the dark spots of the eyes and nostrils and the tiny depressions of the ears."

Susan dabbed the transducer into the gel and began moving it around. She looked back at the screen and continued making circles on Sara's stomach.

Sara watched the black and white image on the monitor. She could make out a sac and what she believed was the baby's head and curled body but that was her unskilled assessment. Her pulse sped up. "That's my baby there, isn't it?" she asked.

"Mmm-hmmm."

The tech continued fiddling with some knobs and looked back and forth between the transducer and the machine. Sara hoped she was taking pictures.

Susan placed the transducer on a little shelf alongside the screen. "I'll be right back," she said.

Sara watched her leave with dismay as she didn't think Susan behaved very professionally to leave a patient on the table in the middle of the procedure. The seconds stretched into minutes and the room took on an eerie quality: cold, still and silent. Finally, the door opened and Susan and Dr. Carr walked in.

They didn't say a word as Susan again began moving the transducer around on Sara's belly and they both stared at the image on the screen. Sara felt a growing concern and her heart ticked louder, the sound reverberating against her eardrums.

Dr. Carr took off her glasses and leaned alongside the table. She switched her gaze directly to Sara.

"I'm sorry, Mrs. Tilson, but your baby has no movement. And there's no heartbeat."

Before Danny left the hospital for the day, he made late rounds on his group's patients. It was already 6:00 p.m. and he had saved David for last. Perhaps he'd find that the CT and other tests had all been wrong and he'd see the young man signaling to unhook him from the ventilator.

But that's not what he found.

Annabel sat on a chair, her head and arms resting on David's mattress; some of the therapeutic treatments that Danny had ordered for his brain edema pulsed through the IV attached to his limp arm.

"Annabel," he said softly.

Like a rag doll, she raised her head up and looked sideways at her father. Her dry eyes looked as if they'd expended all the tears she was capable of and her complexion had turned sallow.

"I couldn't go to any classes this afternoon, Dad. I had to come back."

"I can imagine … it would have been difficult to concentrate."

"I really can't believe this. I keep thinking that none of this happened and it's all a figment of my imagination."

Danny stood next to her and touched her shoulder.

"I mean, it wasn't as if he got tackled by a swarm of big football players."

As he thought of how to console her, the IV pump made a tiny bleep every few seconds. David lay motionless with no change in his condition so Danny knew he shouldn't offer her any hope right now.

Annabel slowly got up and pushed the chair back to the wall. "You didn't make it clear enough," she said curtly.

"What are you talking about?"

"You weren't emphatic enough! You should have told him not to lift a finger. You should have told him he was grounded to do anything, even hold a basketball."

Danny reeled from the accusation … from his daughter, no less. He opened his mouth, ready to start defending himself. But as Annabel made her way to the doorway, he realized it would be pointless. She would believe the way she construed it, especially now during the denial and anger phases of what happened and also when there was someone to lay blame on.

But her own father? This was hard to take.

And now that she had planted the seed into his thoughts, had he really been strict enough? Had he done his best to make David realize the importance of his post-concussion orders after his first fall on the basketball court?

Getting out of his Lexus at home, Danny wondered which entrance to go into first. Sara could be with Casey and Mary upstairs; he could check on his friend and his finger if he went in the main entrance. Most importantly, however, he wanted to see the ultrasound pictures that Sara would have from her appointment.

He gambled that the babysitter would have left and that Sara, Nancy, Julia and Dakota were downstairs. He opened the door as his rambunctious dog trotted towards him.

Danny jostled with Dakota down the hallway until he found Nancy and Julia hunched over in the big room eating ice cream.

"Hi, girls. That sure looks good."

"Hi, Dad," Nancy said.

He sat on the coffee table and rubbed Julia's head.

"How was your day?" he asked Nancy.

"Good. Do you want to put Julia to bed soon? I still have homework to do."

"Sure. Is your Mom around? She went to the doctor today."

"She's in the bedroom. She's kind of quiet and didn't even take Dakota for a long walk when she came home."

"I'll go say hello and then I'll put Julia down and see how your Uncle Casey is doing with his finger."

"That's really terrible what happened. He's acting like it's no big deal."

"He's a trouper." Danny frowned as he felt he was somewhat responsible for Casey's accident, too.

"Did you talk to your sister today?" Danny asked.

"No, should I have?"

"David is in the hospital. He had another head injury this morning and it's serious."

Nancy held her spoon in midair and then lowered it back into her bowl. "I'll call her. She doesn't have to talk to me if she doesn't want to. That's pretty terrible."

"It is. And she's taking it hard." Danny looked towards the bedroom door. "I better go see your Mom and see how things went for her this afternoon. But first …" He smiled at Julia, picked her up and twirled her in the air. She giggled as he put her back down. "You're almost getting too big for that, pretty girl."

Danny walked away towards the bedroom and, with each step, he broadened his smile. He had to greet Sara and her news with enthusiasm as her pregnancy was a beacon of light during a string of misfortune.

"Sara?" Danny peered into the dark bedroom. Although he couldn't see her face, she had the covers wrapped around her and she didn't stir. It's early to go to bed, he thought, and it was unlike her. He wondered if she was truly asleep … perhaps she was having an evening episode of nausea.

He quietly went alongside her pillow and crouched down.

"Sara?" he said softly as her eyes opened. "What's the matter?" he asked, gently moving a strand of hair away from her cheek.

She took a deep breath, the bedspread rising and falling with her effort.

"Our baby didn't make it."

Danny's breath froze. His heart stopped; he wasn't sure when it started to beat again, or if it did. Did she really say and mean what he just heard? As the silence continued and he grappled with the truth, he realized this is where a doctor would normally tell a patient the usual rhetoric under the circumstances. They would tell the patient that the fetus's demise was for a good reason: it may have been malformed; it probably had a genetic problem and its death was necessary; and the patient could always have another.

But he didn't verbalize any of that. Their 'fetus' would have gone on to be another child and member of the Tilson family. To love and to be loved by them all. Their unique baby could not be replaced by any other and it deserved their mourning.

He slipped off his shoes, pulled back the covers and slipped into bed. He held Sara for what seemed like an eternity until she fell fast asleep.

The chocolate ice cream must have given Julia extra energy so Danny read her two books before her arms and legs stopped squirming. He finally kissed her and left her to fall asleep. He ambled up the cellar stairs, knocked on the upstairs door, and cracked it open.

"Hey," Casey said from the couch while turning the television volume to mute. "Come on in."

Danny unbuttoned his top shirt button and went around to the front of the couch where he found Mary lying down, her head on her husband's lap.

"I don't mean to disturb you two so late," he said.

"You look tired," Casey said, "but you also look like you've lost your best friend."

"I haven't lost him but I did come to check on him," Danny said while sitting across from them.

Mary turned sideways, adjusting her robe over her hips, and faced her brother. "He has a hand surgeon's appointment in a week," she said, "and then they'll decide when he can go back to work."

Casey stroked Mary's thick red hair. "I talked with Mark again and he's worked out a plan. The new medic who will be replacing him starts tomorrow in my place. When I go back, Mark is going to take the opportunity to leave and the new person will work with me. Mark will enjoy the break before med school. He said he'll train his replacement so that whoever it is can drive me crazy."

Danny nodded.

"You're not laughing," Casey said. "That's not like you."

"After you were discharged today … well, you weren't the only casualty."

Casey squinted his eyes as Dakota came from the stairwell and sat in front of Mary.

"David decided to play ball with some buddies and had a second blow to the head. He's in the ICU in a coma."

"Oh, no," Mary said, raising up on an elbow.

Casey swallowed hard and shook his head. "Why did he go against your orders?"

"I don't' have a clue. Maybe peer pressure."

"And Annabel?" Mary asked.

"Practically in shock. She's even placing some blame on me."

"She'll see clearly in a few days," Mary said, rubbing Dakota's neck. "Give her time."

"We're all fond of David," Casey said. "This is terrible news."

"That's not all. There's something else, too."

"Uh-oh." Mary bent her knees and sat up. "What else went wrong? We were wondering why Sara didn't come upstairs to see us after she came home today. We were expecting to see ultrasound pictures. Is everything okay?"

"No. She didn't go into details, but there must have been no signs of life. The ultrasound news must have been like handing her a death certificate; it had to be awful."

"Oh, Danny. I'm so sorry."

"Sorry to hear it," Casey said. Shielding his eyes, he stroked his eyebrows with his good hand. "You two must be disappointed. We are, too."

"What happens now?" Mary asked. "I don't understand."

"It means that she just happened to have the ultrasound within this awful timeframe. In the next few days, she would have aborted. She's probably scheduled for a D&C."

"It could have been worse," Mary said. "If you had both gotten pictures last week with a living fetus, it would have been sadder had she aborted in the next few days."

Danny squinted his eyes and bowed his head.

"But in any case," she asked, "why is the man upstairs you've been talking to so annoyed with the Tilson family? Even after you brought God back into your life?"

"I wish I knew," Danny responded. "But I'll still keep my faith. Prayer can't hurt a thing."

Casey nodded. "Put in an extra prayer for me. I'm going to talk to your attorney about this." He wiggled his bandaged finger.

"Mark already knows about Rachel," Danny said, "so it shouldn't take long. But he'll tell you that legal proceedings involving morally-bankrupt people are never easy."

Chapter 8

Danny woke extra early, hoping to see David in the hospital before going to the office.

But he still didn't know what Sara's plans were for the day and he wanted to give her the support she may need after yesterday's tragedy. He contemplated calling Bruce Garner, the previous head of the group, to fill in for his appointments. Bruce worked there a few hours each week, so he may be willing to help Danny out.

As he pulled on a pair of trousers, Sara stirred. He zipped up and sat on the edge of the bed as she rubbed her eyes.

"Can you bring me into the hospital this morning with you?" she asked. "My obstetrician wants to fit me into her schedule since I need a D&C and it's a quick procedure. I can't eat or drink before going in."

"Yes. We'll go together. I'll stay with you as much as I can. I'm going to call Bruce and ask him to fill in the entire day for me."

"I have to call school, too," she said, sitting up.

Putting his arm around her back, Danny pulled her in close. "I'm sorry," he said. "I was looking forward to another child, too."

"I know you were. We both were."

When Danny called Bruce, he was happy to help out. Sara contacted the principal to request a sick day and then they both headed to the hospital. By mid-morning, Sara donned a surgical gown and was soon groggy with sedation. Danny kissed her good-bye as they wheeled her back to the OR and then he went upstairs to the ICU to check on David.

Danny brought the chart inside the room where the respiratory therapist was fine-tuning ventilator settings. "The morning's blood gas is back, Dr. Tilson," he said, handing him the sheet.

"Thank you," Danny said as he scanned the lab values. "You can keep the present settings. His CO2 is as low as I want it."

After looking at all the nurses' notes from overnight, Danny scrutinized every aspect of David's care. The youth's lab values were decent and the early morning's CT scan on the computer looked no worse than the day before. David's physique was still robust, his arms nicely toned, and his legs muscular from playing sports. He felt rather sad because he knew the longer David stayed bedridden in his present condition, the more likely he would look more aged and sickly.

When Danny finished his exam, he stood against the sink and called Annabel on her cell phone. At least he hadn't found her in David's room; perhaps she'd gone back to class today. There was no answer so he left her a message … the second one of the morning.

"Sara did fine and she's ready to go home," a nurse told Danny when she exited the recovery room. He followed her back where he found Sara failing miserably at getting dressed behind the curtain.

"Let me help you," he said. "You're probably still groggy." She sat in a plastic chair; Danny crouched down, gathered her pants at her ankles and slipped them up. She held onto him as he pulled them over her high-cut underwear. "Let's go home," he whispered in her ear.

A volunteer wheeled Sara to the lobby entrance and Danny helped her into the car. The clouds hung like soggy cotton balls and a misty rain washed the car as they pulled away from the front door.

After they rode in silence for half the trip, Danny finally spoke. "Are you okay?"

Extending her left arm, she looked at him. "I didn't tell you but I had names picked out."

"Would you like to tell me what they were?"

She shrugged her shoulders. "It doesn't matter now. I think I'll keep them to myself."

"Okay."

"By the way," Danny said, "Mary and Casey give you their love and condolences; they said for you to come home to them. Mary can keep her eye on you this afternoon. I'd like to go with Casey to see Mark Cunningham about his accident."

"I couldn't ask for a better sister-in-law, could I?"

"Maybe since we're not married, she's not technically your sister-in-law but we could change that."

"I do consider her as good as a sister-in-law. She was before and she still is. That's a sneaky way for you to try and have us remarry." She gave him a small smile.

Danny took her left hand and gave it a squeeze. "I'm sorry. You know I love you, don't you?"

"I think so," she said, pressing back. "Yes. I'm sure of it." Her smile grew wider. "And yes, let's visit with Mary and Casey when we get home," she added.

Danny left Dakota and Julia downstairs with the babysitter while Sara rested on the upstairs couch. To be close to her, Mary sat on the floor and quietly sketched on a canvas propped against the coffee table.

By mid-afternoon, Danny and Casey left for Mark Cunningham's office. The rain had let up but the roads were still wet. They dodged a puddle of water outside of Mark's building and went upstairs.

As usual in his attorney's waiting room, Danny glanced at his watch every five minutes. "It's better to meet Mark over a meal," Danny said. "He shows up on time."

"In all these years," Casey said, "I don't think I've ever met your attorney except in a restaurant as he left."

"And you've never accompanied me to any of my voluminous court appearances. From a malpractice case, to divorce proceedings, to child support issues, to being accused of going against visitation rules and keeping Julia, to who knows what else. I've put Mark's kids through college."

Casey ran his hand over his crew cut and laughed. "And this is the first time I'm ever seeing a lawyer. I guess the more powerful you are, the bigger target you make so that's why you need to keep an attorney employed."

The door opened and a woman hurried through the room, the man behind her trying to keep up. "I don't know why you need a pre-nup anyway," she said.

"A guy can't be too careful these days," he said as they exited.

Danny laughed. "They're starting off on a slippery slide."

"Well, there you go," Casey said. "They're not even married yet, he hasn't had an affair yet like you, and they already have a lawyer." He poked Danny in the arm.

"Exactly. Mark gets business no matter what. I bet the bad economy didn't even put a dent in his cash flow."

"It probably made it better," Casey said.

"You can go in now," the receptionist said, looking over the counter.

With quick baby steps, Mark came around his desk when they entered his office. Over sixty years old, his full head of hair was now showing its first sprinkling of gray.

"Any friend of Danny's is a client of mine," Mark said, taking Casey's outstretched hand. "I hear you're a paramedic and the brother-in-law."

Casey nodded as Mark pointed to the two leather chairs.

"I was just telling Casey how busy you are," Danny said.

"No different than the both of you. We're all in the business of putting people's lives back together, no matter how you look at it. And the worse they've fallen, the bigger our jobs."

"But Mark," Danny said, "most of my patients have a definitive end point in their care and I don't see them again. Divorce court and custody issues, depending on the nastiness of one of the parties, can go until a child turns eighteen or twenty-one. If a child is two when the parent's divorce, it can be upwards to eighteen years that one of them will be paying your bills."

Mark smiled as he lowered into his chair. "You're correct. And to be candid about it, most people don't know that when they file for divorce. Not only that, but look at your situation. Rachel is a noose around your neck and you never exchanged vows. Like I said a long time ago, men should keep their dicks in their pants and not be putting them where they don't belong."

"But never mind," Mark added. "You can always go to law school if you want. I'll write either of you a letter of recommendation."

Danny laughed. "That's generous of you but I think I'll stick with a surgical drill."

"Suit yourself. Now, I understand you need my services," Mark said, looking at Casey.

Casey raised his bandaged left hand. "I lost part of a finger under a hood of a car. The driver who started the car and caused this showed no empathy. It was but an inconvenient moment in her charade of a life. I'd like to recover my medical bills."

"I'm glad to hear it wasn't your fault." He slipped a legal pad in front of him. "Let me get a few basics. What's your full name?"

"Casey Hamilton."

"And what's the finger-chopper-offer's name, the respondent?"

"Rachel Hendersen."

Mark sat tall. "Oh. I take that back. It was your fault. Any man who sticks one of their appendages into anything of hers is asking for trouble."

Casey frowned and Danny put his hands over his eyes.

"You never told me," Casey said when they left Mark's office, "what an interesting character your lawyer is."

"But his humor and bluntness can be painful."

"He says what others dare not say, like an echo of your subconscious."

They both took the staircase and, at the bottom, Casey turned on his cell phone and listened to his voicemail while they walked to the car.

"That's too bad," Casey said after deleting the message. "It was my partner. I won't see him before he leaves. He wanted to tell me that my new partner's name is Tony Dixon and everyone is looking forward to my return."

"That means the health-care females who have anything to do with you."

Casey shrugged his shoulders.

"Have you ever noticed," Danny asked, "that there is just a fraction of a percent of men who reach fifty and age to be more handsome than they previously were?"

"Like a few movie stars."

"Well, ask Mary or Sara and they'll tell you that that's what's going to happen to you."

Rachel left the medical center's children's hospital at 4:00 p.m. When she got to her Mazda, the first thing she did inside the car was to pull out the small calendar in her purse and crossed off the day's eight hours of community service as sentenced by the judge. It was the most pleasure she had derived from this Saturday so far.

After all, she thought, I'm not a fan of helping disabled kids reach out for their toys in the playroom or assist the physical therapists in teaching those with genetic disorders how to walk or wipe slobber off of youngsters with mental problems. Her skills were as an operating room tech making a salary in an outpatient surgical center and this mandate they gave her was just a bunch of b.s.

Yet she'd grin and bear it for three months as it beat going to trial for the offenses she'd been charged with. Phil Beckett had done a good job getting that prosecutor off her back but she had done as good a job in getting the judge to see her point of view so that he had gone soft on her.

She put on her sunglasses and drove away from the medical complex, the sun warming the inside of her car. Tomorrow's visitation with Julia was all set except for the last and most important detail. She wasn't happy about doing it because she'd already gotten rid of one dog – Dakota - in the past few years. However, now the importance of getting another was paramount.

Not very far from her apartment complex was the county shelter. Dogs get recycled, she thought, no sense in finding an expensive purebred this time. If she got a dog that had an unstable history already, the happier it'll be just to sit in her apartment during her long working days; it will be there mainly to enamor Julia anyway.

Rachel pulled into the small parking area in front of the building. For a community shelter, it wasn't too shabby. Some rich person had probably screwed their bratty kids, she thought, and dumped their trust money inheritance right into the pet facility.

That's the kind of thing that she should do. Find some terminally-ill guy dreaming of a woman – one who stupidly believes she would want to help him into his chair and think he's magnificent. She would be as good a charity for some man's will as any.

All she did was open the front door but it created a cacophony of barking in the room behind the front lobby.

"Hi," a booted man said as he restocked pamphlets on a table. "We're closing in an hour. Are you here to look at cats or dogs? Or donate supplies?"

"I'd like to see your dogs. If you have something that a cat didn't just drag in here, I want to surprise my little girl tomorrow."

"A dog's for life, though." He gave her a questioning look.

"Sure. I know that." She tapped her foot.

"Come on then. Happy to oblige." He led her to the back; kennels lined the right and left walls, twelve in all. Some had two dogs to a pen.

"Looks pretty clean in here, especially for me dropping in unannounced."

"We try. Walk around. I'd bet most of these dogs would make a fine pet."

"I don't want anything too big. My daughter is small and I live in an apartment." She walked down the right side. Pitt bulls, terriers, big dog retriever types, and a mixed poodle either ignored her or barked. Halfway through the other side, she stopped.

With pleading eyes, a white, brown and black dog wagged its tail at her. "Looks like a beagle," she said.

"It may even be a purebred. She's a beauty. Gives us no trouble. We've only had her three days."

"Where from?"

"Showed up on a man's farm without a collar. He had enough pets to take care of."

Rachel stooped down and put her hand through the bars.

"She's just short of a year old. Almost fully grown at eighteen pounds. The breed is easygoing and she'll make a nice family addition. She's fixed, too."

Rachel stood up; the dog sat down but didn't take her eyes off of her.

"All right. Good. She may be the perfect thing."

"You mean dog."

After the two adults took care of the paperwork, the wide-eyed little dog took a car ride home to Rachel's apartment.

Chapter 9

Danny helped Julia put on leggings and a cotton dress while Dakota laid nearby, his head between his paws. "Are you ignoring Dakota these days?" Danny asked.

Julia grimaced and turned away from the dog.

"Dakota loves you. I think he misses being your good buddy."

The dog pounced up and nuzzled his head into both of them.

"See?" Danny said.

As she started walking away from Danny, Julia extended her elbow into Dakota.

"Please don't push Dakota away like that when he's being good." Danny patted the dog on his head and followed his daughter. "Let's go to church now and then you'll see your mom."

"I don't want to go to church," she mumbled.

"That's where we're going, sweetheart." Outside the bedroom, Danny handed her a jacket and then carried her to the car.

With such a terrible week, Danny was going to Sunday mass no matter what. Once there, he lit a votive candle for David Bell. When he finished, he put his arm around Julia; she'd been fidgeting the whole time.

"Daddy, I want to light that one and that one," she pointed. "Mommy doesn't just light one candle."

"I thought you two didn't go to church," he said questioningly.

Julia clammed shut and Danny shook his head. Maybe that's another reason to call this age the 'terrible twos,' he thought; they're impossible to figure out. He added three people to his prayers: Sara, Annabel, and Julia.

Danny realized Sara had gone through mourning for her unborn baby and, although she'd gone back to work by the end of the week, she was still depressed.

And then there was the issue with Annabel. He had left several messages for her but she was ignoring his calls. It seemed like she wanted him to feel guilt over David. But he refused to doubt his innocent role in her boyfriend's injury and Danny would not allow his teenage daughter to convict him otherwise.

Next came Julia. Although Rachel was her mother, she was still a Tilson and he didn't like her newfound attitude of shunning the family.

Clasping his hands together in prayer, Danny whispered, "I'm sorry. I have a plate full. But all my prayers are for others. He smiled; he was praying like he did when he was a little kid. Interesting, he thought. He guessed it was common for human beings to go back to their roots.

Rachel lingered outside in her carport waiting for Danny to drop off Julia for visitation. She wanted to sweep her daughter away from him without much of a discussion, especially anything to do with her private life in case he asked.

She was glad Danny knew nothing about the charges that had been brought against her after Leo Ramsey's conviction and the grand jury case, or that she was 'serving time' with community service. It had been easy to keep it all quiet. Lucky for her, it all stemmed from Knoxville and not Nashville. If she implemented her plan, she couldn't afford for Danny to get wind of it or he would use any or all of it against her.

The Lexus pulled down the street and Danny got out. He unstrapped Julia and she immediately scrambled out of the car. "I think she's looking forward to the visit," he said as he approached Rachel. "You look tired," he added, noticing her more carefully. "It's not like you."

"You'd look tired, too, if you had as many problems as I do."

Danny bit his lip. What did she know about his problems anyway?

"See you later, sweetheart," he said as Julia gave Rachel a hug. Danny left as mother and daughter headed towards the apartment.

"I have a huge surprise for you," Rachel said when Danny was gone. "I found the most fun four-legged playmate for you ever!"

Julia's eyes grew wide as saucers, and she jumped up and down as Rachel opened the door. The beagle Rachel had bought ran across the room to both of them.

Julia giggled with delight as the dog excitedly wagged its tail and curiously sniffed her shoes.

"It's a girl dog," Rachel said, "and since she's yours, you should give her a name."

"She's mine?" Julia asked in near disbelief.

"All yours."

The dog's attention went to the youngster's face and quickly darted out her tongue, swiping Julia's chin.

After a stream of giggling, Julia wrapped her arms around the dog's neck and squeezed. "She's little like me."

"And she's all potty-trained just like you, too. You both are big girls. So … what would you like to name her?"

"Mommy, she's like Charlie Brown's dog. Can I name her Snoopy?"

"Ask your dog."

"Snoopy?" she said, looking into the dog's alert eyes. In a moment, the dog licked her face again.

"I think you made an excellent choice," Rachel said. "She likes that. I think Snoopy is going to be your own lovable pal for a long time."

"I hope today is a better Monday than last week's," Danny said as he joined Casey in the parking lot. They had both left for work at the same time, Casey earlier than normal to meet his new partner and hopefully have a cup of coffee with him.

"I'm lucky I was cleared by the surgeon so soon," Casey said, "and I'm happy to get back." He looked at his newest bandage, a thin wrap with a small strip of Velcro meant only as protection until another hand surgeon's visit as the end of his finger had healed nicely so far.

"And I hope that my new partner is as easy to get along with as Mark," Casey added.

"Since you're easygoing," Danny said, "you shouldn't have any problem."

The day was warming up quickly and, as Casey unzipped his leather jacket, they neared the rear entrance. The back door of his ambulance was open and someone wearing a paramedic's uniform was hunched over a clipboard looking inside.

"You must be Tony," Casey said.

"Yes, I surely am," said Mark's replacement with an unmistakable southern drawl.

"Oh," Casey said when the person straightened up and was unmistakably female. "You must be a Tony with an 'i.'"

"Yes, Toni with an 'i.'" She shook his hand firmly.

"Nice to meet you. I'm Casey and this is Dr. Tilson, one of the neurosurgeons here."

Danny smiled. "Good luck with your new job. You'll be working with one of the finest."

She took her foot down off the back bumper and Danny figured her to be a full-figured size ten, maybe thirty-two years old. She wore a clip in her hair, stylish and unique, but her primary asset was perfect white and straight teeth; a smile she wasn't shy to display as she shook his hand.

"I better get going," Danny said, "if I want to get a cup of coffee on the run."

"We'll be quick behind ya," Toni said. "Can't work with Mr. Casey until I've downed some myself."

Danny walked through the double doors, wondering what his best friend was thinking about his new partner.

Danny admitted it to himself: He'd been giving David Bell preferential treatment. Maybe not totally preferential, but certainly more attentive time. He had even skipped one night he was supposed to go to the gym with Casey and, instead, spent an hour in the ICU scrutinizing every detail of David's care. When he went home, he poured extra time into researching new neurosurgery and neurology information on comatose traumatic brain-injured patients.

He stopped in the ER coffee room after leaving Casey and his new partner, displaced the coffeepot, and let the dripping brew fall into a cup. As he took a sip, he remembered why he was addicted. It was, by far, a liquid drink better than Tennessee whiskey and the glory of it was you could drink it on the job.

No one was in the room so he leaned against the counter and thought about his next step with David. His patient was young and medically healthy except for the present circumstances but the time had come to consider full nutritional replacement for him; he could stay in a coma for a long time and his metabolic needs needed to be replaced.

Danny decided his first chore after seeing the young man was to start a central line or very large IV into a main vein where they could infuse TPN. The total parenteral nutrition could help ward off too much weight loss; if David lost even thirty-percent of his weight, statistics indicated his chances for mortality increased.

When he finished half his coffee, his pager beeped; he returned the call to the ICU from the main ER desk.

"Dr. Tilson, this is Charlotte, taking care of David Bell. His eyes opened within the last half hour and he's responding to commands."

"What?" he asked in amazement.

"David Bell is aware of his surroundings."

He could hardly believe it. David would defy all odds if it were true.

"I'm on my way," Danny said.

After dumping out the remaining coffee, he hurried up the stairs. When he entered David's room, the ICU nurse was adjusting new tape to an IV on his arm and talking to him in a reassuring tone.

David's eyes were only slightly open as if he craved sleep. He looked at Charlotte, they gave each other a tiny smile, and she stepped to the side.

"David, it's Dr. Tilson." Danny put his hand into the youth's left palm. "Squeeze my hand."

David's fingers weakly enclosed Danny's and slightly pressed.

I'll be damned, Danny thought. He could swear this qualified as a medical miracle.

"Very nice," Danny said. At the bottom of the bed, he asked David to wiggle his toes. After checking out reflexes and being satisfied, Danny finally allowed himself to really smile.

"David," he said, leaning close, "I have to evaluate your condition slowly this morning but, perhaps in a day or two, we can take out that breathing tube. You have had a brain injury and you've been here more than a week. Bear with us, keep optimistic, and let's get you better."

With renewed vigor, Danny walked out and over to a private corner. He pulled out his cell phone and dialed Annabel. "Hi, honey," he said when he reached her voicemail. "I'm cautious, yet optimistic. David has opened his eyes. I know you are not talking to me but I just wanted you to know."

Next, Danny went to his patient's chart. He opened it up to the personal information and called David's parents. Mrs. Bell picked up and Danny gave her the same cautious update on her son's condition.

"Mrs. Bell, at the moment, David's waking up is extraordinary. It's the turnaround we've been waiting for so let's say a prayer he continues making progress."

The outpouring of warmth and gratitude from Tara Bell made Danny lower himself into a chair and savor every word. He listened as she expressed newfound hope like grabbing onto the last life jacket on a sinking ship.

After finishing all his work in the ICU, Danny strolled to the chapel. It was one thing to pray for help but a different thing all together to give thanks for prayers answered.

Before going home, Danny called ahead to ask everyone to dinner.

"Let's get last week's bad luck behind us," he told Sara. "I'll spring for anywhere you all would like to go."

After speaking with Sara, Nancy said she would stay home to mind Julia. His littlest girl was going on three years old but her 'terrible two's' were getting worse instead of better and it wouldn't be fun if she acted out during their dinner. Danny always tried to give her slack because she had been abused but, after coming home from Rachel's last night, she had been mean-spirited with Dakota and he didn't know what to make of her behavior.

At seven o'clock, Danny met Sara, Casey and Mary in the front entrance of a southern-style restaurant.

"Did you have a nice day?" he asked, taking Sara's hand.

"I actually did. It was a test day for my students and I've already started grading their papers."

"Glad to hear it. And glad this date worked at the last minute."

"And glad you both could make it," Danny said to Casey and Mary. A waiter signaled for them to follow and they asked for a window table.

After they ordered and a bottle of wine arrived, Casey made a toast. "To the two of you. We're sorry about your recent miscarriage. Don't worry. Since we're all growing older together, there will be lots of happy times ahead."

With water for Mary and wine for everyone else, they clinked glasses together. Sara put her elbow on the table and motioned with her hand. "I was miserable last week but I feel a lot better now. Support from you both has helped and, of course, you too, Danny."

Danny put his arm around her shoulder and squeezed. "That's the first time I've seen you smile since last week."

"So," Danny said. "I have big news. But Casey, you come first. How did the first day go with your new partner?"

"Yes," Mary chimed in. "You haven't mentioned it yet."

Casey leaned towards his wife, admiring her; she wore her hair loosely tied with a scarf and seemed to glow.

"You won't believe it," he said. "I've been paired with a confident and energetic woman. I think work has just gotten more interesting."

"A woman?" Mary asked, putting her glass down.

"Toni with an 'i,'" Danny responded.

"You met her?" Sara asked as both women looked at him.

"I did."

"All right," Sara said to Casey. "You and your partner are synonymous to cops in a patrol car. You spend a lot of time together. So … what does she look like?" Sara glanced at Mary. She was asking the question for both of them.

Casey finished a sip of wine. "Do you all remember at all," he asked in a hushed tone, "what Marilyn Monroe looked like?"

Sara and Mary exchanged serious looks as Casey tapped his glass.

"She doesn't look like her at all."

"Oh, Casey Hamilton," Mary said, poking his arm.

"Don't worry, ladies. I love you two the most and no sassy paramedic can take your place. As long as she can pull her weight and do a better than average job, that's what's important."

"It's not like I was jealous or anything," Mary said. "I'd rather know the situation right now before I'm blindsided. Plus, it's time to make a toast for your future paramedic teamwork."

Chapter 10

"So how far along is Mark Cunningham with the litigation against Rachel?" Danny asked while a waiter placed étouffée down in front of his brother-in-law.

"We're in the paperwork stage," Casey said. "I'm gathering the medical bills for him."

"When and if you go to court, I'd like to go," Mary said. "It's bad enough Danny suffers with her all the time but now she's impacted the two of us. It's horrid … you losing most of your finger. Even if she didn't plan on doing it, I'd like to see an empathetic judge give her hell."

"Dear sister, don't get your hopes up," Danny said as he stirred together shrimp and grits.

"I agree with Mary," Sara said. "She deserves more than the broken face she got last year. Why don't you claim post-traumatic stress disorder from the trauma of the accident? You could be so afraid to put your hand anywhere that you can't do your job."

"And then you would have to take a permanent medical leave from being a paramedic and sue her for future wages," Mary said.

"My, my," Casey said, "how do you women come up with these schemes? But then what would I do?"

Sara shrugged. "Well, for one, you two can start having babies. Better late than sorry."

Grinning, Mary shot a glance her way.

"Oh … is that smile for a reason?" Sara asked.

Mary gave Sara and Danny a sheepish look. "We didn't want to tell you both yet."

"We felt so bad about your miscarriage, we just couldn't say anything," Casey chimed in.

"But we're the first to know?" Sara asked.

Mary nodded affirmatively and Danny put his fork down. He stretched his hands over to Mary and clasped hers in his.

"Congratulations, sis. Congratulations to the both of you."

Beaming, Sara waved her hand at Danny. "You're going to be an uncle and I'm as good as an aunt."

"Only if the upcoming months go well," Mary said. "As we know, a pregnancy doesn't necessarily mean it will go to term."

Danny still held his sister's hand. "It's going to go fine; I can feel it in my bones. If only … if only Mom and Dad were alive. They'd be thrilled."

Mary's eyes twinkled. "I could see them hoarding time with our baby so I wouldn't have enough time with it myself."

"They were something else with the girls when they were small," Danny said.

The waiter stopped at their table. "Satisfied with your food?"

Everyone nodded. "Yes," Danny said, "very nice."

"Good. Let me know if you need anything else," he said. When he stepped away, Mary went back to her salad and bourbon chicken.

"So, I have fantastic news from today," Danny said. "David Bell woke up from his coma."

"Didn't you say his chances were poor?" Sara asked with surprise.

"As bad as they get. But it's not like he's wide awake; he's had a major brain injury. His progress now will be so unpredictable, I have pins and needles just thinking about it."

"Nice work. But how did you turn his outcome around?"

"I treated him with all the usual tricks in the bag to decrease brain edema - hyperventilation, osmotic diuretic." Danny looked up. "Sorry, ladies, that's more detail than you need."

"That's okay," Mary said. "That's like when I tell you how I use certain techniques and mixture of colors on my canvases and you have no idea what I'm talking about. With all our fields, what matters to others is the end result, not the journey. Like David's parents, they won't know the skill or decision-making you used to cause their son to wake up. They just care that he has."

"This is true," Casey said.

"I agree," Sara said. "And besides David's parents, does Annabel even know this news since she's not talking to you?"

"I called her but she didn't pick up," he said, dabbing a piece of bread in the sauce. "I left a voicemail which is an impersonal way to tell her. I wish I knew what's going on in her mind."

Danny glanced at Sara. "Is she talking with you?"

"We talked over the weekend. She sounds despondent but I assured her David was receiving good care. All she said was, 'Yeah, the same care that got him in the ICU to begin with.'"

Danny grimaced.

"I'm sorry, Danny," Sara said. "Our daughter, or people in general, will perceive things from their own perspective and sometimes there is nothing you can do to make them see the light. It's like trying to drive through a brick wall."

"Was Julia polite with you tonight?" Danny asked Nancy when they got home.

Watching TV and eating potato chips, she looked over from the couch. "She was overbearing, Dad. I thought about dropping her off at your table in the restaurant."

"I'm sorry to hear that."

"When I put her to bed, she said she wanted to go home to her mother's. Did you know she has a new dog at Rachel's? Its name is Snoopy and she made a big deal that she named it."

Her parents exchanged glances. "No, I didn't know that," Danny said just as his cell phone rang.

"It's Annabel," he said and answered right away. With Sara following him, he walked into the bedroom.

"I got your message today," she said softly. "I'm just leaving the hospital. I've been sitting with him. I just wanted you to know."

"I bet you perked up his spirits."

"He shouldn't be where he is to start with," she said, annoyed. "But what do you think is going to happen to him?"

With just a slight shake of his head and a frown, Danny let Sara know that Annabel was still holding a grudge. "It's hard to say but I never expected him to come out of a coma this soon, if at all. Keep your fingers crossed or, better yet, say a prayer."

"I don't have a choice," she mumbled. "Tell mom I said hello. Bye."

When Danny hung up, he put his wallet and things on the dresser. "At least she's talking to me," he said.

"She's being hard on you and she better straighten out."

Danny sank next to her on the bed. Putting his hand across to her opposite shoulder, they both laid back. "Are you back on birth control?" he asked.

"I am."

"Good. I guess now we'll leave the baby-making to Mary and Casey."

"Yes. That may be for the best, although they're no youngsters anymore either."

They lay on their sides facing each other and entwined their legs. Sara moved closer and grasped Danny for an embrace; after they kissed, each article of clothing came off one at a time. Danny turned off the nightstand light and they burrowed under the covers.

"This is going to be the perfect ending to a long day," he said.

Sara brought her hand down to his thigh and then inched it over to his hardness. Their mouths joined again while Danny pulled her closer. In a few minutes, he whispered in her ear. "I'm so grateful for the day I met you."

By the time they fell asleep, he no longer thought about the possible problems Annabel's boyfriend would be facing.

As soon as Danny walked out of an exam room, Cheryl stopped him.

"Matthew's on line one," she said. "He has more good news about David Bell."

Handing Cheryl his last patient's chart, he hurried to his office and picked up as Matthew was in charge of hospital rounds that morning for all their patients. "Matthew," he said, "what's going on?"

"We extubated him a little while ago like you were hoping. So far, he's doing fine breathing on his own. He said to also thank you for helping him get rid of that breathing tube."

"Perfect, thanks. Please order arterial blood gases. I'll make evening rounds so I can see him myself."

As he hung up, Cheryl walked in. "Want some lunch when you quit concentrating on your daughter's boyfriend?"

"Glad you said that. Getting too close to any patient or treating David differently could cause me to lose my objectivity."

The parking lot closest to the ER as well as the entrance itself looked unusually quiet as Danny stepped onto the curb alongside Casey's ambulance. He'd gotten out of the office later than he wanted and walked briskly. With a gentle breeze in the air and fading sunlight, he wished he could stay outside longer before going into the ICU.

A waft of smoke blew out from behind the open door of the ambulance. As he came around, Toni sat on the bumper, cigarette in hand and Casey sat inside on the bench, writing on top of a clipboard.

"You both must be three-to-eleven," Danny said. "What? Nothing to do?"

"Hey, Dr. Tilson," Toni said. "Nothing official. Doesn't mean I'm not amusing your friend, though."

Casey looked up. "She may be a newbie partner but she has the lingo down."

"Did you know," she said to Danny, "that the beat for "Staying Alive" is the optimum speed for doing CPR?"

Danny laughed. "No, I didn't. But believe it or not - as a neurosurgeon - I can't remember the last time I had to do CPR. Probably as a resident and that was eons ago."

"Casey will soon learn I need CPR every day."

Danny shot a glance Casey's way.

"Yeah," she said, blowing out more smoke, "my CPR is how I function adequately. It stands for coffee, Pepsi and Redbull." She flicked her cigarette and ground it out with her shoe.

"We know about energy drinks," Danny said, wincing at her habit. "Especially ones that can get you into trouble."

"I'm happy to report I've never touched the stuff … nor the cigarette habit," Casey said.

"Wow," Danny said. "You two sure seem like seasoned partners already."

Toni glanced back at Casey and smiled. "Casey is such a cool partner; I can act like myself and speak my mind."

Danny raised his eyebrows. "I hope that's okay with him."

Casey reached over for a bottle of water. "She has her own way of doing and saying things. But she has passion for the job and that's what counts."

Toni shrugged her shoulders. "I already have it figured out. I love the job but I'll never let it weigh me down when I go home.

There's only so much we can do and, no matter how much that is, people will eventually die anyway."

"I guess what the three of us usually do is prolong life," Danny said.

"And as far as that goes, how is David doing?" Casey asked.

"Full of surprises," Danny said.

"We both know there's no such thing as a textbook case," Casey said.

Danny laughed. "At this point, maybe he's better than a textbook case."

"I've heard it said around here that you work miracles," Toni said, adjusting the clip in her hair.

"That's a tall order to fill," he said. "Nothing but preposterous rumors."

A call came through from the front radio and Casey scrambled between the two front seats. "Time to break up this party," he said.

"See you tomorrow," Danny said. "Bye, Toni. I'm off to the ICU. Have a good ambulance run."

"Thanks," Toni said. "We're off to another site where most bleeding stops no matter what we do ... for better or for worse."

Danny turned and went into the hospital thinking that Casey now shared eight-hour shifts with a polychromatic character.

Besides David's nurse, there were two more people in scrubs and a respiratory therapist in David's ICU room as Danny came alongside the glass window. That was not the patient-health care ratio he expected to see and a worried look crossed his face as he rounded the corner.

"Dr. Tilson, I was just going to call you," the head nurse in the ICU said. "Several of the staff have been busy with your patient who just had a terrible seizure."

Danny slipped between them to stand at the bedside. Practically lifeless and somnolent, David had an ashen color and his limbs looked spent and exhausted.

"I monitored his airway," the respiratory therapist said. "It remained patent the whole time."

Danny glanced at the caretakers. "You all did a marvelous job. How long has it been?"

"Only about five minutes," someone replied.

"David?" Danny said. The young man stirred but hardly let out a mumble in response.

Danny glanced at the monitor with David's arterial-line blood pressure readings and noticed they were higher than normal. He grimaced, knowing the ramifications of a young man having new-onset seizures. The event wasn't a total surprise as it was a possibility after a brain injury but, nevertheless, he had hoped David had been through enough.

Chapter 11

"There's one more thing, Dr. Tilson," the ICU nurse-in-charge said. "Just before David had the seizure, his parents showed up for a visit. We sent them to the waiting room."

"Please tell them I'll be out to talk to them as soon as possible."

As Danny wrote orders at the bedside, a tech rolled in the EEG machine. He attached the electrodes to David's scalp, connected the wires to the electrical box, and then the box to the EEG machine. After turning it on, Danny stood and watched as his patient's electrical activity traced across the paper in a series of squiggles. Not only had David's rhythm slowed after his head trauma but, as expected, it now exhibited more slowing due to the seizure.

When Danny finished, he wrote an order for a consult. Although he had spoken informally with his neurologist friend Penny Banks about his patient, it was time to officially call her in on the case. Sharp and thorough, she'd be able to concur or disagree with his further choice of seizure medication for David.

An evening news show droned in the background as Danny entered the lounge and sat at the Bell's table. Both parents rose but Danny signaled them to sit back down.

"Such good and bad news," Tara said. "First, David wakes up and gets off the breathing machine but now he's … he's had a seizure. I don't know if I can take the emotional roller coaster anymore."

Floyd Bell put his hand behind his wife's back and rubbed. "Dr. Tilson, tell us about the seizure and how he's doing."

"I arrived too late to see it myself. The staff did an excellent first-aid job and gave him the care and comfort needed. He's very drowsy but right now he has no recall of the event. That's not uncommon. His brain is recovering from the trauma of it."

David's parents exchanged soulful glances and Danny let them absorb what he had said. "Even though David's been on medication which would stifle the occurrence of a seizure, chances are that he'll have more. We can count on their unpredictability. I've now asked a neurologist to be more active in his care."

Floyd glanced at his wife again. "We don't know what to do, doc," he said. He looked back at Danny, shrugging his lopsided shoulders. "We've been avoiding the decision but it looks like he won't be able to finish the semester. Should we take him out of school and the dorm?"

"I'm sorry to echo your concern. Yes, after the first and second head trauma, it would be too much for him to continue with school work. What his brain needs is rest. And, of course, sports are out of the question."

"This is terrible," Tara said. "It's his first year of college. And all of this because of a stupid basketball game." She closed her eyes as a tear slid down her cheek and her silver-blonde hair fell forward as she bent her head.

Floyd continued consoling her, his hand staying behind her. "Honey, they were accidents. You can't stop a young man from being active."

Danny leaned over the circular table. "Mrs. Bell, your son woke up from his coma. That in itself is spectacular, especially so soon."

Her eyes stayed shut and she took a deep breath. "Thank you. I will try to take solace in that."

"Dr. Tilson," Floyd said, "how is your daughter? We don't expect her to continue coming to the hospital to see David. She has her own life and education to worry about. Please let her know that."

"She's a big girl. Annabel isn't talking to me much these days but she'll figure out what to do. I hope you both will support her decisions."

"Absolutely," Floyd said. "She's a sweet girl and we want what's best for her."

Tara took a tissue from her purse and dabbed at her eyes. "Do you … do you think we could go see him now?"

"Yes," Danny said. "Please be very calm and comforting with him. And quiet. Also, I need to warn you. This is his postictal period. That refers to the time after an epileptic seizure when a patient has an altered state of consciousness. It can last up to thirty minutes so he may still be confused. He can have a host of symptoms such as a terrible headache like a migraine, or feel nauseous, or be disoriented." Danny looked from one to the other. "Okay?"

Tara nodded affirmatively, moisture welling up in her eyes again.

"We understand," Floyd said. "I think, based on what you're saying, we may need a crash course in seizures by the time we're finished with all of this."

Danny rose slowly. "Me or my colleagues, or the hospital staff, will help you both with anything you need."

The next day, Danny barely had a break between his surgeries. Hospital staff seemed primed for a marathon. He wished all days could go so well and, by the end of this one, he smiled because it was over and he wasn't on call.

Danny went straight to the office. He unlocked the front door with its classy group practice sign and turned on the lights; everyone had left for the day. He strolled into the kitchen to fetch a snack and began tidying up around the counter. Rinsing the dregs someone had left in the coffeepot, he refilled it to begin brewing French Roast when the office opened in the morning. He opened the refrigerator, slapped cheese and turkey slices on white bread, and sat down.

Danny wasn't in a mood to rush home. Everyone right now had their own recent problems to think about and work through. The only two left unscathed seemed to be his sister and Nancy. Even though Dakota had the life, he had a dog's problem; he had been made into a target, the victim of Julia's newfound dislike of him. Danny frowned just thinking about it as Dakota adored that little girl.

After eating half a sandwich and gulping down a glass of water, his cell phone rang.

"Danny, it's Penny Banks. You don't happen to still be around the hospital?"

"Actually, I'm in the office."

"It's late for that but I have to drop by upstairs anyway. Can I come by to talk shop about David Bell?"

"Sure. Door's unlocked and I'm in the kitchen."

The proximity of other specialists in the same building, including Penny, was a perk Danny appreciated. Any of them could always meet quickly besides calling each other.

Within fifteen minutes, the silence broke when Danny heard a soft voice and the patter of high heels in the hallway. His eyes were fixed on the door.

"That's a weary smile," Penny said with a soft voice and a Boston accent as she entered. She was in her thirties and doggedly committed to her field.

"Reflects how I feel. How's life treating you?"

"Can't complain at the moment," she said.

"How about a non-gourmet sandwich?"

"I'll pass. What else do you have in that fridg?"

"Fruit medley in a plastic tray. Help yourself."

Penny placed down her leather bag, pulled out the container, and slid some cantaloupe onto a flat plate. "I just came from the ICU. Your partner, Jeffrey Foord, was making evening rounds so I told him I would fill you in."

As she sat across from him straightening out her skirt, Danny noticed her crooked nose which gave her eyes the appearance of being slightly crossed.

"As you must be aware, David Bell had a seizure early today. However, he just had another one this evening. Dr. Foord and I were dismayed at the intensity and length of it, Danny. I would think anti-epileptics would have subdued or prevented them by now but I'm going to keep reaching into my armamentarium of older and freshly-marketed drugs."

Danny felt a twinge in his stomach as a forlorn look of hopelessness registered across his face.

"The nurse said something about your daughter knowing this young man," she said.

Danny nodded, realizing he'd written an order for Penny's consult but that he had not filled her in on the personal nature of his patient.

"David is my daughter's boyfriend. The one in college. You may have read my original history and physical on him. The first blow to his head occurred at a home basketball game. The second one happened while he was supposed to be on head and body rest."

"So much for that," Penny said, then speared a piece of cantaloupe and put it in her mouth.

"It's a tricky age. They're old enough to drink and drive and pick out their career choices for the rest of their lives but their common sense isn't yet grounded. And advice from older adults is perceived as lecturing."

Penny smiled. "I have yet to have one that old but there are exceptions, I'm sure."

"Yes, there are. But my daughter is being sulky and partially blaming me for not being more forceful about David's orders to rest with no physical activity."

"Danny, in that respect, you can't win. Take heart. This too shall pass." She swung her long brown braid behind her shoulder and smiled. "So, being that David's two seizure medications should have therapeutic blood levels by now and he's still having them, it looks like this regimen is a failure. There is a new pharmaceutical release which I'll start him on tomorrow. Let's see how he does on it."

"In the meantime," Danny said, "I can't consider moving him out of the ICU."

"I understand. But statistics show that the majority of patients around the world who suffer from epilepsy can be treated by anticonvulsant drugs. And there are 50 million of them. Pessimistically, however, a handful of patients do not respond to standard treatments."

Danny grimaced as the two of them locked eyes.

"And that's where you'd come in," Penny said.

"Yes, that is where I'd come in. And we both know what that means."

Having not been on call, it was late for Danny to arrive home. Only the dull light over the stove guided him through the hallway where he stopped outside the bedroom door, hearing the low volume of the television. A few steps later, there was only quiet from Julia's room. Nancy's door was slightly ajar; she faced the wall with a sheet strewn over her shoulders.

Danny went upstairs and stopped at the landing facing the closed door. Although he heard no voices on the other side of the door, he heard the low hum of the dishwasher. Turning it on was often the last thing Mary or Casey did before going to bed. In any case, he realized he wouldn't have been in the mood to talk and he headed back downstairs.

At the bottom, the shrill of his cell phone on his belt startled him. Almost nine o'clock. He wondered if it was Annabel with a problem but, on unclamping his cell, Rachel's name appeared.

"Hi, Danny. It's Rachel."

"Is everything all right? It's late to speak to Julia. She's fast asleep."

"Then I wouldn't think of having you disturb her. I bet she's having the most angelic dreams."

These days, Danny didn't think so. He waited a moment during her silence. "Yes, then?"

"I rarely request extra visitation which I am entitled to. But can I pick up Julia Thursday night and bring her back Saturday night?"

"Do you have safe arrangements for her when you work on Friday?"

"Actually," she said, "I have no commitments on Friday and I'll be spending the day with her."

"Sorry, I didn't mean to imply …"

"Yes you did," she snapped. "It will be a lovely day," she added, softening her voice. "As you know, she's growing so fast. We have to capture the memories while we can. They are but fleeting and must be savored."

Danny blinked. Sounded like a bunch of malarkey since it came from her. "I don't see a problem with that. You can come by Thursday evening."

When he hung up, Danny entered the bedroom. The TV was now off and Sara seemed to be sleeping so he avoided turning on the overhead light. He took off his shirt and tossed it in the bathroom hamper and showered. Before getting under the light covers, he sat and leaned over with his head in his hands. A soft hand touched his shoulder.

"Are you okay?" Sara asked quietly.

He turned his head. "The question is are you?"

"I asked you first. I'm wondering if you're the one being burdened with too much."

"It's not the first time." He took her hand in his.

"But each scenario is different. It doesn't mean you have to stand up like the Rock of Gibraltar every time you have multiple problems at the same time. You're only human, Danny."

"So what do I do about how I feel?"

"How do you feel?"

"Despondent."

"Well that's a start."

"What's a start?"

"Telling me how you feel. Men are notorious for not sharing their feelings."

A silence ensued. "I have an idea," Sara said. "How about going to the lake house this weekend? Maybe we could leave Julia here with everyone and have a peaceful retreat."

Danny squeezed her hand. "We could go Friday night and come back Sunday morning. Since Julia will be with her mom until Saturday night, everyone here would only have to put her to bed when she gets back."

"See, sometimes things do work out," she gently reassured him.

Chapter 12

Casey loaded the last plate into the dishwasher and glanced at his watch: 8:30. He knew Danny hadn't been on call and he hadn't heard his car pull in. It was rare for them not to talk for a few days. They'd seen each other at dinner when Mary sprang her pregnancy news and then when Casey introduced his new partner outside the ER but, other than that, nightly talks had diminished.

He closed the door and pressed the power button. Mary had gone to bed and, not wanting to disturb her as she fell asleep, he waited awhile before heading upstairs. He sat in the recliner, book in hand, as the sound of streaming water filled the dishwasher and made background noise.

With an easy maneuver of each foot, he slipped off each deck shoe and moved the ottoman under his legs. He settled back into the leather chair and spied his paperback. Instead of opening it, he placed it on the adjacent table. He closed his eyes and folded his hands on his lap, aware of the absence of a distal digit.

At first, thoughts roamed to Danny. He knew him too well and his friend and brother-in-law didn't seem his usual optimistic self that week. Sara had even mentioned that Danny's laughter seemed to have gotten scarce. He decided to be more attuned to Danny as far as watching for signs of depression. Sara's miscarriage had been a sad loss and dealing with Annabel and her boyfriend as a patient, and Julia and her mother, were a handful. And he couldn't imagine the stress of his practice and cases. Although he always handled those well, they were enough in and of themselves for anyone to deal with.

Casey began drifting to sleep, caught between wakefulness and the blackness of not being aware. He still had the ability to choose his thoughts so he allowed his mind to shift far back to when he was a boy of eight years old; his younger brother, Tommy, was six.

Around home, it wasn't unusual for Casey and Tommy to be stuck to each other as if one belt surrounded both their waists and was cinched with a buckle. It was inevitable as the Hamilton household didn't function that smoothly, something more obvious to Casey when he spent time over at the Tilson's residence with Danny.

Most of the time, Casey's father Wendell was away from home. His career as a salesman, Casey had learned, was different than what people called a 'traveling salesman.' He didn't lug products around in his car and go door-to-door pitching them; instead he had 'areas' where he had to market farm equipment and often went to meetings in distant cities. His father was but a brief visitor in their home, someone who wasn't good with kids but stood as a decent authority figure and had the respect of the two boys.

It was Elizabeth Hamilton, Casey's mom, who stayed at the house especially since working had been out of the question. Besides the fact that Tommy was a far cry from being a healthy child, she suffered from frequent migraines which often made her hide away in the upstairs bedroom, isolating herself from activity, sound and light. The only escape from her headaches was sleep - the ultimate refuge from the pressure in her head, the tense grimace on her face and the nausea which forced her to the toilet to throw up her last meal.

With the scant inclusion of his parents in their lives, Casey was not only Tommy's big brother but he watched and protected him. So he fended for himself at an early age and also learned early on how to be a caretaker.

Within the first year of Tommy's life, his parents suspected a problem with his health. The baby lagged behind in weight gain and growth and had two lung infections almost back-to-back. After the pediatrician sent them to a specialty clinic, sweat and genetic testing confirmed the diagnosis of cystic fibrosis.

It was around the house or outside that Elizabeth asked her older son to "mind your brother." Casey loved his curly-headed sibling who had a sweet disposition and he learned the skills to become a caretaker of someone ill. He became used to his brother's breathlessness with exertion and his constant stuffy nose, always carrying the tissues Tommy may need.

It was a pleasant early summer day when Elizabeth Hamilton forced herself to make the boys a late breakfast of boiled eggs and toast, sent them outside to play, and retreated back upstairs with a growing migraine. She closed the bedroom door and struggled to keep down the small amount she had eaten. She reclined in a chair instead of lying back in bed, hoping the migraine pill would settle her stomach; luckily, she slept for a while.

Outside on the porch, Casey picked up a blue plastic ball from a rocking chair, and he and his brother sat down on the top step in front of the walkway. The sun was bright but not hot, the small lawn was neatly mowed, and honeybees hummed in the bushes flanking the front porch.

"If Mom left the dishes in the sink, I'll help you wash them when we go back inside," Tommy said.

"Maybe you can dry them," Casey said, scrutinizing him. "Your nose looks sore. Were you blowing a lot this morning?"

"Yeah," he said shrugging his shoulders. He leveled the bottom of his sneakers on the top step and hugged his legs below his knees. "Whaddya wanna do today?"

Casey stared at his shoelaces. "If you're feeling okay, we can play ball for a little bit. But I have a piece of chalk in my pocket. Do you want to play tic-tac-toe on the sidewalk instead?"

"Okay," Tommy said, rocking back and forth. But neither boy made an attempt to move. The quiet of the morning was broken up by the slamming of a distant house door and a car radio blared for a few seconds and then became faint.

"Look," said Tommy, "there's Pumpkin. Is she afraid of something?"

Casey saw the deep-orange neighborhood cat slink out beneath the parked car in front of their house. From the other side of the vehicle, a rangy-looking mutt appeared and hightailed after her.

Both boys stared and their eyes widened as the two animals darted along the sidewalk, the dog gaining ground in hot pursuit.

"Here," Casey said, "hold this."

He rose, dropped the ball into Tommy's hands, and took off. Three houses down, the cat ran between houses, the dog practically on its tail. Since Pumpkin had one lame leg, Casey worried for her safety. He also knew the nasty reputation of the stray dog.

The three of them cut through a backyard, passed a swing set and several more yards, and ended up facing a porch from a house on the street behind them. Which was fine with Casey because it was where Pumpkin lived. The cat scampered up an apple tree while the dog planted itself at the base of the trunk and barked incessantly. Barely out of breath, Casey ran through the thick grass right up to the scrubby dog.

"Go away," he yelled. "Scoot!" He waved his arms and, within a few minutes, his efforts paid off. By intimidation, the dog finally grew weary and put some distance between them.

Casey sat on the nearby picnic table looking up at Pumpkin who sat on the lowest branch. Her tensed-up hair started to look less raised and she fixed her eyes on him with approval.

"Come on down," he pleaded. He stood up and reached for the branch but he wasn't tall enough so he pulled the picnic bench over and climbed on top.

"It's okay, girl. I'll rescue you from that mean dog." He cupped the side of her head and stroked behind her ear. Seeming to have her trust, he grabbed the cat and cuddled her close, then got off the bench and walked between the rose bushes to the back door of the McKinley's house. After knocking several times, the door opened.

"Why, if it isn't Casey Hamilton," Kelley McKinley said, "the best and most grown up boy in the neighborhood." As she spoke through the screen door, she opened it up and smiled at him. "Is Pumpkin okay?"

"Not so much, Mrs. McKinley. A dog chased her up your apple tree. I got him to leave her alone while I rescued her. But he's not too far away. Here," he said, extending his hands to give Pumpkin to her owner.

The elderly woman pointed into the kitchen with her wrinkled hand. "Please come in and set her down in here where it's safe."

With the soft feline in his arms, he followed her inside and she shut the door.

Little Tommy watched his brother beeline after the dog and cat like his legs were in flight. The three made a riotous sight especially due to their small, medium and large sizes. Even cartoons weren't as entertaining as that. Several houses down, they made a sharp right turn and fled through the dark green grass where Pumpkin appeared lower in her surroundings. The cat's orange color bobbed up and down from the verdant lawn until he couldn't see them because the three of them disappeared between two houses, headed for backyards.

Tommy's amused look faded and he glanced down at his shorts where the ball was lying in his crotch. He swiped his annoying nose, picked up the ball and rolled it around in the palms of his hands. After some thought, he decided it would be more fun to play ball with Casey when he came back, especially since his breathing at the moment wasn't too bad. He stopped making circles with the ball, tossed it lightly into the air, and caught it effortlessly on its return. On the third attempt, he gathered more confidence and threw it higher. It spun farther out, he missed catching it, and it bounced on the path in front of him. It began rolling and picked up speed on the decline; faster and faster it rolled as the youngster got up and followed its course down the path and across the sidewalk.

The ball dropped off the curb into the road between two parked sedans and stayed on its straight course beyond the trunk end and front grill of the two cars. Tommy stepped down and between the vehicles. He had to get it before it rolled under the cars across the street.

With the ball now in the middle of the road, the youngster was out in the open as he hurried to scoop it up.

A pickup truck was coming and, seeing the rolling ball, the driver slowed to avoid it. But he didn't fully apply his brakes as a child lurched out from between parked cars.

As he leaned forward trying to hurry, Tommy saw the large bulky grill of a moving vehicle came at him before it impacted his small frame, throwing him to the ground. With smashed internal organs, his head also crashed on the tar road.

As Tommy looked straight up from where he lie on the pavement, his view of the clear blue sky faded as well as his thoughts and consciousness … and then his beating heart stopped.

Upstairs in her bedroom, Elizabeth Hamilton propped her elbow on the tall dresser and rested her head into the palm of her hand. She closed her eyes. Better than any meteorologist, she could predict weather changes with accuracy as significant fluctuations of barometric pressure signaled the onslaught and continuation of her migraine. And today she was in for a doozy.

She opened her strained lids and spied the prescription bottle in front of her. After taking care of the child-resistant cap, she dropped a pill into her hand, walked to the bathroom, filled a cup with cold water, popped the drug into her mouth, and swallowed.

Thoughts turned to the rest of the day as she walked back out into the room. Spying the unmade bed, she figured it was where the remainder of her day was going to be spent. On the nightstand there was a novel she had recently started but she doubted if any pages would get read today. She stepped over to the closest off-white blinds and closed them; walking around the dresser, she went to the other window to do the same.

She looked out and spotted a blue ball rolling along the path between the two patches of their small front lawn. Her precious Tommy rose from the front steps and, in his own lanky style, hastily followed it. But as he slithered between cars, her view was better than her own child's. A jet black vehicle headed down the street as the ball kept rolling. She gasped, realizing the inevitable was about to occur. As she watched, her fingers tightened into her hand, her nails piercing her flesh.

The driver quickly slowed but not enough as it slammed into her son and tossed him forward like it had hit a dog.

With no recollection of it later, Elizabeth Hamilton was out of the bedroom, down the stairs, and at Tommy's side so quickly she almost beat the male driver to the carnage. She knelt, pulled at her son's shoulders, and leaned back with him in her lap. In complete shock, she rocked back and forth like he was a babe in her arms and softly repeated, "Tommy, Tommy, Tommy."

The distraught driver knelt beside her. Trembling, he looked up and down the street to ask someone, anyone, to call the police. When he saw a middle-aged man taking out his garbage, he shouted, "Please, call the police! There's been an accident!"

Chapter 13

After stroking her one more time, Casey put Pumpkin down on the floor and Mrs. McKinley motioned for him to sit at the round kitchen table.

"I can't thank you enough," she said, "for rescuing my little sweetheart. She's all I have left after my husband passed away."

"It's okay," Casey said, fidgeting with the placemat. "It's just that I like animals but my mom says we can't have any."

"I rarely see your mother but I know she often doesn't feel well."

Casey absent-mindedly nodded while he looked around. A kitty litter box was in the corner of the room, some of the pellets scattered on the tile floor nearby. A flowered teapot sat on the stove and several stoneware mugs lay in a dish drain by the sink. He wondered if she had any grandkids that visited her.

The elderly woman pursed her chapped lips. "I know just the thing. After all, it would be polite to offer you something after helping out with Pumpkin. I made the most delicious vanilla pie yesterday." She opened the refrigerator and pulled out a covered dish.

After placing the pie on the table, she fetched a plate from the cupboard along with a knife and fork from a drawer.

Casey thought about his predicament. He hated leaving Tommy too long by himself back at the house. However, even though his mother had taught him not to really take things from people he didn't know well, this seemed like an exception. He thought it may be ruder to not accept her offer than to get up and leave.

Kelley McKinley sliced a piece of pie and slipped it onto the plate and put it in front of Casey. "Here's a fork," she said, then turned to pour him a glass of milk.

"Actually, I have a secret," she said as she watched Casey take a bite. "That pie is sinful and all I did was make a box of pudding and put it into a store bought graham cracker crust."

Casey managed to smile. Since his mom didn't fuss too much with baking either, it was the kind of dessert he was used to. "Mmm. It's good," he said.

The phone rang somewhere beyond the kitchen. The old woman got up as if arthritis had just stiffened her up and she headed out of the room.

Casey occasionally heard her voice respond as he polished off the vanilla pie, leaving the best part – the crusty side – until last. When he finished, he drank the milk but then wasn't sure if he should put the dishes in the sink or continue to sit there. When the elderly woman returned, however, he had to tell her he must leave.

Kelley McKinley walked through the doorway with a frown on her face. She nervously wiped her hands on her blouse, took Casey's dishes and put them on the counter.

"That call was from your house. Your mom wants me to drive you over to your friend's. They are expecting you."

"That was my mom?" Casey asked.

"Not exactly. But your mom made the request." She went to the sideboard and picked up her purse.

"But I left my brother, Tommy, outside."

"They said not to worry about him; he's with your mom." She motioned him up from the chair and towards the front of the house.

"Are you taking me to Danny Tilson's?"

"Yes. He must be a very good friend. And they told me you know the way. You can show me, all right?"

"Okay," Casey said following her through the living room and out the front door to her car.

Casey had already been in the same elementary school class with Danny Tilson for two years. They'd become best friends and the only thing that limited Casey from spending more time with him was either because he had to mind Tommy or because he needed a ride to Danny's house. Sometimes Danny's mother or father would drive Casey home with them after school or sometimes Elizabeth Hamilton would feel well enough to drive him over and keep Tommy at the house with her.

The Tilson's home was a far cry from the situation Casey had at home. The big house and the surrounding property were like visiting a palace. The two boys could get lost and even lose track of time playing beyond Donna Tilson's magnificent gardens and trees, or playing board games, or talking in any of the numerous bedrooms. He respected Greg and Donna Tilson and never minded their soft approach to scolding the boys when needed, and he also never minded Danny's sister Mary when she joined them.

Mary was three years younger and had striking red hair and blue eyes. They would tease her about her funny gait; her right foot turned inwards. If she wasn't tagging along with the boys, they would spy on her; she was usually off somewhere with a pad of paper, drawing what she saw in front of her.

On this strange summer day, it was Kelley McKinley who drove Casey to the Tilsons as he directed her down the last long street with large verdant gaps between houses. When they pulled into the double driveway, he jumped out of the car although the woman took her time following him up to the front door.

With much exuberance, Casey knocked and the heavy door was quickly opened.

"Casey, welcome," Donna Tilson said and tenderly cupped his head, pulling him towards her slightly. She let go and pointed. "Danny and Mary are in the kitchen." As Casey walked down the hallway, he wondered why she'd given him a little hug for just walking in the door.

Danny stood at the kitchen table near Mary who sat bent over a large sketch pad. "Wow, Mom said you were coming over," he said. "Cool."

"Yeah, that's what I thought." He went closer to them and realized Mary had drawn the bowl of fruit in the middle of the table.

"Danny and I don't even know what we're going to be when we grow up," Casey said to Mary, "but you already have it figured out. And you're littler than us!"

"She'll be making people happy looking at paintings but we'll be helping people by using our hands, too."

"How?" Casey asked.

"Well, I don't know. In medicine, I guess."

Casey turned around to look down the hall again where Donna Tilson and Kelley McKinley stood close to each other, a whispered conversation in progress; they both had concerned looks on their faces. Finally, Mrs. McKinley patted Donna's shoulder and left.

For three days, Donna Tilson gave Casey some of Danny's clothes to wear and he slept at their home. The second afternoon Danny's father took the three children to their *Downtown Italy* restaurant where they sat at a back corner table and ate spaghetti and meatballs and garlic bread while Greg worked.

After taking a customer's payment at the cash register, Greg walked over. He pulled out a chair and sat down, his long legs extending under the table.

"How long am I staying with you all?" Casey asked. He didn't know why he had been sent, especially since he hadn't requested a sleep-over. Not that he minded; he was having a great time but now he was curious.

Greg Tilson's thick dark eyebrows scrunched closer as he leaned over the table. "Your mom told us to tell you that Tommy's cystic fibrosis has acted up. His lungs have made him sick and the doctor's need to take care of him. She doesn't want you to worry while you're with us. You are going home tomorrow."

Casey wiped some sauce off his mouth with a linen cloth. He stared into Greg's eyes, his look of pleasure fading to sorrow. "Poor Tommy. He's always getting sick. I wish I could help him."

"I heard that you often take care of your brother, even when he's not well. You are a young caretaker, Casey Hamilton." Greg got up, reached over, and lightly patted the youth's head. When he left the table, he went into the kitchen to glance at the chef's preparations.

"I hope he gets better," Mary said.

Casey nodded.

"And just so you both know it," Mary added, "I'm doing stuff without you this afternoon when we get home."

"Good," Danny said. "You've been like a stray cat hanging around us."

"Shut up, Danny."

"I will," he said.

Late in the afternoon the next day, an unlikely breeze stirred through the neighborhood as Elizabeth Hamilton drove up and rang the Tilson's front bell. Upon entering, she spoke with Donna for some time.

Donna went upstairs to Danny's bedroom where Casey was sprawled on the floor and Danny lay on the bed, each with a book; Casey was reading "Anne of Green Gables" which Mary had offered from her collection.

"Casey, your mom is here to take you home," Donna said. She sat at the edge of the bed, speaking softly in her usual pleasant way. "You may borrow the book if you'd like."

Casey popped up. "Okay, I'd like to. Bye, Danny. See you soon."

Danny rolled onto his back. "Okay. It was fun."

"You are welcome any time," Donna said as they walked out the door.

As Elizabeth drove Casey home, a silence enveloped the car. He had questions for her but she seemed more upset than normal. Perhaps she had a killer migraine in which case he would be wise to avoid talking to her. Instead, he thought about his brother and hoped that his cystic fibrosis flare-up had gotten better.

When they got to the house and went inside, Casey didn't have time to look for his brother as his father called to him from the small living room, a surprise since his father shouldn't have been home. His dad pointed for him to sit at the end of the couch while his mother followed and sat sideways on the coffee table.

Mr. Hamilton stoked his mustache, considering his words, and Casey prepared to get scolded for something he'd possibly done wrong. He tried to avoid his father's gaze.

"We have some very, very sad family news," Wendell Hamilton said.

Casey relaxed a little bit. It appeared he wasn't in any kind of trouble.

"You know how difficult Tommy's medical condition was. The doctors had told us he probably wouldn't live many, many years like all of us will." His father let that sink in for a moment before he continued.

"Your brother hasn't done too well in the last few days and … he's passed away, son."

The gravity of what his father said registered slowly as if he was in a slow-motion dream. "You mean, he's … he's dead?"

"Yes. He's no longer with us. God has taken him early."

For the rest of the day, Casey clammed shut, not fully accepting it. But as the evening progressed and Tommy's bedroom took on an eerie quiet, the emptiness of not hearing his brother's voice set in. He must have been really sick, he thought, for his bedroom and toys looked the same as the day they were on the front porch together and he went off chasing the neighborhood cat.

The next morning, the funeral parlor visitation room swelled with families familiar with the Tilson boys through school. They outnumbered friends and relatives of Tommy's parents who were scarcer in number due to their private lifestyle.

Several times, Casey stared blankly at the wooden box that housed his brother. It was 'closed,' and he was glad he didn't have to see Tommy like he had seen an old, dead relative in a coffin one time.

After most people left, a few folks remained and were part of the funeral procession to take his brother to the cemetery where a heavy humidity hung in the air. With his parents on one side, and Danny and Mary on the other, he watched the casket disappear into the earth.

There was nothing in Casey's childhood that changed his life as much as Tommy's death. He tucked the memory of his brother deep into his soul and had trouble with the empty void he felt in their home. And talking about his brother with his mother and father became less and less.

Although Elizabeth Hamilton had to take an occasional sick day due to her migraines, eventually she was able to take a job as a waitress, especially since Tommy's absence and not dealing with his medical condition seemed to unburden her. Since she now wasn't home as much, Casey spent even more time at the Tilsons. Donna didn't seem to mind since the two boys were like close brothers and she treated him with warmth and thoughtfulness.

Casey's arm slipped off the leather chair's armrest, causing him to wake with a start. He rubbed his eyes in the darkness and looked at his backlit wristwatch which read 1 a.m. His entire dream surfaced and he couldn't believe it; such detail of Tommy and his most potent childhood memories. He hadn't given it all that much thought in at least a year.

Nowadays, the most thoughts he had of his brother were when he visited his failing mother in a nursing home. She had been in a retirement facility when she attended his wedding but had since been moved to the full-care part of it.

He lingered in the chair, the quiet comforting and the blackness causing him to search his soul. After a big sigh, he whispered his brother's name. "Tommy," he said, "I hope you're enjoying heaven."

Casey took his legs off the ottoman and got up, his eyes scanning for the nightlight back by the kitchen. As he walked through the center hall, he realized Mary must be sleeping so well she didn't miss his coming to bed. He chuckled to himself, wondering if he had ever finished the book she had lent him long ago as a child.

Chapter 14

It had been a long day in the OR. Rachel walked into her apartment, dropped the mail and her purse on the kitchen island, and leaned over to acknowledge Snoopy whose tail circled like a portable fan.

"You sure are jollier than the stuffed shirts I deal with all day," she said, although her day in the eye room hadn't been that bad. Ophthalmologists didn't chitchat that much about nothing because their quick, yet tedious, cases required concentration.

"I better let you relieve yourself before I pick up Julia."

She glanced at the top piece of mail; it was from Mark Cunningham. That's odd, she thought, as she hadn't initiated her legal shenanigans yet. So why was she hearing from Danny's lawyer? Normally, his attorney sent papers to her attorney first so it wasn't usual for her to receive any legal matters directly. Maybe there had been some kind of a mistake.

She tore open the envelope. Passing over the letter, she recognized a familiar format on the legal size documents. What the …,? she thought.

Casey Hamilton vs. Rachel Hendersen.

Casey didn't have anything to do with child support or Julia or Mark Cunningham, so what was this all about? Ignoring Snoopy who kept running back and forth to the door, she picked up the cover letter.

Dear Ms. Hendersen,

Enclosed please find notice of a legal lawsuit against you for Casey Hamilton's medical bills. These charges were incurred due to the almost complete severance of his left middle finger due to your negligence.

In case you've forgotten about this matter, please refer to the specific details in the enclosed court document. I am assuming you will be contacting your attorney, Phil Beckett, about this. I look forward to hearing from him.

Yours truly,

Mark Cunningham

Rachel pursed her lips with anger. I've always disliked that Casey Hamilton, she thought, and wondered why he was such a loyal friend to Danny. She never could understand it. But why should she suffer any consequences for his stupidity?

Snoopy bounded back to her, stopped, and piddled by the corner of the counter.

"No! Bad dog!" she yelled. She pushed the dog gently with her foot and then picked her up. Walking over to the door, she grabbed the leash and clipped it on her collar. They headed towards the dog run as she mulled over the new legal intrusion in her life.

By the time Snoopy did her business and Rachel let her run in the fenced area for a few minutes, her indignation had subsided. She looked up at the billowy clouds and pondered that Casey was stupider than she thought. Why would he bother to bring a lawsuit if he didn't have anything to gain, like a profit? Even if he received back the money for his medical bills, he'd have lost part of an appendage. If it were her, she'd have put a large price tag on that.

Going back to the apartment, she lightened up. If this debacle ended up with her having to chalk up cash for his bills, she could always work in some more hours at the outpatient facility, especially after her community court-appointed service was done and over with. However, she wasn't resigned yet. Phil would have to get involved and she'd have time to come up with a good 'defense' and try to sidestep the whole matter.

For now, she had to get ready and pick up Julia for the more extended weekend visitation she had planned.

Danny came home from the office to have dinner with Sara and also give Julia to Rachel. Luckily, he had had free time before making evening rounds for the whole group. He brought in a pizza and Sara made a salad while Nancy set the table; Julia sat and waited with more patience than Danny thought possible. He slid slices onto the plates and then cut Julia's into manageable pieces.

"Your dad and I are going to the lake house tomorrow after work," Sara said to Nancy. "Casey and Mary will be around."

"Sounds like I'm not invited."

"We could use an alone getaway," Danny said.

Nancy reached over for the salad bowl. "That's fine but, next time, please take me especially if you bring Dakota. He is so much fun when he gets near the water."

Dakota bounced up from the floor and nuzzled her hand.

"My dog Snoopy is funner," Julia said.

"You mean to say 'is more fun,'" Nancy said. "But that can't be because Dakota is the best."

Julia slapped her fork on the table. "Is not," she said.

"Yes he is."

"Okay, girls, let's not argue," Sara said. "Most dogs are wonderful."

Danny shot a glance at Sara and shook his head. "I am looking forward to the weekend."

"No school, no medicine, and no weekend chores at the house," Sara added.

Danny folded a slice and ate silently. He watched Julia as she ignored the salad and ate most of her pizza without the crust.

"Are you finished?" Danny asked.

Julia nodded and he wiped her hands and mouth.

"Your mom will be coming in a few minutes so let's go outside and wait," Danny said. He gathered her things and he held her hand as they went to the front porch. On purpose, he told Dakota to stay inside; he'd had enough comparisons made between him and Snoopy.

As Danny sat on the front step, Julia walked around in circles on the grass. After several times going fast, she fell on the lawn.

"Are you making yourself dizzy?" Danny asked.

She giggled and got up as Rachel's car pulled into the driveway; the door opened and she yelled for her daughter. Danny walked over with her little suitcase.

"I'll take that," Rachel said after giving Julia a kiss. "And don't come any farther. God forbid you touch anything over here of mine or you'll be suing me, too. You two are a sorry lot."

"Sorry lot," Julia mimicked.

"Just be back at a reasonable time with her on Saturday," Danny said. Shaking his head, he turned and walked to the house. No wonder Julia was misbehaving.

When he got back in the house, Sara and Nancy were both finishing more pizza.

"If you both are finished," he said, "I'll put the box in the refrigerator and have another slice later when I get home."

He gave them both a kiss and left for the hospital. The last rays of the sun disappeared to the west as he put his headlights on and wondered if Julia would be more pleasant when she got a little older. In a few years, he hoped her conduct would change for the better and she'd become a sweet and smart five-year-old.

Danny scanned the print-out of his and his partner's patients as he stopped in the hallway. A nurse took the last chart from him and stood it upright on the rolling cart that had accompanied him. All their patients had been seen except for the two remaining in the ICU.

He thanked the nurse who had been conscientious coming on the evening shift; she had helped him out a few minutes before she even needed to clock in.

When the automatic doors of the ICU shut behind him, the isolation and coldness of the unit made him shudder. A fluorescent light fixture had burned out, the central area grayer than normal, and a nervous quietude hung in the air. How many times had he walked into this large arena and yet, on each occasion, it took on a life of its own? He looked to the right at David's open door. The young man was now sequestered from society as if quarantined from his peers and the normalcy of life; whatever that may be.

Danny stepped into the room where the light was also subdued as if David had been tucked in bed for the night. An RN was alongside his bed taping the tubing from a small infusion bag into a heplock on his hand. Across the room, Annabel sat on a chair in the corner, her face puffy and her hands clasped on her lap; she had been crying.

"Dr. Tilson," the nurse said. "I knew you'd be making rounds this evening. David had a seizure an hour ago. We spoke with Dr. Banks and she switched one of his anti-seizure medications again."

"Thank you," he said and nodded to Annabel.

Danny first examined David, who looked spent and deeply tired and didn't stir when Danny jostled his shoulder. He listened to his heart and lungs with his stethoscope, flickered his penlight into his eyes, and checked his reflexes. After scanning his vital signs again on the monitor, he stepped to the counter and leaned against it.

Annabel glanced at him with moist eyes. He realized how far she'd come from being a tomboy with a crooked tooth and a baseball cap to being a more feminine young woman with a straight, white smile and a shiny curl to her hair.

But within a few seconds, she practically gave him a scowl. "All the muscles in his body contracted," she said, as if accusing him. "I watched him convulse and distort. And then he lost consciousness."

"A generalized motor seizure is a frightening experience when seen for the first time," Danny said. "Especially if it's someone you care about."

"I mean, he ended up looking rigid and he could hardly breathe and saliva drooled from his mouth …" She whimpered and put her head in her hands. "They had to escort me out of here," she mumbled. "How am I going to get that image out of my head?"

Danny put his hand on her shoulder. "Come on. Let's find a private place to talk."

She shrugged his hand off but got up, grabbing her satchel from the floor. Walking past him, she exited the unit while making sure she kept a distance from her father.

Outside the door, he pointed to the elevators. "We'll go to the doctor's lounge."

"I'm not exactly a candidate," she said.

"It's after hours and there won't be many people there, plus it's fine. You are going to be there someday yourself, aren't you? Is med school still on your agenda or has that changed?"

"I plan on applying," she said and didn't offer any more information. They rode down in silence as the elevator creaked and groaned more than usual and then went straight into the lounge. There were only a handful of doctors; Danny nodded at those who looked over.

"I had dinner at the house," he said. "Why don't you make yourself a sandwich?"

Annabel shook her head but stopped at the counter nevertheless. She took a scoop of chicken salad and a package of crackers, then poured an ice tea. Danny deliberated at the coffeepot; it looked fresh enough, so he poured a cup.

He pointed to the couch where Annabel kept the plate in her lap and put her drink on the side table. Danny sat in the separate leather chair and took a swig of lukewarm coffee.

"Before we talk about David, I need to know about you," Danny said. "How is school going? Are you getting your work done while still managing these visits?"

"I had some exams earlier in the week so I'm kind of caught up. That's why I decided to come tonight." She tore the cellophane off the packet and crumpled it on the table.

"I never tell you this but, if there's anything I can help you with as far as schoolwork, just holler."

"I'm not a little kid, Dad."

He let the remark slide and took another sip of his weak coffee.

"What you should be helping with is getting David out of this predicament." She tossed a glare at him then quickly averted her eyes and scooped chicken salad onto a cracker. What is it with girls, Danny thought. Is raising boys this difficult?

"Spare me the accusatory tone," he said. "I don't deserve that. Dr. Banks and I have tried to avoid it but it's now inevitable. David is not responding to standard treatments. I'm going to arm you with more knowledge about what's going to happen."

She took a bite and held his glance.

"What we need to know," Danny said, "is the region of David's brain that is the source of the epilepsy so that I can remove it."

"Oh my God. Really? Brain surgery?"

Danny loosened the top of his shirt and nodded. "But this is easier said than done. There is a very complex and highly invasive first step, a pre-surgical phase. I would have to perform a cranial operation to implant electrodes on the surface of his cortex."

Annabel scrunched up her forehead. "A surgery before you do the surgery?"

"Yes. And after the wound is closed, David would have to remain in the intensive care unit. It gets worse. He would have to stay there for several weeks with wires passing through his cranium."

"What on earth for?" she asked, putting the plate aside and wringing her hands.

"For that extended period, the electrodes are connected to a recording machine which will identify the source of the epilepsy during the seizures."

"No! That is insane. We're living in the twentieth century. We can turn up our house heat remotely and soon we'll have smart cars that can parallel park by themselves. Our cell phones are remarkable and can tell us the price of gas in our vicinity. In the scheme of things, this sounds barbaric. It's like something from the nineteenth century. You surgeons and researchers have gotten lazy and haven't technically developed the process any further!"

She stopped her tirade but he'd never seen her so passionate about anything before.

"Annabel, I can't change what already is and I have to do what is best for my patients."

"But a college student being imprisoned in an ICU for weeks on end? That's torture. His health and his schoolwork and his whole life will be changed, maybe forever. He'll lose his friends, he may never get to play basketball again, not to mention he'll be bored to death."

Danny winced. "I deal with the reality of the neurosurgical issue and what I have at hand. I cannot control those things."

"Ha. Some neurosurgeon."

"Excuse me, young lady?" Danny said, his blood starting to boil.

She blinked and turned aside. "I'm sorry. I know you've had outstanding accomplishments because of your work with that pandemic two years ago and then that issue with that potent drink last year. You're apparently a big deal when it comes to neurosurgeons."

Danny held his tongue; at least she apologized which was more than he expected.

"But still," she said, "what you're proposing as the current course of treatment, this pre-surgical phase as you've termed it, is archaic. I guess I just called you out as you are a better neurosurgeon than that."

Annabel got up. "Are we finished here? If so, I'm going back to my dorm."

Chapter 15

With ridiculous zest, Julia ran circles around the kitchen island in pursuit of Snoopy. The dog caught the gist of the game in no time flat and was more than accommodating to stay out of her arms reach. Julia plopped down around a corner but Snoopy kept going. When he looped back around, he plowed into her.

"I tricked you!" she squealed. But the dog loved it even more and showered her face with her wet tongue.

Rachel watched with a smile on her face. It was the perfect way for her daughter to start the morning before the appointment they had; one which was the main reason she needed Julia on this week day.

"You two get along like a butterfly and a wildflower," Rachel said. "She is so attached to you."

Julia put her arms around the dog and squeezed.

"Stand up, sweetheart. Let me brush your hair and put on this ribbon clip."

Rachel finished and said, "It's even the color of your shirt. You look so pretty."

"You're pretty," Julia said.

"You're prettier." Rachel squatted and looked into her daughter's wide-set eyes. "We're going somewhere this morning. You can talk with a nice lady and she may help you out because you can tell her how much you want to live with your mommy. Okay?"

Julia wrapped her arms around Rachel and squeezed.

"That's a good girl. Now I have to make a phone call and then we'll be leaving. You can play with Snoopy again for a few minutes."

Rachel stepped into the bedroom and called Beckett and Livingston in Knoxville.

"Phil, it's Rachel."

"Miss Hendersen. To what do I owe the honor? How is your pediatric hospital service coming along?"

"It's lots of fun, Phil, except that I prefer time with my own daughter at home a lot better."

"I'm glad she stirs that motherly instinct in you. Now, what can I do for you?"

"I'm putting legal paperwork in the mail to you today. It's from Mark Cunningham but it does not involve Danny Tilson."

"I'm not exactly following you."

She rolled her eyes. "Danny must have referred his attorney to a buddy of his. This friend, Casey, wants to take a bite out of my purse strings because of a little mishap he had under the hood of my car."

"Is this guy a mechanic?"

"No, but he thought he'd play superhero and get my car started."

"Sounds like a Good Samaritan. You know that under that law he is legally protected if he was giving you assistance because you were 'injured, ill, in peril, or otherwise incapacitated.'"

She took a deep sigh, rolled her eyes again, and mumbled "nitwit" under her breath.

"Since you're my attorney, you should know I'm not going after him for trying to help me; he's suing me."

"Well, that's a switch."

"Call it what you want. Why don't you just read it when you get it and spare me explaining it to my own lawyer?"

"It's your salary being put to good use," he said. "I'll look forward to receiving your envelope. In the meantime, have yourself a good weekend."

Rachel grasped Julia's small hand in her own and guided her down the pleasant strip mall's sidewalk; there were holly bushes and an occasional redbud tree in a patch of dirt. They passed a women's salon and a local favorite lunch spot. She stopped at the next storefront with black and gold lettering on the glass door: The Family Therapy Group.

She entered into an inviting area with a matching black and gold rug; it had directional marks on the tufted fabric like it had just been vacuumed. She signed in, then sat on a chair next to a mat with books and toys. While she answered the questions on a form she was given, Julia watched a little boy talking in Spanish to his mother.

Soon the other client was called to the back and another woman in her 20s opened the door again. Rachel and Julia followed behind her slender figure and went into a small room with a large bookcase, a desk, and a chair and a couch. The curtains were half open to the rear parking lot.

"I'm Miriam Kelly," the woman said, shaking Rachel's hand. "And this must be Julia." She squatted and smiled. "It's nice to meet you, young lady."

Rachel made herself comfortable while Julia giggled and jumped up on the couch next to her.

Miriam sat down on the chair. She wore three large rings on her right hand and, as she glanced over Rachel's form, her straight black hair fell forward. "So you work in an OR?" she asked.

"I do. I am the one performing the necessary evil of keeping surgeons sane by handing them what they need under the tensest circumstances. But I also keep them sane with my chitchat," she added and laughed. "Just like you must diffuse a lot of antsy family situations in this room."

"That's so true," Miriam said. "So, when you're not in the OR, what do you do for fun?"

"Besides my job, I gain a lot of fulfillment with the volunteer work I'm doing at a children's hospital. Some of those kids with chronic conditions and a history of multiple surgeries need all the love and attention they can get from volunteer groups like the one I'm in. Other than that, the most pleasure in my life is from this pretty girl right here. Right, Julia?"

Julia shifted on the cushion, cuddling into Rachel's lap.

"Excellent," Miriam said. "Well, I've read your notes on the second page so the best thing now would be for me to talk to Julia alone. It sounds like there are some things troubling her or she would like addressed. She and I can have a nice chat and perhaps I can make her feel better about things."

"I sure would appreciate it," Rachael said. She gave Julia a kiss on the top of her head and got up.

"By the way," Miriam said, "has Julia's father done anything like bring her to a counselor or therapist?"

"Him? He doesn't have time for that sort of thing, even if he did think of it."

Miriam grinned with acknowledgement, Rachel left the room, and Julia and the counselor warmed up and began talking.

Friday afternoon, Danny finished dictating his last patient's visit just as Cheryl popped her head in the door. "Do you want to talk to David Bell's basketball coach? He's on line two."

Danny nodded while he picked up. "Lester, what a pleasant surprise."

"Dr. Tilson, I hope you don't mind my calling to find out how David is. We just had practice and the team was talking about him. Some of them have visited David in the hospital but we don't know or understand how he is from the neurology or medical standpoint. I know you must honor his privacy but maybe you could shed a little light so I can report back to the team. We all miss him."

"No, I'm glad you called. What happened is an integral part of the team's history and it could have happened to any one of the players. As you know, he surprised us by waking up and by doing it so soon. The players must have heard from the nurses that the main problem now is seizures."

"That's what they are telling me. Can we be optimistic they are going to go away? Will he ever play for the school again, even if it's next year?"

"It's not looking likely. He's still in the ICU because we may need to do some drastic measures to get them under control."

Lester sank into the chair in his small university office. "The injuries are one of the few thorns in this otherwise fun and rewarding job of being a coach."

"I bet," Danny said. "And by the way, have the return-to-play medical guidelines been restressed at any university meetings?"

"Yes. David's situation has brought the subject back to the table."

"Good. University sports programs have a duty to these young players. The first hit to the head is problematic but the second or third impact can cause permanent long-term brain injury. Cumulative sports concussions can increase this likelihood by almost forty percent."

"Any other information I can bring to the next meeting?"

Danny considered and was grateful for the question. "A couple of points can be reiterated, such as the athletes must always have information readily available about the potential for serious head injury; the games must have a medical professional present to asses a head impact, which you're doing; and we must keep up and review impact measurement data. The standards must be held high."

"Appreciate that. And we all want you to have a season pass to our games. One is in the mail but I'll put you on a list to receive one every year."

"Thank you. And Lester, please feel free to call me any time. I can share overall information about David's progress if it's okay with the family and then the whole team can be updated."

"Appreciate that."

When Danny hung up, both Cheryl and Matthew Jacob walked in. Matthew planted himself on the couch.

"I'm headed out," Cheryl said. "I just wanted to say have a nice weekend."

"You, too. Sara and I are planning on going to the lake house but I'm feeling guilty about that. Work is coursing through my veins trying to keep me in Nashville like gravity pulling me to earth."

"But Dr. Jacob is on call," she said, pointing to him.

"Since I'm a fanatical runner," Matthew said, shifting his gaze to Danny, "you know I qualify as a good sport. I'll give up my weekend call to help out a colleague any day."

Danny laughed and Cheryl beamed. "I haven't heard you laugh in a while, Dr. Tilson. It's about time."

"That's because there hasn't been much in my life recently to be amused about." He grinned. "But I'm afraid you're stuck with it, Matthew. My thoughts are straying to other neurosurgical areas than direct patient care."

Matthew raised his eyebrows. "Is there something I can help you with? I would be honored to even be remotely involved with something you're working on. Through indirect sources, I heard that last year you were being considered for the 'Physician of the Year' award by the Tennessee Medical Society."

Danny's face registered surprise. "Why?"

"For your significant contributions over the last two years, all due to your persistence in getting to the root of medical dilemmas."

Cheryl's face lit up. "I didn't know that but it makes sense."

Danny waved his hand in the air dismissively. "Well then, there's nothing to write home about because I certainly wasn't picked."

"You're so modest," Cheryl said. "I wish a lot of other doctors were like you. But there's only one of you and that's why I work here." She turned to leave. "And you're okay, too, Dr. Jacob."

"I'm just a regular, normal doc," Matthew said as he looked out the window. Moving his long brown hair further behind his head, he looked at her with a trace of a smile. "But I'll take that as a compliment."

"Okay, bye y'all," she said.

"Have a great weekend," Danny said.

"Ditto," Matthew added.

Danny got up from behind his desk and sat down again catty-corner to Matthew. From his shirt pocket, he pulled out his folded piece of paper and handed it to him. "Here is my list of hospital patients for rounds tomorrow. Please pay extra attention to David Bell," he said, leaning in close with a concerned expression. "My main neurologist consultant is Penny Banks and anything she suggests for his care is a go."

Matthew leaned over the sheet on the table and scribbled something. "Don't worry, Danny, we'll take good care of him. You spend some quality time with Sara and leave all thoughts of your patients here."

One medium-sized suitcase lay open on the bed as Sara stacked two sets of clothes and toiletries inside. Danny stood at the other side of the mattress.

"I already have a drawer full of clothes at the lake house," Sara said, "but I'd rather just bring stuff back and forth this time. You can share this suitcase with me."

As he thumbed through a neurosurgical equipment magazine, Sara stared at him.

"Earth to Danny," she said.

"Huh?" He looked over. "I'm sorry. You were saying?"

"I'm not using all this space so feel free to put your things in here," she said pointing to the bottom of the travel bag. "If you're coming, that is."

He closed the bulky advertising monthly but held it close. "Why yes, for sure."

Sara cocked her head at him as Nancy poked her head in.

"Mom, Casey and Mary are coming downstairs to say hello before you both leave."

"Good. I'm finished here." Sara eyed Danny and left the room.

"I'm coming," he said as he put several T-shirts and blue jeans in the empty side. He took several steps towards the door deep in thought but then retraced his short course and packed the magazine under his clothes. Dakota showed up at the door and woofed.

"Okay, okay … did you come on your own or did they send you after me?"

When Danny joined his family, Mary was sitting with Sara on the couch, Nancy was on the floor waiting for Dakota to come back, and Casey was comfortable on a kitchen stool facing them.

"There you are," Casey said, his sneakers propped on the rungs.

"You headed to the gym?" Danny asked, noticing Casey's athletic clothes.

"I am. Too bad you can't make it but maybe next week sometime."

"I may take a rain check."

"Mary and I were wondering if there's anything we can do for you both that we're not aware of."

"You two are already going to help out with Julia tomorrow night. And maybe Nancy wants to spend tonight or tomorrow night in one of the bedrooms upstairs. She likes to pal around with you two when we're not around."

"No problem on either count. Now I have a favor to ask you. I talked to Mark Cunningham today and he assures me we're going to court within the next two weeks regarding my Rachel lawsuit. I'm not skilled in courtroom testimony so will you come with me if possible?"

Danny furrowed his brow in thought. "I'll do my best. I just hope that, when you need me, I'm not buried in a lab somewhere. Otherwise, I'll have another family member infuriated with me."

Chapter 16

From the upstairs balcony, Danny and Sara had a good view of the full moon and the rippled effect of light on the lake. They had unpacked the small supply of necessities they had brought and, since it was too chilly to sit outside very long, they sat on a bench inside admiring the scenery from the large upper windows. Dakota was lying at Danny's feet, his eyes closing whenever their conversation waned.

Danny finished the last sip of wine while Sara occasionally swirled her glass.

"I talked to Annabel this afternoon," she said. "I called her to let her know where we'd be this weekend."

After Sara repeated herself, Danny pulled his eyes from the natural satellite and looked at her directly. "Was she civil or did she have any wisecracks about me?"

"Perhaps I shouldn't say. You two need to patch things up."

"I haven't instigated anything. But really … I'd like to know any snippy remarks she made."

"She alluded to your coming here when you should instead be looking into patient care. I took that to mean David."

He shifted position and gripped his glass tighter. "It's been a long day. How about we go to bed?"

"How about not just sleeping? Since my miscarriage and D&C, I've been lackadaisical, not too perky. Maybe some romance will do us both some good."

He placed the glass next to him and took her left hand. The absence of their wedding ring often upset him. "Your sadness upset me as much as our miscarriage. I hope you're feeling better."

"Time heals most things but, thanks, my mood is starting to lift."

"Let's go then," Danny said and walked ahead to the bedroom. As he turned on the overhead light recessed in deer antlers from the previous owners, he admired the furnishings. It was as if a logger and carpenter were one and the same as the bedroom set appeared to have been hand-carved from a mountain forest.

He peeled off his clothes while Sara went into the bathroom, pulled back the patchwork quilt, and got into bed. Resting his head in the palm of his hands, his thoughts drifted to his daughter. She was in the throes of the grooming process for medical school and, since she'd always been bright, her potential to be admitted was average or better.

Danny realized that, by admitting to himself Annabel was a smart girl, some of the things she'd been saying to him must carry some weight. He couldn't remember how she'd phrased it, but her observation was that the methods Danny would use to pin point David's epileptic foci were antiquated. And, as far as he knew, the magazine he'd packed advertised all the usual equipment already familiar to him for his specialty.

Sara had gotten into bed and he rolled over, placing his hand on her hip; she had the softest skin. She brought her head in closer and their lips joined … moist and soothing and erotic at the same time. They joined together; although his thrusts were solid, they were seemingly distant.

What would it be like to be in the prime of your life - in college - and yet imprisoned in a stark ICU for weeks or perhaps months with wires passing through your cranium? The isolation from social activities or hanging out with your peers would be depressing if not hugely disabling of your whole college experience and education. Would someone even get back on track after that?

He finished and rolled off of Sara. She looked to the side, watching him as he tried to not close his eyes. He may be troubled by Annabel, she thought, but perhaps he wasn't getting away from work this weekend after all.

Late Saturday afternoon, Danny fried two hamburgers while Sara tossed together a salad. He got two plates, slid the burgers onto buns, slapped cheese on them and brought them over to the table. Sara got the condiments and two soft drinks, then they sat down.

"Yum," she said after taking a bite. "This is the best cheeseburger I've had in a long time."

"Yes, that hits the spot." Danny served himself a salad and smiled. "I'm glad we came. But I think I better make one work-related call."

"Which means you've been thinking about whatever it is," she said.

He shrugged his shoulders. "Sorry about that. But actually I just want to ask Bruce if he can fill in some of my office hours this week."

She poured salad dressing and looked at him questioningly.

"I'll keep my surgery schedule the same," he said, reassuring her.

"Good. People count on their surgeon, especially if it's you."

They finished eating and Danny quickly washed the plates while Sara dried. He then dialed Bruce's number on his cell.

"It's a Saturday evening so I'm wondering if this is a work or social call," Bruce said right off.

"Can I count on you to add more hours in the office to the few you'll be pulling this week?" Danny asked.

"You taking a holiday?"

"Actually, Sara and I are on the lake this weekend so that should tide me over. I need to get to work in the lab; I don't really have a plan but I have to start somewhere. Call it research."

"I trust you. You say the word and I'll do what I can. My wife's honey-do list will have to wait."

"Thanks, Bruce. I have surgeries three mornings this week. How about you take over my afternoon appointments in the office those days?"

"Consider it done."

Even though Danny anticipated getting home on Sunday morning, it was Sara who darted towards the front door with Dakota, deciding to see Mary and Casey first before going to their own place. Nancy opened the door.

"How was it?" Nancy asked, twirling her hair in front of her ear without letting Sara pass as Dakota slipped through. "You two look like lovebirds ... my own mother and father acting like honeymooners."

"Hmm. Sometimes neurosurgeons have other things on their mind," Sara lamented. "But I enjoyed myself nevertheless. There's nothing like the sight of a natural body of water to renew your soul."

"Okay, that answers that," Nancy said, stepping aside.

"How were things here?"

The two women walked into the kitchen as Danny stepped in and closed the door.

"Mary is painting and there's Casey and Julia," Nancy said, pointing to the big room.

"Uh-oh," Casey boomed. Dakota trotted into their space on the floor. The monument of toy building bricks they'd been playing with collapsed as the sorrel retriever nudged into both of them and his excitement waved his torso back and forth. Julia squealed and Casey rolled onto his back, grabbing Dakota from underneath and wrestling him.

"It's good to be home," Sara said. "It looks like Julia got back from her mother safe and sound."

"And thanks for minding her," Danny said.

Casey smiled over at them. "We weathered some sulkiness but that's over, isn't it young lady?" He tickled Julia's side and she dashed away from him laughing. "It was our pleasure. I hope you two had fun."

Between his two Monday morning surgeries, Danny raced up the stairs to the ICU. After he read every chart note Dr. Banks and Matthew had written over the weekend, he went into David's room.

"You're looking refreshed," Danny said.

David sat up in bed, his shoulders straight. With his short brown hair neatly combed, he looked quite good for being bedridden in an ICU.

"Hi, Doctor Tilson. I feel fine but I am bored out of my mind. What do they call it when patients just get up and storm out of a hospital? And don't come back?"

Danny looked him up and down wondering if he was considering it. "An AMA. Against medical advice." He patted the side of the mattress. "Do you mind if I sit?"

David shook his head so Danny sat, his left knee bent up on the bed, his posture relaxed. "Annabel mentioned how difficult it would be, you're being in here. I can see that. Sometimes it's virtually impossible when someone is going through tough times to see that things get better down the road. Later is when you realize you had to go through that necessary passage of time and events that got you to a better place." Danny rubbed his chin. "Going AMA is not a good idea."

A few seconds elapsed before David spoke. "Like not shooting some hoops again with my buddies after you warned me."

"Yes, and I'm so sorry it happened."

David nodded. "That Dr. Banks was by again this weekend. She explained to me again what you might have to do. That I'd have to go to surgery. And Annabel came by yesterday afternoon. I told her she doesn't have to come by anymore if she doesn't want to."

"She's a big girl. You two will figure out where the relationship is going, especially if you don't put pressure on each other."

"Dr. Tilson, I think we're becoming even better friends."

"A true friend is a rare thing. The best ones can last a lifetime." Danny thought of Casey. Not only that, he thought, but it also means protecting a friend in unusual ways even without their knowledge.

David smiled. "So we can be old like you and be sharing work stories and pictures of our kids?"

"There's a good chance," Danny said.

After his next intracranial surgery, Danny strolled over to the medical campus still wearing his white coat. He had called ahead to the research center and they had recommended one particular individual. With an engineering degree and a PhD in neuroscience, he didn't think he could collaborate with a more skilled person, at least on paper, for what he thought about accomplishing.

Danny rode the elevator to the top floor and got out. The hallway was empty and he couldn't hear a peep from the rooms that he passed. At the last door, Lab 608, he turned in. Most of the tables around the edge of the room were spotless but the middle area had signs of disarray where Danny found a tall man hunched over an EMG machine.

"Dr. Saxton?"

The man still tinkered at his project and Danny now noticed a small screwdriver in his hand.

"That's me," the man said. "What can I do you for?"

"I'm Danny Tilson, one of the local neurosurgeons."

Vance Saxton put down his tool and stood straight. "Name sounds familiar. Yes, I've heard about you. Nice to meet you."

"Likewise," Danny said noticing his dark yet searching eyes and felt automatically comfortable when shaking his hand. "The research department gave me your name."

Danny figured him to be around forty. He was bald, although not from premature hair loss; he was one of those men with remarkable facial features so that he could shave his head and still have a handsome, rugged appearance. With a weathered look, he either had weekends filled with outdoor activities or had heritage that rendered him a tan complexion.

"I was wondering if I could discuss something with you," Danny continued.

"Do you mind talking here or shall we go across the hallway? We have a room there with a couch."

"Here is perfect. As a matter of fact, time is of the essence."

"You're heightening my curiosity," Vance said, pointing him to a stool.

Danny shook his head and leaned against the counter. "My first question comes with two parts. Can I have access to this campus lab to work on a project? And, secondly, would it be possible to incorporate your help? If not, however, I'd still go ahead solo." He wrung his hands as if itching to dive into whatever he was thinking about.

Vance studied Danny's intent. "Unequivocally, yes. But I take it you can't just drop out of your practice to be here eight hours a day; nor can I help you that much or my other projects would suffer."

Danny smiled. "Wonderful. And you're correct, although I have Bruce Garner - the former head of my group - who is going to fill in many of my office hours.

"That's fortunate for you. Whatever it is you want to examine doing must be pretty important. So how long are we talking about?"

Danny gritted his teeth. "Ideally, within a month. At the outskirts, two months.

Vance raised his eyebrows. "Do you want me to install a cot in here for you to sleep?"

"No, that's okay."

"Really, I'm not joking. I've done that myself before when I'm possessed by an idea."

"I have a feeling I've stumbled onto a good partner."

"If you have the brainstorm along with a novel concept, then I will be your assistant and not technically your partner."

"If you wish," Danny said.

"So, are you going to enlighten me?"

"I must warn you this may sound like a crazy idea."

"You must not be aware of what Albert Einstein said."

Danny's eyes sparkled and he laughed wholeheartedly. "We must both be fans. I have an autographed book by the genius. I believe you are referring to 'If at first the idea is not absurd, then there is no hope for it.'"

"Perfect," Vance said. He walked around Danny, pulled in the stool a little bit and sat down. "Now, tell me."

When Danny finished explaining the notions and concepts he had in mind, Vance remained silent. Finally, he nodded.

"When do you want to start working?" Vance wanted to know.

"Right now."

Chapter 17

Danny lost track of all time. Vance had left, he kept tinkering at the bench, and then realized how tired he felt. He could go home, possibly wake someone up, or he could sleep in a hospital call room. Instead, he walked across the research building's hallway to the couch and, after rolling up a towel to substitute as a pillow, he laid down and easily fell asleep.

His pager on the table woke him up and he started fumbling for it as he spotted the time on a wall clock. If he were in the hospital, it would be buzzing with activity but not a sound was to be heard at 7 a.m. in the lab. These researchers probably come in at eight, he thought. People with normal lives.

The ER was calling. No matter how he altered his office hours or surgeries in the near future, his call schedule was firm. And today he was 'on.' Strange, however, to be contacted immediately. He returned the call and found out a head case was on its way, actually almost there.

Danny stopped in a bathroom for a few minutes, freshened up, and then made the short walk to the ER. Casey's ambulance was at the curb, the back door open, and a bloody sheet draped on the bench. He pieced together Casey's schedule in his mind and realized he must be 11-7 this week.

Stepping into the ER, Toni steered a dirty stretcher into the hallway from the trauma room. Her crisp paramedic uniform was worse for wear and, when she saw Danny, she acknowledged him with a slight nod towards the door.

They walked in side-by-side. All necessary hands were over the patient, monitors and equipment, while Casey was in the process of giving the ER doc a report. Danny jockeyed his way in to make them both aware of his presence.

The young man on the stretcher had lacerations like he'd been in some kind of martial arts sword fight. A bloody mess was the only description Danny could think of but he also knew there had to be a head injury since they had called him. He stepped around Casey and the respiratory therapist oxygenating the patient's lungs to check his pupils when the ER doc shouted 'clear' while trying to shock him out of ventricular fibrillation. Danny stood back as they continued with the resuscitation.

He shook his head; the patient had to be as young as David Bell. And what had gone wrong this sunny morning that he found himself at death's door? Then an image flashed in Danny's mind of what had been partially sitting on the soiled sheet in the ambulance … light-weight helmet.

The EKG was flat-line despite the staff's best attempts to make it otherwise. The ER doc finally held his hand up like he was stopping traffic. He grimaced, the bags under his eyes more noticeable. "I'm calling it," he said. Looking at the clock, he added, "7:46."

About a third of the staff disappeared out the door while everyone else tended now to the lifeless body, the gathering of personal information from tattered clothing, and the endless paperwork and chart notes for the short time he was in their care.

The physician in charge continued working while glancing at Danny. "You got here quick," he said. "And sorry about this."

"I'll fill him in, doc," Casey said.

Danny, Casey and Toni walked into the hallway. "Do you want to go outside?" Casey asked. "We're off so we can start getting the ambulance ready for tonight's shift."

"Sure," Danny said.

"But a quick stop here," Toni said, pointing to the lounge. They followed her lead knowing it was coffee they all craved; after they poured three full Styrofoam cups, they went outside.

"Whatever it was, it was a horrific way to die," Danny said. "We'll never know what the rest of his life would have been had he survived. I would imagine his head injury was as bad, or worse, than his external and internal injuries."

"In all these years," Casey lamented, "this was the first. And to tell you the truth, I never even heard about this before."

Danny held his coffee without sipping and looked questioningly at him.

"A deer versus a scooter or a version of a motorcycle," Casey said. "Full impact."

"That young fella," Toni said, "that deer carcass, that bike … all mangled around each other. It was awful."

Silence ensued until Toni stepped up into their vehicle, set her coffee down and started putting things away.

"I got a text before from Mary," Casey said. "Sara was leaving for work after the babysitter got there and asked her if she knew your whereabouts. She was real concerned because you apparently hadn't come home. Neither of them thought you were on call last night."

Danny's shoulders sagged. "I didn't mean to worry them. I'll give them a call."

Toni shot a glance their way. "You know what a woman would be thinking if her man doesn't come home, don't you?"

"She's right, you know," Casey commented. "And you've been down that path before. Why don't you fill me in so I know how to defend you? But also because I am curious and concerned."

"The only thing that lets a man get off sleeping beside his woman," Toni said, "is if he has to work in a different time zone or is ill in a hospital. And if he's on the job nearby, he has to have witnesses."

"Sounds like he has to be handcuffed to her bedpost," Casey said.

"No, that's a bit too restrictive or kinky. Locked in the house is more like it, with alarms that go off if someone tries to leave in the middle of the night."

"I'm glad we agree on the kinky part," Casey said. "I'm beginning to understand why you're not married."

"You betcha," she said. "The last guy I dated told me he was going fishing one weekend and I came to find out his last girlfriend was not totally out of the picture. He called the status of that relationship 'the photo finish' – as in, when an old girlfriend was fading out as a new one broke through the winner's banner. Anyway, he had spent another night with her."

"So what'd you do?" Casey asked.

"What any female paramedic would do. I told him if I ever gave him mouth-to-mouth again, I'd bite off his tongue. And that wouldn't be the only appendage I'd bite off."

"Uh, I hate to interrupt," Danny said, "but are you two finished?"

"Oh, yeah, sorry Danny," Casey said. "So anyway, I'm on the way home and I can reassure Mary you were at the hospital. But Sara must have left already." He eyed him cautiously. "But were you here all night?"

"No. I was across the way in R&D. And I did have to sleep there for a little bit because my eyes were slamming shut. It may not be the last time either if I am going to invent a ground-breaking method to handle epileptic patients."

Toni paused as she listened to the confidence behind Danny's words; Casey's face grew serious and he rubbed his hand along his crew cut. "If there's anything I can do to help you, either at home or over in the lab, just let me know. I believe it's David's recovery that is foremost on your mind."

Mid-afternoon and without knowledge of any incoming emergencies, Danny decided to head home. But, as he headed out of the parking lot and glanced at his watch, he decided to take a chance. Sara should still be at school and, in recent years, he couldn't remember ever paying her a surprise visit.

He suppressed a yawn and flipped on the windshield wipers for a couple of swipes. An earlier shower had left droplets on the window but now the sun began even evaporating the small puddles as he drove east.

The stately brick building already showed signs that classes had been dismissed as after-school activities had begun. When he drove slowly around the front, he glanced over the vehicles and finally spotted Sara's car. Since he felt so tired, he sighed with relief that the trip was not in vain.

He parked his Lexus and went to the door where he had to be buzzed in by the front office. The school has more security than a hospital, he thought, which was somewhat reassuring since both his ex-wife and daughter spent their days there.

Inside the office to the right, Danny poked his head in. One woman was feeding papers into a fax machine. "Where can I find Sara?" he asked.

"Dr. Tilson," she said, "we haven't seen you in forever."

Danny laughed. "That ends right now. Forever is a long time."

"She's probably still in her homeroom. Make a right down the hallway and it's at the end. Room 8."

"Thanks so much."

Danny saw that the door to Room 8 was closed so he peered in the window and, sure enough, class was dismissed. Sara sat at the head desk and a man sat ninety degrees off to the side in a wooden straight-back chair.

He knocked and waited for acknowledgement before going in; the man looked over and Sara's face lit up. As she rose, she waved for him to enter.

"Danny, what a surprise," she said, smoothing the black and white floral dress she wore. A belt accentuated her waistline and her lipstick must have been refreshed during the day. She still made his heart thump, especially when he encountered her in unfamiliar places or situations.

"Please have a seat and meet Ross, our principal. We're just discussing budget concerns. There's never enough money to do what we'd like."

Knowing the head of the school had been interested in Sara in the past, Danny stiffened. He held out his hand. "Nice to meet you."

"You must be the lucky man who used to be married to one of our finest teachers," Ross said.

"I am fortunate that we are still a couple," Danny said with sincerity, noting Ross' thin frame and sparse beard and mustache. He didn't seem like the bereaving widower that Sara had described to him.

"I was worried about you," Sara said, her tone changing as she sat back down.

"I was just leaving," Ross said.

"No, that's okay," Sara said.

"With an assistant's help," Danny said, "I started a new project over at the medical campus yesterday. It may consume time which I already don't have." He laughed lightly.

"Danny is very dedicated," Sara said, "as we all are."

Danny had to agree, especially looking around at Sara's impeccable classroom: A large world map covered the side bulletin board; a circular table near them had a lone microscope with what looked like an exhibit of small reptilian species laid out all around it; one blackboard had her writing, fluid and sweeping with biologic terms and short definitions; and her desk had a black and white picture of Darwin sitting with a notebook on the Galapagos Islands. Underneath it she had taped, "Always be thinking creatively thinking. Solve biologic puzzles."

"We have a student here that saw a doctor over in your campus's neurology department," Ross said. "He's doing quite well."

"Right now, one of my most vexing patients is almost as young as your students."

"I bet you can understand an older person having difficulties," Ross said, "but a young person with serious health problems is a different story. But actually, our student is doing quite well. The school had a fundraiser and, with the money we collected, we were able to help him get a service dog. The dog, Melbourne, now alerts him as well as his teachers that a seizure is imminent."

Danny's unrest over Ross's presence with Sara faded. "That's exactly what I'm concentrating on - epilepsy. And a service dog for seizures is an idea I haven't had experience with. I think, down the road, the same type of dog may be a helpful addition for my patient. Thank you, Ross, for your input."

Ross's pencil-thin eyebrows rose and he smiled. "Sure thing. Any time." He absent-mindedly got up. "I better leave you two alone. See you tomorrow, Sara."

The principal walked out, snapping shut the door behind him.

Sara began putting away pens and sorting papers on her desk for the next day. "You certainly did surprise me and I'm glad you came by."

"Me, too. It's been too long. The principal seemed more together than I imagined him."

"He's come a long way. He's getting over the grief from his wife's passing and is a lot more whole. He asks me for advice about women once in a while since he's taking baby steps back into dating."

Danny smiled. "Since that dating doesn't involve you, I wish him lots of luck."

When Sara got up, she led the way out. In the hallway, she closed the door and wrapped her fingers around Danny's. They walked out hand-in-hand like the corridor was a wedding aisle.

After another few days of surgeries, office work and extensive tinkering in the lab, Danny hoisted Julia onto his shoulders, called Dakota, and went outside. Wearing light jackets and carrying a tennis ball in his pocket, they went up to the main backyard porch. From there, Danny put Julia down, dug the ball out and threw it as far as he could. Dakota took off like a bullet and Julia slowly ambled down into the grass.

The French door opened and Casey stepped out. "I was going to hunt you down," he said, stretching his arms over his head then behind him. "I know it's short notice, but how about coming to court with me tomorrow? It's for the finger-debacle issue."

Danny eyed his stretching maneuvers. "Despite your muscles, you sure stay limber. Yes, I think I can arrange that because I'm already jockeying my schedule around. I don't think I want to miss it."

"Good. We'll leave at nine and meet Mark Cunningham at the courthouse."

Chapter 18

Danny and Casey quickly walked up the wide courthouse steps. They both wore suits and shoes like Wall Street businessmen and looked more refreshed than the haggard lawyers rushing past them. Inside, they stood in a short line for security where everyone moved quickly, familiar with the process.

Their assigned room was upstairs so they took the steps and waited for Mark on a bench. Casey wrung his hands and rotated his wedding band.

"This is a whole different world," he said. "I guess I'm uncomfortable with it because I don't know enough about what goes on. When I hear about seemingly bad people getting off without much punishment, I don't understand the law. And I sure couldn't work as an attorney." He watched a lawyer walk by with a woman who scowled at him after an innocent glance. Her hardened appearance almost made his skin crawl.

"I agree," Danny said.

"You're a seasoned veteran already," Casey said. "I hope this is my first and last time in a courtroom."

"If you don't attract trouble, it should be. By the way, how is Mary feeling?"

Casey stopped fiddling with his hands and flashed a wide smile. "Fine, and her appointments are going well, too." On purpose, he didn't mention their first healthy ultrasound pictures.

The heavy doors opened to their left and a cascade of people left, including two young children being dragged by an adult. From among the group, Mark emerged and stood before them, reshoving his briefcase closed due to its overstuffed contents.

"Good day, gentlemen," Mark said. "I just had another case. Rare to have a to-follow in the same room. It must be my lucky day.

You can go in unless you have any questions." He cocked his head and they both shook their heads 'no.'

"I'm taking a bathroom break," he said and shuffled down the hallway with short steps.

Casey peered around the doorway into the big room. "Just like TV," he said and rolled his eyes.

Danny stood. "Come on, let's go in and get seated, especially before her highness shows up."

Casey rose and straightened up his shoulders; his heart rate ramped up a bit as he went in and sat with Danny in the front row. Danny decided not to tell him that he'd be sitting up closer as Mark came back in and signaled for Casey to follow him to a front table.

They all heard the clicking of high heels as Rachel and Phil Beckett came up the aisle. "Hi, boys," she said as she sat with her attorney at the other table; she had on a mauve pantsuit with a floral pin on the lapel and matching earrings.

Danny watched both lawyers and clients from behind. The time for attorney-client discussions was over at this late date and all four were quiet and expectant of the judge to be announced.

"All rise," said the bailiff. "Judge Underwood presiding."

The black-robed judge ambled in from the back door and sat down. With broad shoulders and a square chin, she looked like a retired heavy-duty sports player. Rather than once again inspect the briefs she had put on the desk, she scrutinized the new group in her courtroom.

"Mr. Cunningham," she said with a husky voice, "according to your brief, your client is fine with a judge deciding this case. I will let him reconsider a jury trial one more time before we begin."

For appearances sake, Mark glanced next to him. Casey shook his head and placed his hands on the table.

"Your Honor," Mark said, "my client does not want to tie up the court's time or attention on this matter. As you recognize, he is only asking for due monetary compensation for the medical bills he sustained. We will decline a jury trial and ask for your consideration and verdict."

Mark believed the woman at the bench had a reputation of being a no-nonsense judge so he held his tongue and didn't pitch into a theatrical discussion about the horrors of Casey's accident. On the other hand, unless Phil was good at reading people, he was at a disadvantage since he primarily worked in Knoxville and was not too familiar with the Nashville judges.

When Mark finished, the judge narrowed her eyes at Casey and then looked over at Phil and Rachel. "Mr. Beckett, I hear that is a fine law firm you have over in Knoxville. Welcome to our city." She cracked a small smile and Rachel relaxed with a deep breath. "Are these medical bills a financial burden for your client to pay?"

As Phil deliberated his reply, Danny thought it was nice for a change that he was a spectator and not in front of the judge himself. But how he hated that his best friend had to be in court at all.

"Your Honor, the accident in question occurred after my client had checked her oil. She was at a house where she was waiting for her daughter to come out for visitation. She simply still had her car hood open when Casey Hamilton came out with her daughter. She didn't ask him to stick his hand in there and look at her engine."

Although Rachel had explained the situation as he just told it, Phil thought they had a judge who was a big 'women's libber,' so he continued with one more thought. "Sometimes men think that women aren't capable of taking care of their own vehicles."

"So true, Mr. Beckett," she said, but her tone was indecipherable. "However, you still have not answered my question. Are these medical bills a financial burden for your client to pay?"

Rachel nudged Phil with her elbow. "May my client address that question?" he asked.

"Go ahead, Ms. Hendersen."

"Your Honor," she said, getting up and slightly drooping her shoulders. "I am a single mother doing the best I can to make ends meet. Mr. Hamilton has an extremely lucrative field in the medical profession. For me, all bills are a financial burden. But despite my hardships, during the miniscule time I have left over for myself, I volunteer at a children's hospital taking care of the most invalid cases."

Rachel knew the volunteer work was a nice ploy but she also knew the real reason she was rushing to Knoxville was that she was due in court because of her involvement in Julia's child abuse case. If they ever knew that, she'd be in big trouble.

Listening to her, Casey wanted to pick up his jaw after it had metaphorically fallen on the floor; he tried to keep his anger from boiling over or to look back at Danny with disbelief. Danny had already dropped his head and closed his eyes; maybe they shouldn't have encouraged Casey to sue after all.

The judge noticed Casey's reaction as well as that of the man behind him and folded her hands on the desk. Rachel lowered into the stiff chair as if she had a backache.

"You can stay seated, ma'am," the judge said. "I understand you were in a hurry after Mr. Hamilton lost much of his finger. You weren't the one to drive him to the hospital?"

"No. I had limited visitation with my daughter and was preparing that day to do this volunteer work. And my car wouldn't start so that's why I couldn't drive him."

"So something was wrong with your car when Mr. Hamilton went to look at it for you?"

"Well, I didn't know that when I decided to check my oil. I didn't know it until I tried to start the engine and leave."

The judge twisted her mouth as if she clamped down on a wad of gum. She looked at Casey. "Mr. Hamilton, please give me your version."

"Your Honor, I brought my brother-in-law's daughter out to Miss Hendersen." He turned his head and nodded to Danny. "He's in the courtroom behind me. Anyway, after strapping Julia in and Miss Hendersen turning her ignition key, the engine wouldn't start. I told her I'd help her and to not turn the engine on while I looked under the hood. While my hand was under there, she started the car and a belt whacked off my finger. She said she was in a hurry and, for her, that was the end of it."

There was silence. The stenographer looked around waiting to take notes.

"What is your brother-in-law's name? the judge asked.

"Dr. Danny Tilson," Casey responded.

"Dr. Tilson, do you pay Miss Hendersen child support?"

Danny stood up, a little relieved to render information. "Yes, I do. However, it's not much because I have Julia most of the time. Her mother has her on an occasional weekend."

The Judge looked down at her desk, scratching behind her ear.

"Your Honor, may I say something?" Phil Beckett asked.

"No, Mr. Beckett."

"Mr. Cunningham," she said, "if you have your client's best interest at heart, I think you did not serve him well."

Mark didn't know what to say; it was rare to be so admonished by a Judge.

Judge Underwood's broad shoulders pulled back as she sat with perfect posture and she looked intently over at Phil Beckett.

"Mr. Beckett," she said, "your client will pay Mr. Hamilton's medical bills, every single penny within the next thirty days."

She shifted her gaze to Rachel. "You are an amazing woman to feed me that volunteer work story. If it's true, then it must be done in as callous a manner in which you treated Mr. Hamilton after the injury he sustained by your mistake. Do you realize you have shown no empathy in this courtroom for him losing most of his finger? He's walked around with that digit his whole life and he was going to use it for the other half, too. Too bad you had some place to go. You are heartless, Miss Hendersen."

Rachel gulped and felt her face turn red. "I …"

Very quickly, Phil put his hand on hers, putting pressure to not speak any further.

"In addition to the medical bills, I am ordering you to pay Mr. Hamilton twelve thousand dollars for pain and suffering. With leniency, I will allow you to pay one thousand dollars a month and have the total paid off in one year." She pounded her gavel, then stood and left the courtroom.

Rachel practically blew steam as she turned on Phil Beckett. "You imbecile," she said.

Simultaneously, they both slipped out from behind the table and walked down the aisle without looking at Mark, Casey or Danny.

"Rachel," Phil said, "that was your undoing."

"My undoing? You're my attorney."

"You run things in the courtroom your own way. I usually don't carry as much weight as your testimony, either good or bad. In this case, bad." He pulled open the heavy door and let her walk out first.

"Do you realize I will need a huge jump in income to pay off that buffoon?"

Casey and Danny had turned around and watched them leave, smiling as they looked at each other.

"Well done, gentlemen," Mark said. "Let's get out of here while we're ahead."

Mark shoved his papers in his briefcase and led the way. When Casey joined Danny in the aisle, they left alongside each other.

Danny suppressed a laugh as he grinned at Casey. "Who would have thought?" he asked.

"Not I," Casey responded. "You can't make this stuff up. Sometimes the world works in mysterious ways."

Another week went by and Danny and Vance sat across from each other at the work bench they'd been using in the lab. The fluorescent bulb on one side of the room flickered in need of replacement so Vance turned the lights off, went over to the blinds and yanked on the string, pulling them as high as they would go.

"I think we've made progress," he said.

Danny picked up the electrodes on the table within arm's reach and looked them over. The intracranial strip electrodes, grid electrodes or depth electrodes were way too big; they were clunky and invasive and the reason he was persisting with his idea.

"Yes, these ten-millimeter electrodes won't cut it."

"But don't forget, Danny. For traditional intracranial electroencephalograms, they are fine. You're just not satisfied with the present state of affairs." Vance stood alongside Danny, took the electrodes with his hands, and placed them out of reach.

Danny rubbed his eyes, trying to feign off the sleepiness he felt. He'd been in the lab since 6:00 a.m. and had only taken a break for incoming phone calls from the office and for a quick lunch in the lounge. Vance, on the other hand, had come in later after much more coffee than Danny and with a half-read newspaper tucked under his arm. Although he was devoted to his projects, he made sure they fit into a 40-hour work week.

Both men eyed their product. Danny's fingers separated them and he nodded his head slowly and emphatically, a pleasurable grin replacing his tired look.

"We did it," Danny said. "At least I think we did. The diameter of these electrodes is less than 100 micrometers?"

"You know they are. You just need someone to pinch you that they are a reality."

Danny sighed. "And the other parts?"

"The engineers made you a microchip, an antenna and a miniaturized station all based on your ideas and theories as to how this will all work." Vance opened a cardboard box and let Danny take out the contents.

"I'm speechless," Danny said. "Thank you and a big thank you to the department."

"You're welcome but you're responsible. They and I just helped out. Putting your gadgets together functionally is your job; the rest of your idea is yet to be put to the test." Vance scratched his bald head in thought but gave Danny the benefit of the doubt.

"Okay," Danny said. "Have I developed a wireless microelectrode system that will monitor David Bell's brain activity without having him be confined to an ICU bed?"

Vance didn't answer the question. If it worked, it wouldn't just impact David Bell but the future of all patients who were in the same predicament.

Chapter 19

Between cases, Rachel sat in the outpatient facility OR break room. She barely touched the microwave popcorn in the bag next to her and fiddled with a pen. Since going to court when that nasty judge ordered her to pay more than what was requested, she had lain low at work and at home.

This new mandated financial payment to Casey felt like an iron anchor sitting on her chest, one so big it could hold in place a mega-cruise ship. Misfortune, that's what she called it. A string of bad luck.

But it was going to change. Her original plan was fool proof. So much so, it was practically 'in the bag.' However, now it wouldn't be enough.

She had recently been relying only on herself and staying clear of involvement with more men, but the more she thought about it, perhaps it was time to change that yet again. A supplemental plan in her back pocket wouldn't hurt. Since she knew a move very far away was imminent in the coming months, it would be possible to tweak the exact location if someone else was involved.

Rachel looked around the small lounge. There were few nurses and orderlies there, and all the doctors were doing surgery or in the recovery room. An effeminate nurse named Tom was sitting on the other end of the black leather couch with her. If anyone wanted to know what went on in the ambulatory center, or with their health care personnel or local physician practices, the best information source, gossip or not, was Tom.

She slid the warm popcorn bag over to the middle of the seat between them. "Tom, help yourself. It's kettle corn which makes regular popcorn taste inferior."

Tom's eyes twinkled as he turned sideways and reached into the bag. "I don't mind if I do."

"Say," Rachel said, "I have a dear friend who is moving out west soon and I'm trying to help her with preliminary details. You know everyone coming and going around here. Are you aware of anyone that's moving out there? If you do, I could ask them a few questions."

Tom finished chewing and crossed his legs. "No, can't think of a soul."

She tapped her pen on her blue scrubs. "What about residents? Third or fourth years should be finishing up and have their jobs lined up. I mean, they take positions all over the place when they are offered the best salaries and spots in good practices."

After scratching into his ivory-blonde hair, Tom took a sip of coke beside him. "I know a bunch of them. Two going to the big northeast cities, although I don't know why. That little female Ob/Gyn resident you see running around here is going down the road to Huntington and the ENT fellowship guy that does the MOHS repairs with the attending is going to the windy city."

Rachel frowned, almost giving up with her questions.

"It's not like you said, ya know," Tom added. "In other words, they may start off with good salaries and spots in good practices but think of the debt a lot of them have."

"That's true," Rachel lamented.

"The only one probably not floating in that boat is Dr. Kevin Mcbride. I was in a room with him about three weeks ago. He hardly comes over here." Tom looked down at the bag.

"Here, you finish them," Rachel said, handing him the chips. "What do you mean about this Dr. Mcbride?"

"If any of them aren't in debt, it's him. He was a CPA for years. One of the partners of the group. He became one of those late bloomers to apply to medical school. You know, it's like one day they wake up and an epiphany strikes them in the head and they can't get it out of their system from then on out. They believe they were supposed to help people and so they become fixated on becoming a doctor." Tom shrugged his shoulders and laughed. "If only they knew what they're getting themselves into."

Rachel smiled. "Yes, if only they knew. So, does he have a job waiting for him and what's his specialty?"

"He's what I call a male Gyner. You know, a genitourinary doc. I know he's accepted a position. Hey, I think he said he's going to California. Yes, I'm sure of it. He's going where he'll be tied up in the ridiculousness of the traffic around the Golden Gate Bridge."

She practically got goose bumps but there was one more thing she needed to know ahead of time. "That's a move that will surely be disruptive to his wife, especially if she has a lucrative job here in Nashville."

Tom licked his fingers and crumpled the bag. "The guy may be older than most of the other residents but I know he ain't married." Tom practically blushed. "I was kinda wondering about him myself, if you know what I mean, but he's straight."

"Thanks, Tom," she said. "I'll be sure to try and track him down. Maybe he can shed some light on the San Francisco area."

"He's usually over in the main OR, especially in the cysto room."

Rachel grew happier that Tom was such a chatterbox and always willing to gossip. "They have a devoted cystoscopy room?"

"Why sure. And it's as busy as seven-year cicadas. I have a friend who works mostly in that room and he's sick and tired of the monotony of it. Guys with big prostates. He says you've seen one, you've seen 'em all."

"Hmm, sounds like something I'd like to do for a while. You know, a change of pace for something easier." She reached for her bottle of lemonade on the scratched table in front of them.

"Actually, my friend loves our outpatient facility," Tom said. "You could ask the head nurse who deals with staffing. Maybe you two can switch your positions around."

"Thanks, Tom," she said. She rose slowly while her heart thumped at the mere possibilities of what she could attain with Kevin Mcbride.

Danny paced in front of his mahogany desk waiting for Penny Banks to return his phone call. He'd only gotten through half of the paperwork clutter that had accumulated during his limited office time in the last two to three weeks but he needed the break. Besides, it was difficult to contain his excitement about the work he had completed with Vance Saxton as it was time to explain it to the people whom it could possibly impact and then test it on David. He'd already discussed his project with his buddies at the FDA, they fast-tracked it, and there was nothing holding him back but to ask permission from the Banks' family for its placement.

His extension rang and he grabbed the phone.

"Hey, Danny, it's Penny."

"Would you like to be in the ICU when I tell David and his parents about what I've been working on?" he asked. "See if they agree to implanting it in David?"

"I wouldn't miss it for the world."

"How about 5:00 p.m.?"

"See you then," she said.

Danny put down the phone. He resumed pacing across the room, not knowing what to do about Annabel. Since she still was behaving poorly towards him and she scowled at David's present medical treatment, he didn't know if he should reach out to her and include her in the afternoon meeting. And what if his new method failed? On the other hand, it was possible that Annabel would be with David in his room later.

He stopped at the window. Activity on the street was dying down as doctor's offices slowed down and fewer patients were walking back and forth between the medical buildings. Deciding that he would only include family later today and not call his daughter, he swiveled the blinds three-quarters shut.

In the nurses' station, Danny joined Penny as she finished writing a chart note. Her long brown hair was tightly braided and she wore a smile as she looked up at him. "I am very excited about your news. But I know it's too early to celebrate until we see how it all goes."

"I am reluctant, too. As a matter of fact, I haven't even told my daughter. We don't know if my method will work. And, if it does, are we then going to be able to pinpoint the origin of David's epileptic activity?"

"Stay optimistic. It's the best shot this kid has right now."

Danny took David's chart and asked a nurse to come with him to witness the signing of the surgical permission form. The three of them walked in where Tara sat in a chair pulled beside David's bed and Floyd stood with his back to the window.

"I'm so glad to have you all gathered for what I'm about to tell you," Danny said after greeting each one of them.

The couple stole a glance at each other while Danny spoke. Tara held David's hand tightly as if he was still two years old; Floyd stepped forward and Danny wondered if he had forgotten to shave or if he was growing a beard. Yet but perhaps it was concern for his son that had put Floyd's personal tasks on hold.

"Since Dr. Banks is intimately involved with David's care, I wanted to have her here as well. We both feel we have given David plenty of time on anti-epileptic medications and it's time to move on to surgical methods. Without much detail, I have previously mentioned to each of you about the surgical methods and technology that presently exists if a patient doesn't respond to medication. I didn't want to alarm you too much that, if we came down to this, David would have to stay in the ICU for weeks on end due to the monitoring. Wires would pass through his skull and electrodes would be connected to a machine. With constant recording, we would be able to pinpoint where his seizure foci are."

Penny nodded as she stood at the end of the bed. "Dr. Tilson is putting it mildly," she said. "Think how annoyed and bored you are now about being here. Can you imagine staying here for at least another month or two?"

"Right now, I'd rather be studying in a library for final exams than laying here," David said.

"We understand," Danny said. "Yet that wouldn't be possible either because of your daily seizures, which I am so sorry to see you go through."

"So what do you have in mind, Dr. Tilson?" Floyd asked.

"I took it upon myself to brainstorm and develop a new system with the help of an engineer and neuroscientist."

"In essence," Peggy interjected, "Dr. Tilson has been living in the lab for the last few weeks on your account."

Floyd's jaw dropped and Tara's eyes grew wider as David leaned forward, waiting on Danny's next words.

Danny waved off Peggy's remark. "It's become apparent that our next step forward is surgery, David. But rather than monitoring your epilepsy with the old methods we'd usually implement, I'd like to do the operation to implant a wireless system. That's what I've been working on."

"Wireless?" David asked, then thought a second. "Like going from a dial-up email connection to a wireless network?"

"Exactly," Danny said.

"Wow! How cool is that?"

"Wait a minute," Floyd said. "This sounds like pure science fiction. I don't want our son being a guinea pig for a technique meant for human beings living in the twenty-fourth century."

"Dad, advancements are already here like robotics and artificial intelligence. Technology isn't taking baby steps like when you were growing up; it is making exponential quantum-leaps."

"Including cloning and genetic engineering," Danny added.

"And GPS in cars," Tara said. "And what about smart phones? They are ridiculous."

Floyd frowned. "I just don't know about this."

"I'm not here to pressure you," Danny said. "I'll give you plenty of time to decide after I explain more. First of all, if my method doesn't succeed, we'll have to go back to the old system. But there are multiple advantages of this new plan such as a reduced risk of infection and the ability to easily extend the monitoring time. We'll be able to more precisely identify the area of your brain causing the epilepsy and, of course, it's wireless so you can go home. Obviously, no matter which method we use, once we discover the area of your brain responsible, then I'll have to go back in to remove it."

Floyd's shoulders sagged as he went over to his wife to reassure her. She tilted her head up to look at him but didn't say a word.

"Have you told Annabel about this?" David asked.

"No. I will … if you'd like me to."

"I guess you or I can tell her later.

He looked at his parents. "I want to try this," he said as he let go of his mother's hand. "Dr. Tilson, when can you do the surgery and where do I sign?"

Chapter 20

Rachel thought about it the rest of the day and couldn't come up with a reason not to ask for a transfer over to the main OR's GU or urology room; she had nothing to lose by asking and perhaps a lot to gain if her request was granted. Maybe helping in that subspecialty would be easier than what she was already doing. And on top of it, her court-ordered volunteer work was completed. She'd even been able to call in sick two times and not have it count as a strike against her.

She waited around after her shift until the head nurse went back to her office where she'd be free of OR distractions. "May I come in for a moment?" Rachel asked after rapping on the open door.

"Sure," the snowy-haired woman said. "Have a seat, Rachel."

"Thanks. I won't take up much of your time. I have a quick question but, believe me, I'm happy in the outpatient facility. I'm only wondering if I could have a change of pace, temporarily or permanently. Perhaps a transfer to the main OR's urology room?"

The woman leaned back. "You're a good tech. I like to keep people happy. It's okay with me. I have enough part-timers backed up that would like more hours."

"Thank you very much. Can we arrange it?"

"I'm quite swamped. Why don't you go over there and talk to staff. Tell them it's okay by me."

Rachel went straight over through the long connecting first-floor hallway and made inquiries at the front desk of the OR. She followed the nurse in charge of personnel into the lounge, introduced herself, and expressed her desire to work in the cysto room. "The outpatient facility has nurses waiting in line for more work, so they would be happy to relocate one of us," she said.

The head nurse looked Rachel up and down. "Robert has been in that room for ten years and he's sick and tired of it. We'll be happy to oblige you. If they can really spare you in outpatient, start on Monday and you can work under Robert's supervision for a week."

"Appreciate it," Rachel said. Even though they would have to go through the trouble of training her into the position, she wouldn't be giving them longevity back in the job. They didn't even know, she thought, how foolish they were being.

Danny left the ICU after talking with the Bells and put David on the OR schedule for Monday. Although he could still possibly join Sara at home for dinner, he contemplated driving over to campus and talking to Annabel. It might be better for him to personally tell her the latest update about David.

He stopped in the doctor's lounge, sat down, and pulled out his cell phone. After dialing and leaving a voice mail that he was headed that way, he left. She must still be ignoring me, he thought. How can his relationship with her be so messed up?

Driving onto the college grounds, he felt twangs of sadness and yearning for his own past history on the school campus. Little did he know it then that life would never be that carefree again. Even though school work had been difficult, the experience of living among people his own age was unsurpassed by any. Other than eating and studying, playing with teens who lived all around him day after day had been special. And this campus had its own beauty. He used to love sitting on a bench alongside one of the paths where big oaks, poplars, and walnut trees lining the walkways and stately mixed architectural-style buildings were set further back. The scattering of water fountains and sculptures added to the serenity.

He drove down a long street, turned right and moved slowly over speed bumps. Turning into the second parking lot, he got out, stood against his Lexus and texted Annabel. *I'm on campus and I'm coming into your dorm. Don't you want to hear about David?*

Watching students pass in the lot and across green lawns, he waited for a reply. A student on a bike with a light backpack came to a stop and gave Danny a nod.

"I'm Annabel Tilson's father," he said as the youth locked his bike with a chain. "If you're going in the dorm, can I follow?"

"I know Annabel. Sure," he answered.

Danny followed and the teen entered his key card to the main door. "The lounge is straight ahead," he said, then headed to the other side of the building.

The lounge was empty but the TV was on. Danny took out his cell phone and texted again. *"I'm in the dorm lounge. I'll wait here about fifteen minutes, then I'm heading home. Hope to see you."*

Annabel was at the snack bar above the cafeteria when Danny's first message came. She headed over to the dorm, curious about what her father would say about David. Maybe there had been a change in his condition though she didn't look forward to a one-on-one with Danny.

The second text came after she reached the dorm and she walked straight to where her father was sitting. He was an odd sight; an older man with blue pants and a crisp white-collared shirt where normally there would be twenty-year-olds with ear buds or text books.

Her face soured when she sat in an oversized leather chair, Danny at the end of a matching couch. "Hello," she mumbled.

"Glad to see you," Danny said. "I took a chance I'd catch you."

"We'll, I'm here. I'm not out tonight like other students who are dating. Some Friday nights I spend in the hospital visiting David."

"I just came from there. I talked to David and his parents about taking him to the OR next week."

"To put in that insane equipment you told me about?"

"There's been a modification to it."

"Yeah, like when hell freezes over. Did he decide to go under the knife?"

Danny dropped the smile he'd worn when she sat down. "Yes, I'm implanting the electrodes on Monday."

"Well, thanks for telling me. I'll make sure I get over there. I'll see if I can cut any classes; otherwise, I'll come over after I finish." She leaned forward and her tone held a finality to the conversation so Danny didn't feel he had an opportunity to tell her about the work he'd been doing.

Two students walked in and noisily started a game of pool on the right side of the room. Annabel looked over and acknowledged both of them.

"I guess I'll head home," Danny said. "I'll tell your mother you said hello. I know she'll ask me ... how are you doing with your class load?"

"Fine. Pretty good. I'm going to get into medical school even if it kills me."

"Don't let that happen, sweetheart. Nothing is worth that sacrifice. And if there's anything I can do, just holler."

He got up and walked out of the lounge. She followed him but veered off up the staircase to her room.

Since it was almost eight o'clock when Danny left the campus parking lot, he called ahead to Sara, letting her know he was on his way home.

"I'm upstairs with Casey and Mary," Sara said. "Come say hello."

"I'm tired but, since tomorrow is a free Saturday and I can get up later, I'll be there."

"In your dreams," she said. "Julia is already down for the count. Since when can you sleep in with someone who's less than four years old around?"

Danny laughed. "Dakota isn't exactly a late sleeper either."

"Well, there you go."

He slowly drove down their long street where a man and his dog were running and one couple was taking a walk. Lawns had greened up during the last month and, as he pulled into their double driveway, he felt happy to leave the hectic day behind and grateful to feast his eyes on the large house and expansive lot.

Dakota gave him a robust greeting when he opened the unlocked front door. He let the dog out and walked with him around the lawn. The Chessie was at his heels when he went back inside.

"Hey, everybody," Danny said cheerfully, "I'm home."

"Aren't you chipper after such a long day," Casey said. Standing at the kitchen island, he nodded at a bottle of wine and a pitcher of iced tea. "What's your pleasure?"

"I'll have what you're having." He went into the family room, kissed Sara, and went over to his sister and pecked her on the cheek.

"How was your day?" Sara asked.

"Besides the usual, I talked with David Bell and his parents late today about my hardware invention and he's going to the OR on Monday for surgery. Then I went to see Annabel and give her an update. But it was only a partial update."

"You went over to campus?" Sara asked.

"I did."

"What kind of reception did you get?" Mary asked.

"Chilly, like a refrigerator."

"Sounds like progress," Casey said, handing Danny a glass of white wine. "At least you didn't say cold as ice."

"Precisely," Danny said and sat next to Sara. He slipped off his shoes and put his feet on the coffee table. "Is Nancy downstairs?"

"She is," Sara said. "And Julia's fast asleep."

"And how was your day?" Danny asked Sara. "Is that principal still hanging around your classroom?"

"What's this I hear?" Mary asked.

"Danny's just egging me on," Sara said. "The principal spends more time visiting me than he should, that's all. I'm kind of flattered but Danny knows he's safe."

"It's true," he said, squeezing her hand. "If I were in his shoes, I'd be doing the same thing."

Looking over at Mary and her growing belly, Danny raised his glass. "I want to make a toast that baby Tilson-Hamilton keeps growing and maturing as healthy as can be."

Casey slid his legs off the ottoman and moved forward in the roomy leather chair. He raised his glass while Mary and Sara did the same. "In that case," he said, "we have to make it a double toast."

"Then you mean a quadruple toast since there's four of us," Sara said.

"No, Danny said baby Tilson-Hamilton," Casey responded.

Danny looked quizzical as Casey and Mary both smiled.

"Am I missing something here?" Sara asked.

"I think what Casey is toasting to is more than one Tilson-Hamilton."

Sara gulped. "Twins?"

Mary rubbed her belly and nodded. Danny put his glass down and got up while Casey did the same. Elated, the two of them gave each other a shoulder grip and then Danny leaned over and gave Mary a hug.

Sara continued sitting and had to fight back the tears. "This is the second best news after the initial news that you were pregnant," she said slowly.

"Congratulations to you, too, Aunt Sara and Uncle Danny," Casey said.

"We have the easy job," Sara said.

Mary switched her rubbing to counter-clockwise. "However … even though two will be a big treat, it'll mean double the work."

"We're a family," Danny said. "We'll do whatever it takes."

Danny and Sara checked on Nancy and Julia when they went downstairs. At their daughter's door, the two adults glanced at each other and smiled; Nancy had fallen asleep, curled up on her side. When they looked in on Julia, Dakota trotted across the carpet and sniffed at her, then turned as if telling them she was okay.

They went to their bedroom and began to undress. "They are going to make the best parents," Sara said while unbuttoning her blouse. "And this is phenomenal. Is there any history of twins in your family?"

"Not that I'm aware of," Danny replied after thinking back to grandparents and great-uncles and aunts.

"It is so exciting," he said, "but I'm going to worry every day until Mary gets near the end of the third trimester or past the time they would be born too premature."

"She'll take good care of herself and we'll be monitoring her, too. And Casey, well, he'll be like her guardian angel protector like he always is for this family. Like you say, although no one talks about it, he was a caretaker of that brother of his. What a loss that was for him."

Danny's expression crumpled and he sat down heavily on the bed. "It didn't happen the way you think it did."

"What?"

"Tommy's death."

"What are you talking about?"

Dakota nuzzled Danny's hands, lying motionless on his lap. He put one hand on the dog's head and rubbed.

"When I was older, Mom told me the whole story. No one was to know. Mr. and Mrs. Hamilton kept the incident quiet but, one day, Elizabeth finally confided in Mom. I guess Casey was spending so much time at our house that she just wanted Mom to know. Later after Tommy died, she even managed to get a job. Besides her migraine headaches, she had to keep busier to divert her sadness."

Sara continued to stand on the side of Dakota and stare at Danny. Afraid of what he was going to divulge, she brought her hands up to her mouth.

"Anyway," Danny said, "Tommy didn't die from his cystic fibrosis nor was he hospitalized for it when Casey was staying with us at the time of his death." He stopped and had to take a deep breath. "That morning, Casey and Tommy were playing outside. As usual case, in essence, Casey was minding his younger brother. While Casey left the front of the house chasing after a cat in harm's way, Tommy went out into the street and got hit by a car."

Sara sank into the bed and Dakota sat in front of Danny. "How awful," she said. "Why was the story changed?"

Danny glanced at her, his eyes narrowing. "Mrs. Hamilton realized the constant responsibility Casey had babysitting his younger brother. And he took it seriously. She knew Casey had run off being a Good Samaritan and hadn't been with Tommy. She also knew that, if Casey knew the truth, he'd believe that his brother got hit by a car because he'd left him and he'd never forgive himself his entire life.

Sara slowly nodded with understanding, her eyes becoming moist. "Are you absolutely sure it's something you should never tell him?"

"Absolutely. I never told him and Mary doesn't know either. That's the way it will be. What good would that information do for Casey except give him tremendous heartache and guilt?"

Sara took his hand. "You're right. And I think your mom made the correct decision to just tell you. And you have my word, I'll never repeat it."

"Thanks. I feel better that you know. Now you understand things better."

"That's an understatement. The both of you are remarkable."

Chapter 21

Another first day at a different work situation, Rachel thought. Transferring over to the cysto room from the outpatient facility wasn't such a big move but she did stop to consider that she was the queen of job hopping. Yet companies and hospitals had no loyalty for their employees so why should she show any allegiance to them?

She changed into dark blue scrubs in the nurse's locker room and looked in the long mirror. Trying on both a blue and a white OR hat, she decided to wear the white one and scattered a little hair alongside her face from underneath it. She put on some mauve lipstick and touched up her mascara. Now her eyes looked their best and she smiled while tightening the bow on her pants.

Having looked at the OR schedule, she already knew that Dr. Kevin Mcbride would be in the cysto room the entire morning. Over the weekend, especially on Sunday while Julia had come for visitation and had taken a nap, she had learned all she could about him from the internet; it was amazing what a person could dig up online.

She walked over to the nurse's lounge and inquired about Robert, the person she was told would show her the ropes of her new position. With shift change occurring, the room was busy with nurses giving reports and checking in. Lots of coffee was being consumed and hands were dipping into boxed donuts. "Does anyone know where I can find Robert from the cysto room?" she asked a group at a table.

"Right there," a male orderly said, pointing at someone leaving through the door.

"Thanks," Rachel said and hurried after him. "Robert, wait up," she said.

He turned around. "Come on, you must be Rachel. Glad to meet you. Let's get you broken in so I can leave for greener pastures." She figured him to be in his mid-fifties and he walked with a limp. She wondered how many more green pastures did he have left.

The main cysto room wasn't that large. There were glass cabinets, counter space, steel rolling tables and the main table for patients. Besides the overhead fluorescent lights, there were lamps that moved and could focus on areas of the patient. A doorway which stayed open had a supply room and counter space as well, basically where Robert hung out with his paperwork or his crossword puzzle when not directly involved with the patient or the docs.

"Basically, we'll have Dr. Mcbride today," Robert said, "and an anesthesiologist, too. Actually both of them are senior residents. Watch what I get, what I give them, pay attention, and you'll be fine."

In a half hour, an orderly rolled a stretcher in with a male patient. With Rachel at his side, Robert verified the name and paperwork in the chart. "You're having a transurethral resection of the prostate or TURP, correct?" Robert asked.

"Unfortunately, yes," the patient said.

After they got him situated on the table, Robert placed a spinal tray on a rolling table for the bubbly anesthesiologist who talked to the man the whole time. After prepping his back with a sterile solution, applying local anesthetic under his skin, and easily placing the spinal needle with further medication, the patient began getting numb from the waist down while Robert positioned him in the lithotomy position.

Dr. Kevin Mcbride entered the room and greeted the patient first while Rachel stayed near the supply room door watching him carefully. She was forty-two years old and she figured him to be late thirties, perhaps thirty-eight or -nine. He had dark features, darker than what she'd expect from the Irish heritage he must have with a name like Mcbride. His eyebrows and hair were black as coal; his eyes were deep blue and he had a sloping tip to his nose. With very white teeth and a flurry of wrinkle lines around his eyes, his smile radiated happiness. So far, so good, she thought. Good looking, but not the most handsome man she'd come across or been involved with.

Kevin turned from the patient. "Good morning, Robert."

"Good morning," Robert said. "This is Rachel. I'm showing her the ropes. She's a tech who is going to be my replacement. I'm asking for a change of pace. Maybe they can teach an old dog a new trick."

Rachel stayed where she stood but focused solidly on the doctor's gaze.

"Nice to meet you," Kevin said.

"My pleasure," she said, her voice as smooth as velvet. "I'm a fast learner but let me know if there is anything I can make better. You've been doing this, I am sure, for years and years so you're apt to find a newcomer's mistakes."

"Actually," Robert said, "Dr. Mcbride is a senior resident."

"Yes, I had a past life as a CPA," Kevin said.

"Really?" she crooned. "You didn't happen to be part of the Janney and Mcbride CPA Associates, did you?"

The doctor nodded with a smile and Rachel followed up immediately. "They were the most respected and dedicated certified public accountants in the state of Tennessee. That's my opinion anyway, especially before they changed hands to Janney and Forrester CPA Associates. Now it makes sense because that must have been when you left."

"To go to medical school," he said, proudly.

"Well, I hope you don't mind my saying that you had a fine career then and a fine career ahead of you now. I wish you lots of luck."

"Thank you," Kevin said watching her another second before taking the cystoscope and inserting it into the patient's urethra.

The patient started to doze with the sedation the anesthesia resident slipped through his IV. Rachel continued to stand behind the doctor.

"Usually," Kevin said, "how long it takes to do a TURP depends on how enlarged a man's prostate gland is."

"I feel bad for older men who get benign prostatic hypertrophy," she said. "The symptoms must be terrible and limit some of their lifestyle."

"You're going to do fine in this room. What did you say your name was?"

"Rachel … Rachel Hendersen."

Tara sat on the stiff chair while Floyd paced across David's ICU room waiting for staff to transport him to surgery. Annabel was going to skip her late morning class and had arrived a short time after them. "Do you mind if I join you?" she had asked.

David waved her over. "I'm so happy to see you," he said, "but you know you didn't have to come." She kissed him on the lips and gripped his hand.

"I want to be here," she said. "After your surgery, I'll still try to get here a lot. But I know you're going to be laid up for a long time. Maybe I can bring some books and come study here once in awhile. I can bring you something to read, too."

"If your dad's invention works out," David said, "then you won't have to study here at all." He smiled and squeezed her hand; Annabel blinked as she didn't know what he was referring to.

A rail-thin nurse came in. "They're getting your chart and paperwork from the desk to take you downstairs," she said, displaying a syringe. "This is a preop sedative ordered by anesthesia. Here you go. Enjoy the slumber." She injected the Versed into his IV and left.

"David," Annabel said, "what invention are you talking about?"

David's eyelids began to sag and she heard concerned murmurs from his parents. She got up and stepped back while staff came in and began unhooking monitors.

"You all can wait out in the lounge or the OR waiting area," his nurse said.

After quick good-byes to David, the three of them proceeded to the empty waiting room. Two pots of coffee sat on a warmer; Tara poured some decaf, stirred in a creamer, and took her cup to a couch.

"David said something back there," Annabel said while lowering into a comfortable chair. "Has the plan for surgery somehow changed? Is my dad using some new equipment or something?"

"I guess it makes sense," Tara stuttered, "that your dad can't tell you everything about his care of patients. He told us of a new system he's developed. It would eliminate David's long stay in the ICU. It's a wireless system for seizure monitoring. But … but … as it's experimental, we don't know yet."

"He made it?"

"Yes, dear. Apparently he's been holed up in a research lab besides trying to manage his practice. It was his creative brainstorm and long hours which may bring this to fruition."

"I didn't know," Annabel said almost in a whisper.

David was Danny's first case of the new week. He'd had a good night's sleep and had gone through the equipment in his mind over the weekend and felt optimistic about using it for the first time. Even though he'd developed it with David in mind, he hoped it would be successful and that the same thing - or a version of it - could be used again and again in future patients.

He stood next to the OR table as his favorite anesthesiologist, Dean, placed the mask over David's face and asked him to take some big deep breaths. "See you in recovery," Danny said.

"Night, night," Dean said as David's lungs filled with oxygen and he injected old-fashioned sodium thiopental in his IV. Dean still preferred its use for neurosurgical cases if there was no contraindication. When David was unconscious, Dean safely inserted the endotracheal tube and the table was moved forty-five degrees from the anesthesia equipment. The top of David's head already had a large shaved circle for where the surgery would take place.

With Dean's nod of approval that his patient had enough anesthesia on board, Danny finished preparing David's head by putting it in a fixed position using a 3-pin fixation device which he bored into the skull

Danny went out to scrub but looked in the window while the nurse prepped David's scalp with an antiseptic. He thought over David's journey to getting here ... the irony of the teen's problem starting at a recreational event - a college basketball game – and, later, suffering a secondary impact. Now he'd have his skull opened up for a brain procedure because of seizures and it shouldn't be the last time either.

Annabel may be involved with David the rest of her life, Danny thought, as he scrubbed thoroughly between each finger. Besides the fact that she already found fault with him, it made him carry a heavier burden than usual for the welfare of his patient.

He pushed the door open with his foot and went back in. Dean still buzzed along with padding David's arm resting on an arm board where he had access to an IV, hanging the Foley catheter bag where he could monitor urine output, and administering the anesthetic.

After the scrub tech helped Danny get gowned and gloved and they applied all the sterile blue drapes, he got comfortable at the head of the table. He asked for a scalpel and made his incision on skin. After completing a long, rounded incised area, he folded back skin, muscles and tissues, exposing David's skull. His heart thumped against his chest; now came the more difficult part, especially since he knew his patient. He glanced at the scrub tech who handed him a high-speed drill and he bored several small holes. With a bone saw, he cut out a flap through the holes.

Danny straightened his posture for a moment and glanced at Dean who was standing with attention. "All's good up here," Dean said. He nodded with appreciation and then removed the bone flap to expose David's brain tissue.

Danny allowed himself a big sigh and Dean sat down to begin his paperwork. "I understand this is a novel case," Dean commented.

"Yes," Danny said. "And let's pray that it works." He reached over to the instrument tray and picked up a network of electrodes which looked like little white, round sticky pads on sheets of cellophane. "These are electrodes which have been whittled down to 100 micrometers in diameter." He smiled under his mask. "Versus 10 millimeters."

"Nice," Dean said, holding a pen between his fingers.

Danny laid the grid back down and suctioned the bloody oozing around the edges of the moist cortex. For the next hour, he worked on electrode placement as if precisely setting up the pieces of a chess game on an open brain instead of a board.

Dean lowered the amount of anesthetic flowing from the vaporizer as the present part of the case was less stimulating. He stood and stretched his legs. "I understand this is the premier college basketball player who had those two head injuries. Have you been taking care of him all along?"

"I have, along with Penny Banks. He's also dating my daughter. If it had been more serious than college dating, I would have considered it a conflict of interest to be caring for him. I couldn't turn my back on him, however; I was even at the basketball game for the first head injury."

"That's a tough one, Danny. But, knowing you, your patient has benefited from your involvement. And I hope your daughter knows what an excellent father she has."

"That's to be seen. Maybe when hell freezes over." Danny reached for the next equipment and held it up for Dean to see. "This is the tiny microchip and antenna which I'll implant right here. So, the electric signals from the epilepsy will be captured and processed under the skin in this miniaturized station."

"And then what?" Dean asked.

"Via wireless power transfer from the outside, this internal device is powered."

"Electromagnetically?"

Danny nodded affirmatively. "Inside here, the system can process a lot of data and then transfer it to an external unit."

"Why not let a mobile phone pick up the data?"

Danny laughed. "One step at a time, one step at a time," he said while implanting the last pieces of the process. He stopped to suction several times and was finally satisfied as he looked down at the living, breathing brain with attached paraphernalia. It made him think of the movie *Matrix*.

"Thank you for not turning the radio too loud during this … you can crank it up now."

As he heard the country music, Danny asked the scrub tech for David's bone flap, put it back in place with some soft wires, then placed a temporary drain for excess fluid.

Finished, he hummed a Blake Shelton song as he left the OR knowing David would wake up just fine under Dean's care.

Chapter 22

Danny shed his OR shoe covers, mask and hat and walked straight to the waiting area where Tara and Floyd were more than anxious. To his surprise, Annabel was there, too. Wearing a school T-shirt, blue jeans, and sneakers, she looked more relaxed than her boyfriend's parents.

Except for the overhead television on a low volume, there were no other distractions in the room. Danny motioned for them to stay seated while Floyd asked how David was doing.

"He's on his way to recovery and he did just fine."

"Thank goodness," Tara said.

"After some time in recovery, he'll go back upstairs. We'll keep you posted when he can leave the ICU and, hopefully in these next few days, I'll send him home. We'll have a chat about that when the time comes."

"Are you happy with the equipment you used, doc?" Floyd asked.

"So far," Danny said.

Annabel lowered her head. There wasn't much she could say in front of the Bells about her father's work on a new system or that he'd developed it.

"Any more questions? Otherwise I better get going as I have another case."

The Bells shook their heads. "No, and thank you so much," Floyd said.

"You're welcome," Danny said. "Annabel, I hope you had a nice weekend. Call the house later if you'd like. We have some news."

"Okay," she said. "Thanks."

Rachel followed Robert around another Monday morning in the cysto room studying every aspect of how to set up for the day. When they were as prepared as possible, he opened up his newspaper in the supply room and took out the crossword page; he folded it into a neat section, smoothed it out on the counter, and took out a pencil from the drawer.

"Good morning," Dr. Mcbride said, walking in and placing down a small duffel bag. "Rachel, you're a nice break from only Robert being here."

"You won't have me to look at much longer," Robert mused. "But then again, you're not a permanent fixture either."

"So true," he said. "A real job waits. West coast, here I come."

"Aren't you dating someone?" Robert asked. "Is she going with you?"

"It's nothing serious. Her job is here and she's not the adventurous type. Once I get out there, a long-distance relationship isn't going to work so I expect it'll sizzle out."

Rachel lost some hope when she heard the bad news that he had a girlfriend but the good news came just as fast. She smiled to herself because hat cinched it. She'd be the bait plus the trap.

"Moving and experiencing new places is good for the soul," Rachel said. "I look at it as a learning experience. After all, you have to start all over."

"So true," Kevin said. "Add a new job and work environment, and you have a big challenge."

"I hear them bringing the patient in," Robert said, looking up from his paper. "So what's the word for a fictitious name?"

"A pseudonym?" Kevin asked.

"Maybe, but how do you spell it?"

"P-s-e-u-d-o-n-y-m," Rachel said.

Robert got up and grabbed a spinal tray. "You two are a team," he said. "Come on Rachel. Let's get this patient ready for surgery."

After the spinal block numbness set in and the patient was also groggy, the anesthesiologist sat down and Kevin began. This time, Rachel kept switching out the empty overhead bags used for the TURP irrigation for new ones.

The patient's prostate was extremely enlarged so Kevin kept chipping away at removing tissue. He stood straight for a moment and took a deep breath as Rachel stood behind his shoulder. "Do you know the risks of all this irrigation fluid to the patient?" he asked her.

"I heard about the paper you co-authored with attending staff so I looked it up," she said, her breath wafting over his neck when he sat down, her body slightly resting against him. "Patients can have their intravascular fluid volume diluted resulting in decreased sodium or hyponatremia. Am I correct about that?"

After adjusting the cystoscope in the man's penis, he glanced around and her aqua eyes were right there, staring straight into his. "Yes … good," he stumbled. "And especially since you'll be in this room, learn what hyponatremia can cause."

"Please do teach me what I don't know. If not now, in the doctor's lounge or somewhere. Even if I have to move out west this year due to a sick relative, I would still plan on working in a GU room. It seems interesting so far," she said. She paused, then said softly, "Plus, I believe the field attracts doctors who are the cream of the crop."

The anesthesiologist raised his eyebrows and gave the patient another milligram of midazolam.

Robert walked out of the adjacent room. "Okay, what's a seedy fruit of the rose family?"

"How many letters?" Rachel asked.

"Ten."

"Blackberry," Kevin said.

Rachel and Robert looked at each other and Rachel shrugged her shoulders. "See? The cream of the crop."

As Dr. Mcbride finished the procedure, Robert waved Rachel into the supply room. "Get him set up with the Foley catheter and bag. You can put the kit on the instrument tray." He pointed to the glass cabinets full of supplies.

Rachel grabbed what was needed, walked back in, and opened the kit; now the patient was less sedated and more interested in what was going on.

Kevin took the catheter and began inserting it. "Sir," he said, also glancing at Rachel for her ears as well, "I'm inserting a catheter to remove urine and blood - or clots - in the bladder. It's only normal that they occur after the procedure I just did. You're going to your own room and, when your urine is free of any significant bleeding, I'll remove the catheter. Your symptoms and BPH will have been taken care of and you can then be discharged."

"Thanks," he said. "You're all welcome to visit me in my room. Just bring one of those crossword puzzles with you."

"It would be our pleasure," Rachel said. "I'll bring you something not too difficult so you have a more pleasurable post-op course."

Kevin watched their interaction; this woman went beyond the call of duty in her job. He liked that. Besides that, she was easy on the eyes. Very easy.

Sara heard the upstairs door open and Mary and Casey both came down. "Nice to have you down here for a change," she said.

"We'd be in your face too often if we came as much as we wanted," Mary said, plucking a cookie off a kitchen plate.

"I had a craving for chocolate chip cookies," Sara said. "And store-bought ones just don't cut it."

"I'll say," Mary said. She went to the refrigerator and poured some milk while Dakota nuzzled her for a greeting.

Casey went over to Julia and hoisted her up into the air while she squealed.

"Hey, everybody," Nancy said, emerging from her bedroom with a dangling headset around her neck and grabbing a cookie.

"Maybe it's my imagination," Sara said, "but you seem to be getting bigger by the day."

Mary rubbed her belly. "I'm not that big … yet. But sometimes I feel that way."

"Julia," Casey said. "See, Auntie Mary has two babies growing inside her. You're going to have special cousins to play with. After they are born, you can show them things, even help them to learn how to walk. Won't that be fun?"

"I have a baby puppy all my own," she said.

"Yes, you've told me."

"Her name is Snoopy."

"What do you think we should name your cousins?"

"Stupid."

Casey gulped and Sara frowned. "Julia, that's not nice," she said. "Don't say nasty things like that, especially about your family."

Julia scowled at Sara. "You're not my mother."

"Okay, that's enough, young lady. I'm taking you to your room where you can be by yourself until we put you to bed."

When Sara returned, all four of them huddled around the kitchen counter.

"She's become an absolute handful," Sara said softly.

"And she's only two," Mary said sympathetically. "And her behavior seems to be getting worse."

"Makes me think I'd never want to have kids," Nancy said.

"That's quite a thing to think at your age, too," Casey said, shaking his head. "But I can tell you that you girls weren't anything like Julia."

"Thank God," Sara said. "I didn't know I had such fine children." She beamed at Nancy and put her arm around her shoulder, pulling her in for a hug as the phone rang.

"Casey, you can get it," Sara said. "Maybe it's Danny again. He's still delayed at the hospital."

He stretched to the wall phone and answered; it was Annabel.

"Yo," Casey said, "how's school?"

"It's okay," Annabel responded. "The year will be finished soon and I'm looking at job prospects for the summer."

"Good for you. What do you want to do?"

"I don't know. Waitress maybe. But I have to shadow Dad a little bit for the extracurricular activities they like to see on a med school application."

"Don't forget, you can always shadow me and my partner in the ambulance sometime."

"Oh, thanks, Casey. That's cool."

"I know David had his surgery today. Have you heard anything?"

"I was there with his parents. Dad said it went fine. I didn't know he invented something for David to use."

"Yes. He's been missing in action at the house for some time, working off-hours in the lab. He really wants this thing to succeed and I hope it does."

"I guess I underestimated him. I feel bad I gave him such a hard time about it."

"You should tell him that," Casey said.

"Mmm …," she said, not sure. "Anyway, is Dad there? He said to call for some news."

"He's still tied up at the hospital. Your mom is here but I'm sure I can tell you the news if it's okay with her."

Sara smiled across the counter and waved her hands at Casey to go ahead.

"It's about our pregnancy. Mary is carrying twins."

"Uncle Casey, that is so cool! Congratulations."

"Thanks and Mary says thanks, too."

"Okay, I better go. I'm going over to the main library to study an hour or two. I didn't get any done yet today." She eyed her desk and began sorting the textbooks she wanted to take.

"And Annabel?" Casey said. "Listen, don't worry about David. He's in good hands. And I hope you don't mind me sticking in my two cents but, in the future, you'll meet many more nice men. David will always be special but you both may go your separate ways. Things will work out the way they're supposed to. I believe that because you're both good and sensible young adults. Again, I hope you don't mind me giving you that advice."

She stuck a notebook in a drawer and looked out the window at a green field lined with trees.

"No, and thanks. Whenever you've told us girls anything, it's always because you've had our best interest in mind. Love you and say hi to Mom."

After transferring David from the ICU into a room and making regular rounds on him, Danny was ready to discharge him towards the end of the week.

He walked down the fifth floor orthopedic corridor, passing two elderly patients hobbling along like broken insects with a walker and a cane. After nodding hello to them and their physical therapists, he continued to the neurosurgical area and to the last corner room.

On entering, Danny smiled. It was the sunniest place he'd walked into all morning. With two sets of blinds pulled up as high as they could go, baskets and vases of flower arrangements along the windowsill looked even more colorful. He inhaled their sweet aroma which made him realize how awful hospital corridors can sometimes smell.

David stood tall near the streaming light, holding a basketball between both hands and rolling it around. Upon seeing Danny, he abruptly stopped and dropped his jaw with a look of guilt. He let the ball rest in one hand.

"Hi, doc," David said. "You know I'm not playing and I won't play. Mom left this with me yesterday because I just wanted to handle it. It feels so good to be out of bed and moving around a bit. I'm not getting into any trouble."

Danny laughed. "I think the fear of another head injury will haunt you so I'm not worried that you're going to go against my orders. Let me see that." He put his hands out and David handed him the ball.

Danny rolled the basketball around and slightly tossed it up and down several times. "I see what you mean. It's therapeutic." He motioned to the recliner for David to sit and rolled the ball onto the bedspread. "Let me take a look at your dressing and scalp."

David sat down and rested his arms while Danny examined his head. "This is all looking fine," he said, "and Dr. Banks is as happy with your recovery as I am. I hinted at a discharge by the end of the week and I'm going to fulfill that promise. Why not call your mom or dad to come pick you up? I'll go write your orders."

"Really?" David asked, the dimple in his chin deepening as he glowed with happiness.

"Yes. I am serious. We'll keep you on the anti-seizure medicine prescribed by Dr. Banks. Your parents have been instructed on first-aid if you have a seizure at home, and I will see you often in the office while the external unit gathers the results we need."

Danny patted his shoulder. "Enjoy the break from the hospital because, as you know, we'll be doing surgery again once we pinpoint the area responsible for your epilepsy. This system, if successful, will be more precise and won't focus on large zones but zero in on as small a number of cells as possible."

David kept smiling. "I know, I know. I think I've memorized everything you've told me and I've learned what comes out of your mouth is important. Does Annabel know you're sending me home?"

"I haven't told her. It's your decision who to tell." Danny picked up the ball from the bed and handed it back to him. "See you in my office on Monday."

Chapter 23

Rachel bundled up the used surgical drapes and smashed them into the big plastic garbage can while Dr. Mcbride fiddled with a new piece of equipment in the next room.

Robert looked up from his crossword puzzle. "Does etiquette have one 't' or two?" he asked.

"I think it's two," she said, glancing into the other room. The attending doctor of the GU service – basically Kevin's boss - had walked in. She lingered by the doorway while the older man talked with Kevin.

"I know it's Friday, but the hospital is going all out tonight for the new cancer center and the unveiling of its sculpture which is in the front lobby. The press will be there, the public is invited, and there is going to be lots of food. Spread the word among the residents. It would be nice to have the support of as many physicians as possible."

"Okay," Kevin said. "I think I can squeeze that in before I go home."

They went on to discuss the next patient's history and then the other man left. Kevin was so close to being an attending doctor himself, he could function almost independently.

Rachel grinned. This just might be the opportunity she hoped for. She'd been trying her hardest to cross paths with Kevin outside the OR and it had been damn near impossible. What she'd have to do now is go home after work and change clothes. Plus, she'd have to do some research online to dig up recent newspaper articles or hospital updates on the sculpture and its artist.

She stepped further back into the room as Robert was erasing one of his entries. "I can't spell today," he said.

"Robert, are you going to this big hospital event this evening for the cancer center?"

"I may. I haven't decided yet but I'll check with my wife if she wants to go. Why? Are you?"

"I'd like to. Just checking because it would be nice if I knew someone there."

"Okay then, I'll go. We won't regret it because the hospital always knows how to throw a good party. Besides, this is my last day and you're on your own come Monday so we'll have a toast to celebrate."

Rachel went straight home and as she walked Snoopy along the manicured grass lining her street, she formulated a plan. Back in the apartment, she unhooked the little dog from her leash, grabbed a large glass of water, and sat at her computer.

She still hadn't looked up something that had been on her mind so she Googled 'physician salaries.' Landing on a U.S. News and World Report money rankings, she found a graph which displayed an overview and a prediction for future M.D. salaries; they were still magnificent and they were still climbing. Of course, she thought, most physicians starting out on their own were straddled with mounds of debt but that would not be the case for Kevin Mcbride. Next, she refined her search for urologists' incomes. She could hardly contain the pitter-patter of her heart when she read Medscape's report that they were among the highest-paid specialists in medicine.

Sitting back and taking a sip of water, she gave the situation much deeper thought. So far, Dr. Mcbride seemed like a fine person. Most doctors who reached his level of training had those do-gooder attributes like being compassionate, sensitive and thoughtful and he was obviously ambitious and devoted. He also seemed to be easygoing.

Rachel set down her glass and licked her lips. Maybe she should consider going much farther this time than ever before. She wasn't getting any younger and perhaps it was time to totally secure her future. And the beauty of a catch like him was that, if ever the need arose, divorce courts would favor her. Letting out a big sigh, she noticed Snoopy's big brown eyes fixated on her.

"I bet you'd like a sprawling, opulent back yard to run in, wouldn't you?"

Clicking her cursor back on Google's homepage, she searched for any information on the opening of the hospital's new cancer wing. Narrowing down the alternatives, she came to two articles which rounded out the information she needed: It was a modern addition with state-of-the-art equipment for personalized, genotype-directed cancers and the bulk of the money for the project had come from huge donor philanthropists.

Although there were no pictures of the sculpture to be unveiled, its description and theme were available. As reported, part of its magnificence rested on the fact that it was sculpted from a humongous blue spruce that had been removed from the hospital's grounds before construction. The complex wood carving was 25-feet tall and embodied the unity of world spirit and science.

Not much was posted personally about the full-time wood sculptor except that Michael Downs had done many major public commissions and that he was middle-aged Tennessee native. She liked what she read; his description and meaning of the work he called 'Love and Hope' would provide her with conversational fodder. Rachel stood up and paced the wood floor, practically memorizing some of what she'd read. Snoopy followed at her heels, thinking it was a game.

The only thing left to do was to choose an outfit to make herself stun as much – or more - than the wood sculpture about to be unveiled.

Several days had passed since David's discharge from the hospital. Annabel's Friday classes ended mid-afternoon so she broke away from campus with a stack of books and drove over to his parents' house.

Their dark brown, older home stood tall on a narrow street with several picket fences. It had three stories; the top floor was a cozy, finished-off loft with a steep pitched roof that had been - and still was - David's room.

Annabel got out of her car carrying books and rang the front door bell. A cat slinked off a porch chair as Mrs. Bell opened the door and smiled when he saw her; leaning forward, she gave her a little hug.

"Annabel! What … what a surprise," she stuttered. "David will be thrilled to see you."

"I called him last night and told him I may be over. I meant to get by a few days ago but finals are coming up soon and the semester is starting to wind down."

"Honey, I understand. Schoolwork comes first." She pointed to the staircase. "You know where to find him. He's in the loft."

Annabel smiled and padded up the two flights of stairs; then knocked on the original unpainted wooden door. When it opened, David pulled out his ear buds and grabbed some of her books. Putting them down on the bed, they hugged … long and hard.

"Oh, wow," he said. "You don't know how good that felt. I feel like some non-human entity being experimented on and devoid of physical contact."

"I'm sorry about that. You shouldn't feel that way, especially since your situation won't last forever."

She looked around the room with its old floorboards and faded area rugs. Two antique chests dotted the room like they'd been lifted off a pirate ship; and a nice desk and chair fit perfectly in the cubbyhole underneath the window. The computer sat on top as well as several unopened books. Annabel sat down on the edge of the brass bed.

David walked around to the other side and stretched out, his head propped up by two pillow shams; Annabel moved the books around her and sat cross-legged toward him, draping her hands over her knees.

"You told me you had a small seizure three days ago," she said. "Have you had any more?"

He nodded affirmatively. "Last night before going to bed. Even though it didn't last long, they are always scary."

"I bet." She looked at the wireless receiver unit on his nightstand and touched the little antennae. "Does my dad think it's gathering information like it should?"

"I see him next week. But whether this system your dad developed works or not, I'll be forever grateful for the way he's looking after me. Across the whole country, I probably wouldn't have received care from any neurosurgeon better than him."

She gazed into the sincere look in his eyes as he rolled to the side and propped his head on his hand.

"You do know that, don't you?" he asked softly.

"I suppose you're right. Yes, he's trying his best. I do know he is very smart but, over and above that, when he makes an extra effort and thinks outside the box extra special things happen."

"He's like a neurosurgeon Einstein."

"Ha. He'd love it if he heard you say that," she said pulling a book towards her. "So, can we listen to some of that music you were plugged into after you help me study a bit?"

"Me help you study? I doubt it."

"Yes, you can ask me a few things which won't be like you're studying yourself and yet it'll refresh some of the biology you learned this last year. That shouldn't go against your doctor's orders."

"Okay, sounds like a plan. And then we'll listen to some new CDs I bought because of the boring present circumstances."

When Annabel left several hours later, drove to campus, and walked to her dorm, she reflected on the time she'd spent with David.

They were well-bonded and tighter than ever … but it seemed to be getting different.

The hospital's lobby was already jammed with people when Rachel arrived a few minutes late. She wanted to assure that Robert would be there as she didn't want Kevin to see her socially conspicuous by herself. She also realized her good fortune that the hospital she worked for was not the same as Danny's; she had never bumped into him in a work-related situation since the time she had first met him.

Off to the right near the floor-to-ceiling window, she spotted Robert with a woman. "Hello," she said, taking his hand for a light handshake. "I believe this is the first time I'm seeing you without a crossword puzzle."

He did a quick-once over of her, his eyes widening. She had settled on a sleeveless black dress which was open from the bust line up to the neck; with one-inch open heels, a small bag, and shimmering silver jewelry, she was classy material well-suited for the stately event.

"No puzzle in hand," he said, "although I do have the appropriate app on my iPhone." He motioned to his side. "This is my wife, Pat."

"Nice to meet you," Rachel said.

Pat smiled. "I hear you're taking Robert's position," she said coldly. "He's happy to move on."

"Yes, I'm glad it worked out," Rachel replied.

"Let me go get you a glass of wine," Robert said and stepped away.

Rachel stood next to Pat and began looking around the room, narrowing her eyes to find Kevin. More people were crowded on the other side where a gray cloth entirely draped the 25-foot sculpture.

Women and men in uniforms with trays and hors d'oeuvres jostled between the people and Rachel took a bite-sized stuffed mushroom, making sure not to mess up her lipstick. As Robert handed her a white wine, she spotted Kevin.

He stood with another man about his own age. Better dressed than his colleague, he wore a blue sports coat; his patterned shirt was open at the top and he wore no tie. Now all she had to do was to move the couple along.

"Robert, look! It's Kevin. Let's go over and say hello." She took a step forward and, when they followed her, she inched her way through the crowd.

She stopped right behind the two senior residents finishing their fellowships, then tapped Kevin on his arm. He turned and, after taking a second to recognize her, he broke into a smile. "It always amazes me how much better health care workers look when they're not dressed in scrubs," he said.

"All health care workers?" she asked, her eyes aglow.

Although the space between them was limited, his eyes roamed over her dress and back to her face. "No. You have a point. And, in your case, you already looked nice and now you look … exquisite."

She took a baby bow. "Thank you so much."

Kevin extended his arm past Rachel, shook Robert's hand, and was introduced to Pat. "And this is another surgical fellow, Burt," he said.

"Nice to meet you," Rachel said.

The hospital CEO standing to the side of the sculpture's platform began addressing the crowd as Rachel sipped her wine. As he droned on about the stellar donations they had received for both the new wing and the commissioned sculpture, the two senior fellows separated the space between them and she now stood with one of them to the left and right of her.

When the CEO finished his speech and photographers poised their cameras, he and a volunteer board member began pulling off the huge drape. When it lay on the pedestal, those without drinks or food in their hands applauded while others exclaimed their approval.

The slim, tall carved wood stood with artistic beauty and was a recreation of the family unit; a mother, father, child and a dog stood twice their height. Each was its own separate piece and they were enveloped in a double helix strand with carved globes of the earth interspersed along the way.

Kevin turned to Rachel, his eyes wide and he smiled.

"A marriage between our planet and the family unit!" she exclaimed. "It's magnificent."

"It is, isn't it?" he said.

"Can you believe the size of the blue spruce from the hospital grounds that was used for this?" she asked. "It's as if it that tree was meant to be this sculpture."

"Really?" Robert asked. "This was carved from one tree that was here?"

"Yes. The artist, Michael Downs, is a full-time wood sculptor and he believes in using trees for their beauty and truth. They dwarf human beings and many people around the world believe forests are spiritual places that have links to spiritual pasts. He loves working with each individual tree knowing that each one has its own character and soul. Just think, he worked over a year on this masterpiece and it will withstand time, giving all who pass it a sense of connection of the family with the earth.

Kevin's boyish smile continued as he watched her and listened; she was not only beautiful but smart and attentive. "We have our own artistic interpreter with us," he said.

"My pleasure," she said. "I must go run my fingers over a little bit of it. Feel the grain and the beauty under my skin."

The flashes of cameras had stopped and Rachel gave her glass to Kevin as she walked forward. He watched her posture and her sway; watched her as she put one trim, toned leg on the step-up stand and ran her right hand along the child's dress.

The others followed and encircled her. It was as if she knew the secrets of sculpture and they were all her pupils.

"Sublime," she said, stepping back into their circle. She took the wine glass back from Kevin and sipped what was left.

Small talk ensued and, after another round of food and drinks, Robert and his wife got ready to leave.

"Lots of luck with your next position," Rachel said, "and thank you for all your help."

"Any time," he said. "And Dr. Mcbride, good luck going out on your own and with your relocation."

"Thanks," Kevin said, "it'll be a major change. It's like starting all over. I better make friends fast."

"You're not taking a significant other with you?" Rachel asked.

"No. Not really."

"That's a shame," she said. She tilted her head and bowled him over with her smile.

After Robert and Pat left, Rachel looked at her empty wine glass.

"Can I get you another?" Kevin asked.

She furrowed her eyebrows. "I'm afraid I've had two and that's one too many. Thank you anyway. Perhaps there is a set-up over there with coffee?"

Kevin and Burt looked over at the tables but they only had the appetizers, soft drinks, and wine.

"I don't see any," Kevin said.

"I think I should go find a cup of coffee before driving home."

"Say, why don't we all go for coffee or even more of a bit to eat?" Kevin asked.

"Thanks, Kevin, but I'm going to split," his colleague said. "Nice party and nice to have met you, Rachel."

"Likewise," she said.

After he left, Kevin focused back on her eyes. "What do you say?"

"Would you mind very much driving me and afterwards dropping me back off at my car?"

"Sure thing and I take it that's a yes," he said. "Where to?"

"Your choice," she said. "You're driving."

"I don't know of any coffee shops open this late but I know a diner that puts on a mean pot of coffee and makes breakfast all hours of the day."

"Eggs and French Roast? You have good taste, Dr. Mcbride."

He gave her a warm smile. "It appears that way."

And so do I, she thought. This couldn't be going along any better than if I scripted it myself.

Chapter 24

Dr. Kevin Mcbride opened the door of his Honda Accord and Rachel got in. Her svelte black dress rode mid-way to her thighs as she positioned her purse on her lap. He went around to the other side, took off his jacket and draped it on the back seat, then started the car.

"So, are you a big art buff?" he asked, pausing to look at her legs before driving off.

"A little bit. I do appreciate good work but I'm more supportive when the artist is local. After seeing his name in the newspaper, I made sure I learned all about him. That piece is extraordinary."

"I agree with you. If ever the need for something like that arises where I am moving, I'm going to recommend him."

"I have all his information. Feel free to contact me for it. I may even be near you if you're going out west to practice. I'm moving to San Francisco."

"Really? So am I."

"It'll be a pretty area," Rachel said casually.

For a few minutes, he concentrated on making several turns. "This place we're going to is known to the residents and fellows," he finally said, "because we're always screwed up with our hours. Getting breakfast at 9:00 o'clock at night is a favorite pastime."

"I wish I'd known about it. I can eat scrambled eggs any time of the day."

When they arrived and sat at a bench across from each other, a waitress appeared like from a vintage television show. With a pencil hanging off her ear and chewing a wad of gum, she drawled out a "What'll ya have?"

Rachel held Kevin's attention with a wide smile, her eyes locking onto his. "Why, scrambled eggs, of course," she said.

The first patients for the day were just being checked in and Danny sat with his colleagues Matthew and Jeffrey in the office kitchen. Besides Cheryl coming in and out to talk about the day's schedule with him, they could hear the buzz of staff from the front desk.

"This is rare we're all here on a Monday morning," Danny said.

"I received late notice that my first surgical case cancelled," Matthew said.

"Well, there's no shortage of things to do," Danny said.

Cheryl stopped on her way out. "You must be anxious to see David," she said.

"I'm excited yet worried about seeing him." He looked from Matthew to Jeffrey. "My first patient is David Bell. I'm nervous as hell about the monitoring he's getting while staying at home. I've invited the research engineer who is working with me on the project to also come in for David's visit. Two minds are usually better than one."

"If your system works, wouldn't you be able to patent it?" Jeffrey asked.

Danny looked at him. "I never even thought of it. I haven't considered anything further than where we are right now."

Jeffrey drained the end of his coffee, tossed the cup into the garbage can, and cleared his throat. "Danny, sometimes you're oblivious to your own worth."

Danny shifted position in his chair. "I'm just a neurosurgeon doing his job; no better, no worse than most neurosurgeons I know, including the two of you. Well ... although I have more experience."

Jeffrey rolled his eyes at Matthew. "Is humbleness a virtue?"

"Don't ask me," Matthew said. "I do know that if he were arrogant or pretentious, I wouldn't be working here."

From the hallway, they heard a front desk secretary tell someone where the kitchen was and then a tall man appeared in the doorway.

"Vance," Danny said. "Come on in and help yourself to some coffee and a donut or something from the fridge. Meet my partners. I told them you were on your way."

Matthew, Jeffrey and Vance exchanged handshakes and Vance sat down. "I hope your patient doesn't mind me barging in on the appointment," he said.

"Shouldn't be a problem. I told the family that I couldn't do this alone and needed the technical assistance."

Vance nodded and poured a cup of coffee while Danny finally selected a glazed donut and washed it down with a glass of juice. If he didn't get satisfaction from evaluating David and the captured wireless system's information stored so far, he'd surely get a buzz from all the sugar he'd just consumed.

Danny opened the door and Cheryl and Vance followed him in where David lay on the examining table with his eyes closed. Looking embarrassed to be in such a comfortable position, the teen sat up; his mother sat swaying her leg back and forth in a chair.

"Good morning to the both of you," Danny said. "You both briefly met Dr. Saxton before. He's helping me along with the equipment. We must make sure it's working like it should. In essence, this is all experimental."

"We ... we can't thank you all enough for giving David such personal attention," Tara said, "even if he is an experiment." She tapped her son's knee in jest and David smiled.

"I'm your only kid," David said. "I've been your experiment my whole life."

"I hope you don't really feel like that," she said and chuckled. "But if you are, I should have had ten more like you."

While they jabbed remarks at each other, Vance and Danny began looking at the receiver until there was a timely silence.

"How have you been feeling?" Danny asked.

"The biggest difference now, Dr. Tilson - compared to before the accident - is that I get really tired. Maybe it's because I'm not doing anything. And that is besides the seizures I'm still getting."

"I'm so afraid when he's upstairs all by himself," Tara said.

"Mom," David said, "you can't treat me like I'm two years old."

"But people with medical conditions sometimes do have to be monitored like they're two years old. It's a fact."

"Okay, you two," Danny said, feeling like a referee. "Let's get to your medical condition, David. Have you had seizures since your discharge?"

"At least three. One of them threw me around as if I was shook up like sodium chloride in a salt shaker."

Danny grimaced. "And you're still taking the anti-seizure medicine that Dr. Banks prescribed?"

"Yeah."

"His father and I double-check that it's taken each day," Tara chimed in.

After Danny examined David's head, listened to his heart and lungs, and looked at his eyes with a penlight, Cheryl handed him a reflex hammer. When he finished, he stood against the counter. "Dr. Saxton, what do you think so far of the monitoring equipment? Are we okay?"

"I'm confident that we are."

"Okay, we can discuss our findings separately and I can get David on his way."

Vance nodded. "Keep taking good care of yourself and your monitors. And good day, ma'am." He stepped out of the room and went to wait for Danny in his office.

204 | Barbara Ebel

"David, I'll collaborate with Dr. Saxton. The way I see it, we'll do one more period of monitoring, compile the data to see if we are still identifying the same areas of your brain that is the source of your epilepsy, and then schedule surgery."

The teen grimaced.

"We're getting a handle on this," Danny said. "And the new system is saving you some major headaches."

"I know and I really do appreciate it. I still feel like a prisoner, though. I can't even drive."

"There are people with seizure disorders that can never drive. I don't see that happening to you."

"Dr. Tilson," Tara said, "we are very grateful. He's just getting frustrated, but he recognizes your hard work."

"I do," David said, letting a smile creep across his face. "Annabel even came by yesterday. We got to hang out."

"Good. I'm glad. Now get out of here. The front desk will schedule your next appointment."

Danny and Cheryl exited first. "Cheryl, you can bring the next patient back. I'll be with Vince."

"Are you as pleased as I am?" Danny asked when he stepped into his office.

"As much or more," Vance said with a smile. "These miniature electrodes are working as well as the rest of the system."

The two men sat down, Danny rubbed his hands together, and they discussed the first set of data.

"It's looking like a small area in the temporal lobe," Danny said. "And if we don't get information next time that shows more involved foci, then I think the chances of surgically removing that tiny area responsible for his temporal lobe epilepsy is good."

Danny's last office patient left by five, making him overjoyed that he'd be leaving in time for the opening of his sister's exhibit hosted by the Nashville Art Foundation. The weekend-long show would begin on Friday night with a wine and cheese party.

He walked the last completed patient's chart to the front desk, slapped it down, and stood there with a grin. "Anyone want to come to the big city art show which starts in a little while? All of the foundation's usual stuff has been cleared out and the participating Tennessee artists each will have their own room. They can display up to ten works and my sister is in it. But if you can't make it tonight, however, it lasts the next two days."

"They have nice events and food at their receptions," Cheryl said. "Maybe a few of us can make it."

"Good. I'd appreciate that. The judges will be there tonight, too."

Despite her best subtle attempts, Rachel hadn't made any personal progress with Kevin Mcbride during the week. Standing next to him while he held patients' penises and inserted instruments into them, or setting up his cases, or making small talk with his patients was one thing. But getting him to ask her for her telephone number or ask her out again after their late-night breakfast had not materialized. And it was already Friday morning. Although she didn't want to, she toyed with the idea of inviting him to something herself.

In the storage and work room, she frowned at the newspaper on the counter. She missed chit-chatting about crossword puzzles with Robert. It was the only reason she had started to bring the paper to work – as a way to engage Kevin between his cases. It had at least proved to be useful when their interactions had slowed down.

Looking at the aluminum holder of paper towels which she used as a mirror, she put on a little bit of lipstick. He was due in about ten minutes but, to her surprise, she heard him come into the adjacent room and drop down his duffel bag.

"Good morning, Rachel." Kevin stood in the doorway, his arms bridging the door frame. "How would your heart and your mind like to accompany me this evening?"

He had tufts of pitch black hair poking out of the head bonnet and wore a sheepish grin; Rachel looked at him as if she was puzzled.

"Oh, I'm sorry. It's an expression. My mom was American Indian and she always asked me to do things with my heart and my mind. My dad, on the other hand, was Irish so he'd ask me to do things for the love of the Irish." He smiled just thinking about them.

"No wonder you're unique," she said. "What an interesting combination."

"I'll take that as a compliment. Anyway, I thought since you are so knowledgeable about artwork, you'd like to go to a big art event tonight. It's short notice but I only found out about it last night. It starts at six."

"I would love to."

"Good. I'll fill you in after the first case."

She hoped so … and now her initial worries about seeing him again outside of the OR were over.

At the front entrance of the foundation's museum, Danny signed the ledger. A well-dressed woman pointed to white sticky labels.

"You can wear a name tag if you'd like," she said. "It makes the event more personable."

He printed his name, stuck the tag on his jacket, and went in search of Mary, Sara and Casey. Almost twenty regional artists were competing and, due to so many qualified submissions, each of the ten rooms was shared by two artists' work. Danny found the room with Mary's name on the outside before stopping in the main room for wine or food.

With outstretched arms, Mary walked over; toeing in her one foot, she gave Danny a big hug.

"Whoa," Danny said. "You and those babies are getting big. Soon we'll be blowing kisses to you over your belly."

"Yes. They're growing like weeds." She grabbed him by the arm and pulled him over to the rest of the family.

Danny gave Sara a kiss. "You must have gotten home and changed into something sexier," he said. She wore a white scarf over a long golden brown dress. Even her nails were polished which made Danny realize she'd gone the extra mile to look special.

"Tonight means a lot to Mary," she said. "And look what's on the wall to the right. It's Julia and Dakota's picture."

"I see that. It stands out and there is a bounty of good work here."

Casey and Mary stood closer. "I've been watching a person over there in the corner," Casey said. "By his name tag, he's a judge. He sure is spending a lot of time in here."

Mary waved his comment off. "There's another artist in here, too," she said.

"Since I see how spectacular this painting is in the correct light and frame," Casey said, pointing to Julia and Dakota's work, "I am wondering if you couldn't do a special request for your husband."

Mary stepped in front of him. "Tell me," she said.

"If I gave you a picture of Tommy and me when we were little, could you paint something like it?"

Sara squeezed Danny's hand and he pressed her hand back

"I would love to," Mary responded. "Maybe someday I'll get to it."

"That's a great idea," Danny said. "We'll be back in a bit. Sara and I are going to look around." When they were far enough away, Danny commented, "Casey thinks about his younger brother more than I thought."

Chapter 25

Rachel signed in for the art event and stood off to the side waiting for Kevin. He had requested to meet her there since, more than likely, he'd be coming straight from the hospital. She realized it wouldn't be wise to date a resident or a doc doing a fellowship. Besides the fact that they weren't earning the big bucks yet and were probably in severe financial debt, their hours were unpredictable. Of course, Kevin would soon be on his own.

She tapped her foot as she waited. This time she wore black dress pants and a Japanese-styled silk blouse. Its crisp collar was open and a round gold enameled flower on a gold chain rested in the depression of her neck. Adjusting the dressy handbag she had on her shoulder, she smiled to see Kevin walk in and spot her.

He slapped his name tag on while walking towards her. "I hope I didn't keep you waiting," he said.

"Not at all. I just arrived. How did all your surgical patients do today when you saw them later for postop rounds?"

"All of them are peeing like race horses and no one is complaining of too much pain." His eyes darted to her blouse and her neck and then settled on her face. "You look very nice."

"Thank you."

He realized what an exceptional voice she had; smooth and seductive. He remembered thinking that only one other time about a woman and it was while watching an old movie with Marilyn Monroe.

Rachel had rested her hand on his upper arm. "Shall we?" she asked, trying to coax him to walk.

"Of course," he said. "How about we check out the artwork and then come back for wine and some of that delicious-looking cheese?" Between groups of people, they could see a huge center table decked out with all sorts of appetizers.

They entered a spacious room with a buffed hardwood floor. Gazing at an oversized painting flanking most of a wall, Rachel was at a loss to comment on it or the artist. After work, the little time she had available was used to find out about the host organization.

"Hmm," Kevin hummed. "What do you think?"

"As my mama used to say, 'If you don't have something nice to say about something, don't say anything at all.' However, the Nashville Art Foundation is to be commended. It's funded by The Carlin Family Charity, The Humanities Forum and The Nashville City Community Institute." She turned from the painting and looked directly at him. "They financially help these aspiring artists. Many of the exhibitors here acquired the skills and knowledge they needed to prepare for a career in the visual arts only because of the NAF. They have to develop self-awareness, too, to make a canvas come alive."

"It didn't help this artist too much." He chuckled and she nodded in agreement as they walked to the other side of the room.

After viewing the next room's paintings, Rachel and Kevin passed the name tags of the artists on the wall for the next exhibit. On one of them was written 'Mary Tilson.' Could it be Danny Tilson's sister?

Her open-backed heels clicked across the floor. She wasn't interested in the other artist as she spotted a work which caught her by surprise and in awe. Kevin lingered close to her.

Her mouth gaped open and her eyes softened. It was what she thought it was from across the room. Julia, her darling Julia. And Dakota, too. Shouldn't she receive royalties or something for her daughter being used in a portrait?

"I'm no aficionado of art," Kevin said next to her, "but that is amazing."

Rachel broke out of her trance as she realized he still didn't know about her daughter. Mothers with children could be game changers, she thought, when it comes to single guys so she knew she had to tread carefully. Although she'd been lucky in that department with men before, she had not had the opportunity yet to mention Julia to Kevin.

"Yes," she said. "This artist was able to engage the child and the dog together as well as pull in the viewer. It's beautiful." She fidgeted her foot, unsure of what to do.

Kevin looked closer at the painting, noting the name of the signature. "I wonder if the artist made this up or modeled it after subjects she knew."

"I have a young daughter," Rachel said. "Come to think of it, this painting looks just like her as well as a dog I used to have."

"Really?"

She didn't know what to say. Did he mean did she really have a daughter or did the painting really look like her daughter?

"What a surprise." A familiar voice sounded behind her and Rachel swung around to find herself face-to-face with Casey. A woman stood next to him.

Casey immediately extended his hand to Kevin and told him his name. Kevin did likewise and then said, "Do you all know each other from the medical field? I'm a surgeon at Rachel's hospital."

"I'm a paramedic," Casey said. "It's a good thing I'm not a surgeon because my career may have been cut short due to a hand injury this year." He stared at Rachel when he finished speaking and raised his hand in front, displaying his missing fingertip.

"I take it this is the artist," Rachel said, interjecting quickly.

"Yes," Mary said. "We've never met," she continued, her voice flat and cold. "But I've heard a lot about you over the years."

Rachel gulped and her pulse quickened. "You are a gifted artist," she said, thinking that she had to catch every verbal curveball they threw and hit it like a fly ball into oblivion.

"Nice of you to say so. What do you think of Julia? You must be overjoyed to see your own daughter in a piece of art."

Kevin Mcbride hung on every word as the conversation had gotten more bizarre by the minute. Since he'd met Rachel, she seemed to know a lot about art. And was she so involved in humanities that Mary had heard all about her *and* had painted her daughter? That was odd, too, that she hadn't mentioned having a child.

Rachel placed her hand on Kevin's arm and turned to face him. "I don't want to be impolite while you're hearing this conversation," she said. "But this is a surprise to me that Julia is so beautifully portrayed in this hanging masterpiece."

"And, of course, you know Dakota, too," Mary said.

"Yes, I do. You have captured the bond between a child and a dog," she said. "This painting is like a testimony to the saying that a dog is man's best friend. And in this case, a little girl's."

"So Kevin," Casey said, "have you met Rachel's daughter?"

"No. I didn't know she had one. But we only work together and have only socially met outside the hospital once or twice. But I hope there will be more things to do together."

"Oh, I'm sure there will be." Casey bit his tongue, stopping himself from adding 'if she has anything to do with it.' "Actually, do you know Dr. Danny Tilson?"

"Oww." Rachel took her hand off of Kevin and held her side under her ribs. "Ouch." She leaned forward. "I have a pain … a gnawing in my abdomen. It's probably best if I go out front and get something to eat."

Kevin draped his arm around her back and crouched near her ear. "Are you okay? Would you like to sit down instead?"

"No. Let me get a small plate and, if that doesn't work, then I better go home."

"That would be a shame," Casey said. "Danny would be sorry to miss you."

"Bye, both of you," Rachel said. "And Mary, it's very nice you dreamed up that portrait of my little girl." She slid her hand into Kevin's and edged him away. After slipping through a group of people, she sighed. Maybe now she was rid of them.

"Rachel?" Danny had a glass of wine in his hands as he almost brushed past her. They were so close, he could discern her faint fragrance which was similar to sniffing a bottle of pure vanilla; it brought back memories of being intimate with her and he shuddered.

Rachel glared at him. "Yes, it's me. I can't stop because I feel famished and must get something to eat."

He felt slightly relieved they didn't have to talk. Sara was following him with her own drink and it always unnerved him when she had to tolerate Rachel's presence.

"Excuse me. You're Dr. Tilson, aren't you?" Kevin asked. "I remember you from a grand rounds you gave a few years ago."

Danny shook his hand. "That's me. I hope my talk left a good impression."

"I'm Dr. Mcbride. It did. I've also read about you since then."

"You can't believe everything you read," Danny said. "Please, meet my ex-wife, Sara."

"Nice to meet you," she said. "And Rachel, good to see you with a free Friday evening like Danny. Julia is in good hands tonight with one of our daughters; she was quite delighted this afternoon when I gave her a new pair of sneakers."

"Fantastic," Rachel said. "She is fond of sneakers. I hope you didn't throw out the blue ones I gave her."

"No," Danny said. "We always send back to you the things she comes with."

Kevin's eyes squinted which made the wrinkle lines on his temple get deeper. The exhibit had turned into some weird exposé of the woman with him and who he'd been working with. He wondered if she was as complex as the art topics she had enlightened him about.

Rachel squirmed, anxious to get away. This town had gotten too small for her to socialize with anonymity from the Tilson family. She disappeared through the crowd without pulling at Kevin's sleeve. Luckily, she sensed, he flanked her heels like a puppy dog behind its mother.

But in any case, it was time to call her attorney.

"Come on," Annabel said to David, "You have another week of monitoring behind you and it's time to get out with people your own age and enjoy the weather."

Putting her hands on her hips, she took two more steps into his loft. "Exams are over except for wrapping up lab stuff and there are two college bands giving a concert on the lawn tonight. I came over specifically to get you."

"You didn't have to," he said, stretched out on his bed with an iPad in his hands. "It's too much trouble to go back and forth to escort me somewhere."

"Your parents even agreed you should get out. I didn't make the trip for nothing, so let's go." She walked over and grabbed his hand, coaxing him to get up.

"It's a little cool so wear something warmer," she said. "I have a blanket and we can spread it out on the lawn. And I know your friends would like to see you."

He slid off his T-shirt, rummaged through one of the antique chests, and pulled out a long-sleeved athletic shirt. She could see that he had lost a bit of his toned musculature as he slipped into it. She grabbed his hand again. "You look great," she said with a smile and led him out the door.

A view of the sun poked between the university lecture halls as it sunk towards the horizon. The verdant campus was alive after two heavy weeks of students being barricaded in dorms and study halls for final exams and a portable stage had been built in front of the massive-columned library where graduation ceremonies were usually held. Young adults threw Frisbees, passed snacks, and played music while a four-member band tuned their instruments.

Annabel carried a rolled-up picnic blanket under her arm as they strolled toward the back corner of the lawn. She stopped and scanned the area. "Some of our friends and your basketball team said they'd be over here," she said. Someone waved and they approached a group they recognized.

"Hey, look who's here," Annabel said while spreading the blanket.

"Yo, David. We're glad to see you. It's been a while," said a young man. He sat on a plastic storage container holding a can in a bag. "How about a beer?"

"No, I better not," he said. "Thanks anyway."

"You missed the hardest damn physics final exam," the woman next to him said. "Maybe next fall when you come back, it won't be so difficult."

David grinned. He didn't even know if he'd be back in the fall; his life was too unpredictable. "I'm sure you all handled it okay."

Annabel patted her hand on the turquoise fabric. She sat crossed-legged and pulled the sweatshirt she'd worn down over her waist. When David lowered himself, he sat close and flexed his legs the same way. As the evening darkness closed in, a light breeze started and the lights came on; they left a subtle light yellow glow, especially over the areas closest to the roads.

"I'm lucky if I got a B-minus," the teen said, "but I bet Annabel ends up with an A."

"Don't sell yourself short," Annabel said. "In any case, I wouldn't be working so hard if I didn't want to get into med school."

The girl shrugged her shoulders. "I refuse to go that route. You're going to spend the rest of your life more buried in books than anything else. My doctor cousin says there are now mandatory exams every few years after you even pass your board exam. It goes on forever." She sipped from a coke can and pushed a bag of tortilla chips toward them.

"Thanks," Annabel said. "Well, there are probably a lot of professions like that. You can't just learn your trade and never expect to keep up with new information."

The girl shook her head. "Better you than me, that's all I'm saying."

The fellow next to her gave her a push. "Let's forget about school right now."

Planting a swat on David's shoulder, two tall male students came from behind and sat on their blanket. "Hey, David. Whenever you're able to, come play basketball with us over the summer. Most of us will be working, but we'll be calling each other when we throw something together."

"I'll let you know," David said.

The band had finished with its short practice session and began a mediocre rendition of a recent pop song. David glanced at Annabel as she wrapped one hand inside the other and bobbed her head to the lyrics. Although he enjoyed being outside and hearing the band, an uneasiness settled in on his bones. Like a child who had sat down in the wrong classroom, he felt uncomfortable; like he didn't know these people anymore and their worlds were not the same.

David thought the music droned on too loud … was the drummer out-of-synch? He couldn't be sure but he felt disoriented and detached. The classmates around him seemed unfamiliar to him and, all of a sudden, he felt confused. The girl next to him patted her hands on her legs. What was that all about? And why were people nearby twisting and turning. Did they think they were dancing?

Over the next few seconds, David stared straight down into his lap. He was falling, he was sure of it. But then it stopped. Now, he felt detached from himself because he wasn't inside his body. Then all the odd feelings subsided.

Annabel pushed up and got on her knees in front of David. "Are you okay?" she asked. He stared glassy-eyed and didn't answer her. One arm began to jerk as he simultaneously slumped flat.

"Oh my God!" one of the teens shouted. "Is he having a seizure?"

One by one, students came closer from the adjoining chairs and blankets. The group dancing also stopped and huddled around them. David's jerking movements increased; now both his arms, his legs … his whole body shook.

Annabel knelt at a safe distance not to be thrashed by an appendage but then realized she needed to be near his neck and mouth if he needed help with keeping his airway open. As she began crawling away, it became obvious that the front of his light blue jeans was darkening with moisture. He had lost control of his urine.

Annabel kept her composure as much as possible. Thinking about the medical seizure steps she had learned, she knew he was in a safe place on the ground as far as location. But the occurrence in front of his peers was the worst place she could think of.

As she supported his head and kept it slightly to the side, she realized no other intervention would help as he was already on the necessary medication. The only thing left to do was for her father to use the information he was gathering from his new gadget and go into David's brain.

Chapter 26

For the ten minutes after David's seizure, Annabel tried to wave away new onlookers but started recruiting her friends for assistance.

"He's drowsy and confused," she whispered. "Almost like his brain is exhausted. I don't think I should try to drive him home. Can someone ask the dorm hallway monitor if I can let him sleep in my bed tonight?" Her roommate made the call while Annabel also took her cell phone out of her pocket.

"It's a good thing you're going into medicine," one of the basketball players said. "That was too scary for me."

She nodded. "He's in the postictal state," she said, "the period right after the seizure. He probably won't remember what happened." She lowered her voice even further. "Good thing, too."

When Annabel's roommate announced they had permission for David to sleep in their room, she called his parents. She counted on them agreeing with her plan.

"Honey," Tara Bell stuttered, "how dreadful. Is David going to be alright?"

"I think so, Mrs. Bell. He's more groggy than I've seen him and we need to escort him to the dorm. Besides the fact that we have his recording monitor, can you please write down tonight's episode in David's seizure diary? He may forget to do it tomorrow after I bring him home."

"Yes, for sure. Please take good care of him … and yourself. I hope you get some sleep."

Annabel said goodbye without telling her she'd be sleeping on the floor and, within the next ten minutes, they escorted David out of the concert.

After sitting David on her dorm bed and being alone with him, she told him a fictitious story about drinks spilling on him and that she needed to wash his clothes. With some cooperation from him, she jimmied his trousers and underwear off and stuck them in a laundry bag. Stepping back into the hallway, she implored her roommate to wash and dry them in the downstairs laundry room. "I'll owe you big time," Annabel said.

By midnight, Annabel had David in clean clothes, her roommate was sound asleep, and she lay on the concert blanket between the two beds. Before sleep came, she figured medical school or being a resident would be a lot worse than this.

Rachel thought about Kevin the rest of the weekend. She took Julia and Snoopy to the park on Sunday and, with the dog tethered to her bench and her daughter running around with another child on the playground, she considered what to do next.

They'd had a social encounter at the hospital's cancer center event, he had taken her to a diner, and then he had asked her to the art exhibit. However, she thought, both evenings still lacked a romantic entanglement or the essence of a real date. If he still planned on asking her for something more conclusive, then the previous nights would not have been a bad social lubricant. However, Casey's and the Tilsons' remarks may have left a sour taste in his mouth.

Should she take the gamble and ask him out? If she suggested having dinner, that may seem too overt. Yet, if she could bridge a formal date request with something more casual like they'd been doing, that would be the perfect blend. She wasn't much of a cook but, the longer she dwelled on it, the more she liked the idea of asking him to dinner at her place.

Julia came running over and pointed at a scrape on her knee.

"I'm glad to see you're not crying," Rachel said. "You're becoming a big girl. Go say good-bye to your friend and let's take

Snoopy for another walk, then go home. We can light some pretty candles before you go back to Danny."

Rachel took the dog by the leash. Tomorrow she'd ask Kevin Mcbride to come over for dinner and, if he said no, she'd forever cross him off her things-to-do list.

Danny had taken Julia with him to church that morning and, after returning her to Rachel, threw a tennis ball down the backyard hill for Dakota. The dog needed the exercise and the attention; Julia certainly wasn't giving it to him.

He turned around and waved at Mary as she walked onto the deck with a mid-day cup of coffee; he waved again when Annabel appeared. She had on a tan baseball cap, reminding him of the tomboy she used to be. But the rest of her, in a slimming pair of tights and long blouse, was very much feminine.

When Dakota trotted back to him and dropped the ball, he slung it low in the air towards the deck and walked that way.

"What a pleasant surprise," Danny said, giving Annabel a kiss.

"I had to come," Annabel said, her eyes moving towards her aunt's belly. "Wow, do you have any room left inside with those two babies?"

Mary laughed, holding her mug tightly. "Barely," she said.

"Dad, I took David to campus Friday night for a concert and he had a terrible seizure right in front of everybody. It was pretty bad. And when he left with me from the dorm yesterday morning, half of the people we passed looked at him like he had the plague."

"I'm sorry to hear that," Danny said. "Is he back to baseline?"

"I think so. But I don't know if he can ever show his face again around his friends, especially since he urinated on his clothes."

Danny put his arm around her shoulder and pulled her close. With his other hand, he stroked her hair like he did when she was small. "A true friend will understand and would never make fun of him for that. And you … did you hold up by being a good first-aid responder?"

She nodded slowly. "But Dad, don't you have all the information you need to do surgery?"

Rachel had a breather Monday morning because the first GU case wasn't scheduled to start until 9:00 a.m. She made a cup of tea in the microwave, then called her lawyer in Knoxville.

"What a way to start a week, getting a phone call from my only Nashville client," Phil said. "I thought we were through for a while … unless you're not making your medical 'finger' payments."

"I'm making them," she grunted. "With much difficulty, I'll add."

"Excellent. So now what?"

"Enough time has passed so now I want the definitive end result."

"Which is?"

"Getting and keeping Julia."

"Except that the child abuse is in the past, how has anything changed that would warrant that?"

"Mountains have been moved. Trust me."

Rachel took some instruments out of the autoclave and finished the preparation needed for Dr. Mcbride's first case. Running a bit late, he entered the room alongside the patient's stretcher and dropped his small duffel bag by the wall. The orderly helped the patient onto the OR table and the anesthesiologist scurried into the room as well.

After morning pleasantries, the elderly man on the table became less chatty after he received IV sedation followed by a spinal block as he lay in the lateral position. As Rachel stood by to assist, she gave Kevin a wide smile.

"I apologize for being a party crasher the other night," she said, throwing the used spinal kit into the garbage can.

"No problem," he said. "What we saw was worth it anyway. I hope you made it home okay considering how you felt."

"I did. And speaking of home and my cutting the night short, I'd like to make up for it. How about dinner at my place one of these evenings?"

His eyes locked on hers and the faint smile crossing his lips was half mischievous, half surprise. "Should I bring red or white wine?"

"White." Oh yes, white will be just fine, she thought; but in essence, it didn't matter. She didn't know what wines went with what foods anyway and it was as unimportant as drinking bourbon from Tennessee versus bourbon from Kentucky.

"White it shall be," Kevin said.

When the case got underway, Rachel stood close behind Kevin's shoulders. Now she understood why Robert had called it quits in the GU room after ten years. How did he stand it that long? She didn't think she could last one year. As a female, who could have imagined that looking at penises all day long was boring as hell? They were so damn flaccid, she couldn't imagine any of the ones she'd seen getting stiff and hard. This room could make a woman frigid, she thought.

However, except for the anesthesiologist, the only other dick in the room she hadn't seen was Kevin's. Hopefully, it wouldn't be a disappointment as she leaned her body against him for a few moments ... especially since their interaction was progressing to a dinner date and, most likely, beyond.

"It's time," Danny said to David and his parents in the office. They had moved up the teen's appointment in lieu of his recent seizure activity; and had reevaluated the wireless system and its data.

"Time to schedule surgery," Danny said, "because we have a fix on the small, precise area of your brain causing all the trouble. At least that's my best guestimate."

The youth's sneakers were planted on the step of the examining table and his hands nervously patted his cargo pants.

"This surgery is going to be a lot different than what you did last time," David said, grimacing.

"I've … been considering that," Tara said. "Dr. Tilson, this is really dangerous, isn't it? You're going to remove part of our son's brain?" Her complexion paled and she shot a look at Floyd.

"Yes. But understand that, with the system we just used, we have isolated the area responsible like never before in mankind's history. I am not going to take a chunk out of David's brain, but a focal patch of neurons."

Floyd put his hands on his hips and let out a big sigh. "If David wants to go ahead, you have my permission here and now," he said. "Everything is a gamble in life but, in this case, you're offering us a shoo-in remedy for his epilepsy."

"I hope I can live up to your expectations," Danny said as he swung back around to face his patient.

"I have been humiliated in front of all my peers, Dr. Tilson," David said. "I have nothing more to lose."

Danny proceeded to tell them all the possible complications and then wrote orders for David's preop labs. "You can get them done this week," he said. "And when you leave, stop at the front desk to have them put you on my surgery schedule. It'll probably be in two or three weeks."

After Danny left, David grinned a lopsided smile at his parents. "I sure lucked out with a girlfriend's father like him," he said.

At the end of the week, Sara had meetings so Danny beat her home. He went upstairs knowing Casey was pulling a three-to-eleven shift, rapped on the door and entered. Not seeing Mary, he called her name from the bottom of their stairs; and heard a door creak open.

"I'm up here in my studio," she yelled. "Come on up."

Taking two steps at a time, he bounded up to see her poking out her head.

"I have to make doubly sure that Casey never unexpectedly comes home while I'm painting this," she said.

"You've started it? The picture of him and his brother?"

She enthusiastically nodded her head and grabbed him by the sleeve. "I decided to get it done without him seeing it. After all, works start from the artist's perspective. Others may see the end product differently but it's the creator who must pull it out of their soul the way they see fit."

"So he's going to be totally surprised?"

"Yes, he doesn't even know I'm working on it. I have another piece going at the same time and that's what he sees whenever he comes in here." She walked him around to the canvas sitting on an easel.

"I don't know what to say." Danny stared at the vertical painting of the two children. The photograph Casey had given her was propped in front, both brothers hamming it up for the picture. The likeness on the canvas had them from the chest up and with less humorous expressions. Danny figured his sister wasn't yet half done, but already the brotherly love between them was evident in their eyes. Casey had his arm around Tommy, draped over his right shoulder.

"Well, you better say something," Mary said.

"If I already love it, Casey's reaction is going to be sheer bliss. The only way this could get any better is when it's finished."

"Thanks."

He looked at the table behind him, her paints and brushes scattered about. "But is the smell of these paints a good thing during your pregnancy?"

"I have the window open and I've been ventilating the room every time I'm in here."

"Okay. Just checking. I have a say with my only pending nephews or nieces, you know."

"I'll let you. Now go get out of here so I can sneak in another hour. And, by the way, your mail is on the kitchen counter. There's a big envelope from Mark Cunningham."

Danny frowned. "Before he puts good news in the mail, he calls me. When he has bad news, he just sends it via the post office."

"Uh-oh," Mary muttered.

Chapter 27

With a sour feeling, Danny opened the large manila envelope sitting on Mary's kitchen counter from Mark Cunningham. The cover letter simply said, "*Just received this from Phil Beckett. Call me after you digest it.*"

The thickness of the paper-clipped enclosure looked ominous and, sure enough, the legal wording in the upper left corner was an official *Rachel Hendersen vs. Daniel Tilson.*

He took the envelope and sat down in the recliner. He had left the cellar door open and Dakota walked across the room, nestled alongside the chair, and tilted his head back to check on him.

Knowing that this correspondence was going to be bad, he briefly closed his eyes; he was absolutely sick of this. How much more could he stand of this woman? His daughter was so young ... was Rachel going to hound him the rest of his life? What made her tick, what made her so persistent, what made her dish out cruelty to others? Was it mostly because she was so self-centered that her vision was clouded and she didn't understand what she did to others? If her actions only affected him, that would be one thing, he thought. But the constant legal maneuvering she dreamed up put stress on the rest of the family as well. And, this year, she even cost Casey part of his hand.

Danny rubbed Dakota's fur. "Sometimes I think I'm not even worthy of your love and devotion," he said softly. "You're as loyal as a soldier who won't reveal secrets under torture." He leaned over and kissed the dog's head as he knew the solace the dog provided was pivotal to his well-being.

Another half hour passed and then Danny had the guts to look at the beginning and end of the court documents. Wanting a huge custody change, Rachel was asking for a trial to make it official. Julia belonged with Rachel full-time, regardless of where she resided.

Feeling drained of all his energy, Danny groaned, leaned forward in the chair, and got up. He heard Mary coming and he also heard activity downstairs; Sara must have gotten home.

When his sister entered the room, he couldn't bear to tell her. She didn't deserve to hear this news. What she needed was constant positive energy around her for her growing twins and her own health.

Yes, he thought, he'd shield Mary from this for the time being. Even though the hellcat had struck again, he didn't need to lay that on others. He gave her a kiss, went downstairs with the envelope and Dakota, and greeted Sara with a big hug.

Casey massaged Mary's shoulders as they sat on a mat in a large room waiting for their Lamaze class to begin. More couples still streamed in, taking their spots on the floor as the female instructor stood quenching her thirst and eating a granola bar. She strutted back and forth behind the table, a lightweight wearing a pair of designer sneakers.

"Relax your back," Casey whispered in Mary's ear. "Begin thinking about your breathing so you can slow it down at will."

"I'm sorry you have to go through this with me," she said. "It's not like you don't know about childbirth."

"Absolutely don't think that way. There are a half-dozen reasons why I should be here as well as you."

"Name them," she said, her shoulders loosening up under his fingers.

"Besides you learning more about giving birth, the Lamaze techniques, and coping with pain, this is a bonding time between you and me. And it's better if they explain to you the available medications and anesthesia if you decide later to use them."

He moved his hands up to the nape of her neck and gently rubbed. "Plus," he said, "I had something to do with this. I'm not going anywhere since these babies were conceived. I'll be available to them from here on in until my last day on this earth. And to you, too."

"But you have confidence in me that I'll be able to do this in the most natural way possible, don't you?"

"Mary, you're a strong and a smart woman. Sure, you can do it. Just know that sometimes Mother Nature has other plans. Whatever is safe for you and the babies will be our plan of action and, in the meantime, these classes will prepare you for whatever might happen."

"Okay, ladies and gentlemen," the instructor said, "let's get the ball rolling this evening. All the babies in here aren't getting any smaller!"

Rachel didn't have a clue how to put together a dinner good enough for a special male guest so she went on the internet to figure out what to do. The most valuable resource available to her anymore was the worldwide web. What *couldn't* she find out on there?

First, she knew she couldn't tackle too big a menu or Kevin would spot her for the novice that she really was. And although she planned on having one or two things prepared ahead of time, cooking something in front of him would serve as a conversation piece.

Stumbling around with search engines, she finally hit pay dirt. Not only did she find an easy recipe, but she found out the best appliance to cook it on so she went to the nearest big box store and bought a small indoor electric grill. She also stopped at an eclectic food market where they sold premade items and selected a package of gourmet cheese-stuffed potato halves. Guys like something heavier than salad to accompany their meat, she thought, and she wasn't capable of making something like that. She bought sirloin steaks and, before leaving, she glanced at the refrigerated dessert section. With many good choices, she decided on a cheesecake with a tempting raspberry swirl. Why do women bake stuff at home, she thought, when stores can fulfill their wildest food desires?

With Friday night approaching, she bought salad ingredients and asparagus. After cutting up lettuce, mushrooms, tomatoes and red onions, she put them in a plastic container and then sliced up the vegetable and stored it as well. Getting any food prep done ahead of time for when she got home from work was crucial because what she would wear and what she would look like would be the most important part of getting ready.

On Friday, Kevin had no genitourinary cases and she didn't see him in the OR or in the hallways. But the date was on and she hurried home and set the table.

When the doorbell rang, Rachel greeted Kevin with a wide smile despite the fact that her heart kept doing somersaults. How and why did people ever invite others to dinner anyway? Throwing food together for one's self or their kids was a snap but why would someone deliberately want to feed others in a manner they didn't use for themselves? She reminded herself of the bigger picture and tried to shrug off the fact that her dinner preparations weren't exactly going along like Martha Stewart's.

Kevin handed her a bottle of wine. He was casually dressed in a striped golf-type shirt and lighter trousers. She decided then and there that she liked his dark features.

"Nice place," he said and walked across the room. "I'm only five minutes away. We have good locations so close to the hospital."

"Smart minds think alike," she said.

"I sleep to the last minute. Then I scramble to get in." After watching her grab a bottle-opener from the drawer, he went over and opened the wine. "I really do appreciate the invite. Existing on hospital cafeteria meals dulls my senses. Once it even made me sick, so it's refreshing to get away from it for a change."

"That way they have more admissions. People visiting their sick relatives eat there and then end up in the ER. But we're being harsh. It's not that terrible."

"You're right. You're kinder than I am. So, I learned the other night that you have a daughter." After a silence, he poured wine into both their glasses.

"Julia's her name. She's a sweet little girl, my only child. She's at her father's place tonight, Danny Tilson's. He and I never married which sure makes my life uncomplicated. Not that I don't ever want to marry, it's just that he's not the right one for me."

Kevin swirled the contents of his glass, deliberating what she'd said. "Sounds like you don't make hasty decisions and you don't want to mess up your life with a bad marriage. Smart ... although Dr. Tilson would probably be better than most available men."

"But there's a thing called love. There better be some chemistry or marriage won't work from the get-go."

"But you both have a child together," he said, looking at her suspiciously. "Are you saying there was no attraction?"

She lowered her head. "Now don't make me blush. We got carried away after a long day in the OR and a difficult late-night case."

"I'm sorry. I didn't mean to make you uncomfortable."

Her aqua eyes penetrated his. "That's more information than I've ever told anyone. But you do know how to bare a woman's thoughts."

"So we're getting ahead of ourselves. I'll change the subject. Let's toast to a nice dinner which you are so graciously hosting."

Their glasses clinked in unison. "Nice choice," she said after taking a sip. "I dislike dry wines and this is not one of them."

After Rachel took off her shoes and padded over to the grill, she prewarmed it and grabbed two frying pans. Into one of them, she put a stick of butter and salt, pepper, garlic and parsley. The mixture was straight from the grill's recipes in the purchase box and was to be poured over the finished steaks. She figured it would splatter all over as it melted, so she covered it with a lid. In the other pan, she set the cut asparagus to sauté as well.

"What can I do to help?" Kevin asked.

She put a finger up, opened the refrigerator, and took out the stuffed potatoes. "Here, I already made these and they just need to be heated in the microwave. Just put them on a plate and cover them. A minute should do."

Kevin did as she suggested as she placed two steaks on the countertop grill, then set out the salad she'd assembled a few days ago.

"We're almost ready," she said.

"You make this look easy."

"I hope so," she said and quickly turned off the heat to the asparagus. She pointed to the table; since it was round and small, she'd set the stoneware dishes across from each other. Kevin took over the wine and waited.

"We can start with salad," she said.

He pulled out a chair for her and then sat as well. Rachel slid the wooden bowl to him first, then served herself and drizzled dressing on top.

They both started together, chewing slowly; yet after two mouthfuls, she tasted something nasty and slimy. She wanted to take whatever it was out of her mouth but that wouldn't look very mannerly. Using her fork, she poked through the salad on her plate.

Kevin looked to be doing the same thing, his expression souring more than hers. Finally, she isolated the thing that must have tasted like snails. Mushrooms ... mushrooms that were apparently not fresh and had turned brown and moist and were covered with a gelatinous guck.

"I'm more of a meat and potatoes kind of guy," Kevin said, pushing the salad plate away.

Hoping to use humor to bail her out, Rachel cracked a smile. "The nerve of a farmer's market to mix up their mushrooms with seafood algae," she said.

Kevin laughed out loud. "Really. You should have bought your salad fixings at a big box store. That'll teach you."

Suddenly, Rachel got up.

"What's that smell?" Kevin asked as he got up, too.

Rachel grabbed the lid off the glaze for the steaks and they both peered at the dry mixture adhering to the bottom of the pan.

"Now that's what's called burnt to a crisp," she said.

"Was that to go over the steaks?" he asked.

"Was is correct. Past tense. It's a good thing meat can taste good all by itself."

"Who needs all that embellishment anyway?" Kevin responded.

She mustered up a smile. So far, she was doing a crappy job of cooking for him but at least he seemed to be a good sport.

"Let's just get to the good stuff." She slid the vegetable into a serving bowl but realized too much time had elapsed for the steaks. The cooking directions had said five minutes so she thought of a tactic to weasel out of overly well-done sirloins. "I forgot to ask you how you like your steaks. I like mine really overcooked so I hope you don't mind."

"That will be fine," he said as she opened the grill. She put one on each of their plates and ignored their black, crispy outer texture. Both of them went back to the table and sat down.

Rachel cut an asparagus piece, or at least tried to. When she did manage to slice it, the pulpy vegetable ended up a wad of string in her mouth and she couldn't swallow it.

With a steak knife, Kevin began cutting his meat. Taking a bite of the tough sirloin, he feigned a pleasant expression but finally just gulped it down. He couldn't cut into the asparagus either.

"What's wrong with it? Did the farmer not grow it enough?" she asked with a straight face.

"It's barely cooked," he said. "On the other hand, the steak is cooked too much."

"Oh no. I'm sorry. Hey, we forgot about the stuffed potatoes, though."

Kevin sprung up. "I'll get them." He opened the microwave, took off the lid, and pulled them out. Bringing them over to the table, he set them down in front of Rachel.

"I'm sorry, too. After all the work it must have taken you to prepare such gourmet potatoes, I think I hit 'one' for a minute but accidentally followed it by a 'zero.'

"Ten minutes?" she asked, looking at the potatoes. Their cheesy stuffing spread out all over the plate like unbaked cake dough and icing all swirled together.

"Yes, ten minutes," he responded.

She let out a big sigh, they both looked at each other, then burst into laughter.

Rachel propped her feet on the coffee table while Kevin leaned deep into the couch with both legs also on the table, crossed at the ankles. Their mood had gotten lighter and lighter, and the two of them had just finished a sandwich and the last remnants of the wine bottle.

She laughed out loud and kneaded her fist into his arm. "That was the best ever. I have never had a peanut butter and jelly sandwich with wine before!"

"See that. I already like your daughter. We wouldn't have had this experience except for the fact that you keep peanut butter and jelly for her."

"Ha! I can go get some animal crackers, too." She got up from the couch but Kevin grabbed the end of her skirt.

"That's okay," he said.

"No, I have to. And I have to get another bottle of wine."

She pulled her skirt from his hand, opened the only white wine she had, and rummaged through the pantry for the crackers; she held the bag under her arm and carried the bottle, squeezing between the table and couch. The crackers began to spill and she tried to hoist them back up but the wine slipped instead, pouring onto Kevin as it almost fell from Rachel's hands.

Like a surgeon catching a bad mistake, he lurched up and righted the bottle. When he put it on the table, they both looked at his clothes and then at each other.

"I'm so sorry," Rachel said.

Wine sank into an elongated path down his shirt and onto his trousers. He shuddered for a second as it hit his bear skin.

"Please, let me take your shirt or pants or both and I'll wash them," she said. "No kidding, that's going to stain."

He unbuttoned his shirt and slipped it off without a second thought. "Here," he said, "it's a favorite and it's got life left in it."

"Your pants?" she asked.

"That's okay. They aren't as bad."

She hurried off to the washer and dryer tucked into a closet. Doing laundry was the second lousiest chore she disliked, she thought, after sewing and doing dishes. Well, the third least favorite thing to do, she corrected herself.

She grabbed a small bowl and went back over to the couch. "Here," she said, sitting down. "The trick to eating animal crackers is to pick out only the ones you like." She poured more than a handful into the bowl, selected a bear, and put it in her mouth.

Kevin took a lion, tiger, elephant and bear and placed them on the table. "But I hate to eat animals I like, don't you?"

"Sometimes humans don't have a choice. Here, taste this. I bet you've not had an animal cracker for twenty years."

"I'm not even sure I've ever had one."

She put one in his mouth and giggled.

"Mmm. Slightly sweet," he said.

"I just realized the only decent thing that we had left from our spoiled meal is dessert. I have a cheesecake if you prefer that over animal crackers."

"I don't know. Sometimes it's the ambience of eating something that's more important than what you eat. Kind of like it's the journey of going somewhere and not the final destination."

"You don't say." She picked up a tiger and with two fingers brought it close to his lips. "Wrap your tongue and taste buds around this baby," she said, the proximity of his bare arm and chest making it easier for her to ramp up her charm.

His lips encircled the cookie but he slid a little further and included her fingertip, then let go. After he swallowed the cracker, he sucked on her finger again.

"Now you give me one," she whispered.

"Which species do you prefer?"

"I can be more specific than that."

He held a cracker in front of her and started leaning back. She followed, their bodies closing the gap. "Tell me," he said.

"An Irish American, American Indian man around six feet tall with skilled hands who works for a living on male body parts. However, what he needs right now is recreational time with only the finest female mind and body parts."

"You don't say."

"I do say."

"Lions, tigers and bears will never mean the same again," Kevin said as he pulled Rachel onto his lap and she pressed her upper body against his naked chest.

Chapter 28

"Casey just got home," Mary said. "Don't any of you say a word to him if you go upstairs."

She hesitated with one hand under her pendulous belly and pointed a finger at them. Nancy sat on the floor amused and Annabel stared from a stool with one ear bud dangling.

"Right now, he doesn't have a clue," Mary continued. "And if he thought I was planning something for his birthday, he'd never suspect a Thursday night."

"What time is the reservation?" Danny asked.

"In two hours, so y'all better start getting ready." She paced the length of the coffee table and stopped again.

"And you're sure you want me to bring the painting?" Danny asked.

"Yes. There it is in the corner. Why don't you head out before us and sneak it into Downtown Italy before we get there?"

"No problem. I can't wait to see the finished product."

Annabel sprung up. "I better get going if I want to make it on time with David. Sometimes his parents talk too much when I get there. And thanks for inviting him, Mary."

"You're welcome. By the way, I asked Casey's partner Toni if she'd like to come, too. She spends as much time with him as Mark did and his partners have a lot to do with how well he likes his job."

"That was nice of you," Sara said. "It'll be fun to meet her."

Mary gave her brother a kiss and, holding onto the banister, went up the stairs.

"I'm glad you agreed to coming here tonight," Mary said as Casey held the door open for her.

"It's not like you wanting to eat fancy on a week night," he said. "But then again, that landscape you've been working on after Julia and Dakota's picture is moving along slowly. Is your pregnancy slowing you down?"

"With Sara around more since school's out and Annabel home for the summer, I'm just more distracted."

"Annabel will start getting busy again with a summer job," he said. "But don't push yourself with the painting and only do as much as you want. We're financially fine with my salary and we don't have a home mortgage thanks to your mom and dad."

They stood inside the entryway at the reception desk. "Tilson," Mary said. The white-haired woman looked down at her notebook and waved for them to follow. "Everyone we used to know here is gone," she whispered. "It's not the same."

"I agree," Casey said. They weaved through tables past a room divider and he blinked. "I didn't know Danny and Sara were coming, or …"

A singing rendition broke out of 'Happy Birthday,' and Casey lightly slapped his forehead; Mary turned around and beamed at him. He put his arm around her waist and looked at each of them: Danny, Sara, Annabel, David, Nancy and Toni. Waiting until they were done to tell them they couldn't carry a tune, they then launched into 'for he's a jolly good fellow.'

He waved his hands, "You all want me to die from hearing you sing before I make it to fifty this weekend."

They finished as Danny patted Casey on the back and David shook his hand.

"This is the first adult surprise birthday party anyone has ever given me," he said with emotion.

"You better enjoy the spotlight tonight," Mary said. "Do you realize that once these babies come, birthdays won't be about us anymore?"

"I never thought about that. Then let's sit down and get this party going."

Making it easier to talk and enjoy themselves, Mary had preordered their food. Danny passed warm Italian bread to David.

"You're on my schedule next week," he said. "Your lab work came back and, from my surgical standpoint, you're good to go. I'm glad you could join us tonight."

"I told Annabel she didn't have to invite me," David said. "But thanks, you all make me feel like a part of the family."

"After David's surgery," Annabel said, "I plan on helping him a little bit over the summer to catch up with schoolwork for the fall."

"You're getting a job," David said, "so don't feel like you have to do that. Plus, we won't even be in the same classes next fall."

"David, that doesn't matter. Good friends stick together thick and thin."

Danny and Sara briefly held hands under the table, knowing what Annabel meant; the two of them were now sincere friends.

As he reached for antipasto, Danny also realized that whatever David's relationship was with his daughter, his medical and surgical care would not change. His own involvement with her college and sport's team had been useful, and maybe some policies and practices would change along with the future of epileptic monitoring. He hoped so.

Across the round table, Toni held Mary's attention. "Do you know how much your husband is focused on your pregnancy?" she asked but answered her own question. "Our seven to three shift takes on a 'morning sickness' quality. I can't eat a donut without him telling me that it's the worst flavor for Mary's nausea. Or that black coffee wouldn't stay down long if Mary drank it."

"I'm so sorry," Mary said.

"Nah, it makes him a better man. If they radio us and we have to pick up a pregnant lady, he's cool, calm, and collected and treats them like he's their Lamaze coach. They're barely in labor and he makes them think they're being driven to Disneyland instead of the hospital."

Mary shot a glance at her husband and he shrugged his shoulders.

"And then," she said, stopping to slurp an oyster, "we get a call about a pregnancy; some frantic female called in. So we get to this house and a middle-aged woman points to the back yard. Casey is hustling faster than I am and I'm holding onto the end of the stretcher. This batty woman follows us and says, 'She's been digging like crazy and she's under the porch.'

"Since we didn't get any real calls for the next hour, I became your husband's assistant to deliver kittens. He rattled off his list of needed supplies. You shoulda seen him. He even cut this long-haired cat's fur around her bottom to make it easier for her to clean up after the birthing process." Toni dunked a piece of bread into an olive oil dip and raised her eyebrows. "Oh, sorry," she said. "I better shut up at the dinner table. Talking about our job isn't standard conversation while eating."

"I want to go into medicine," Annabel said, "so it's okay with me."

"It's not with me, dimwit," Nancy said, rolling her eyes. "Or with Mom or Mary or David."

When the last person was done eating, two waiters cleared all the dirty dishes from the table, brushed off residual crumbs, then put down dessert plates along with clean forks and spoons.

The head chef came out of the kitchen wearing a white apron and hat and carrying a cake. Despite Casey's embarrassment, the group sang again as he blew out the candles.

When they finished, Nancy blurted out, "How old are you, Uncle Casey?"

"It's the big one, honey. Fifty."

"And you two are having babies?"

"Nancy!" Sara exclaimed.

"No, that's all right, Sara," Casey said. "Don't forget, Nancy, your aunt is younger than I am. Plus, I notice I'm not the one who has popped out with a few gray hairs." He looked over at Danny.

"What? Me?" Danny asked. "That's not fair. We're now the same age again."

"Okay, you all," Mary said. "While they cut this exquisite cake in the back, I'm giving Casey his present." She stood and turned around to the back wall. Danny went over to help her. They peeled off the brown paper cover and brought it closer, facing backwards.

"A painting," Casey said. He looked at Mary with admiration as they turned it around and rested it on her chair.

Astonished and overjoyed, Casey dabbed his still dry eyes. The love he felt for his young brother was palpable; the painting the embodiment of their entire relationship and his fond memories.

His wife had done it again. Maybe he was prejudiced but it was the most personal and beautiful portrayal of children he'd ever seen on canvas. He had to cover his eyes because he couldn't contain the tears which welled up like hot water bubbles about to boil.

Danny and Vance sat huddled over a table in the doctor's lounge as a group of medical students filtered in. Their wide eyes, youthful looks, and perky demeanors spoke volumes as to their inexperience. One of them stopped and glanced over. "Can you imagine shadowing or working with him?" he said, nodding towards Danny.

The others nodded while Danny couldn't fathom how they all knew him. Perhaps they recognized him from the infrequent medical grand rounds he presented. He pushed his copy of the day's surgery schedule in his pocket and looked at Vance.

"Don't come over to see the family if you don't want to," he said. "Just meet me in the OR. I suspect Tara and Floyd are going to be nervous wrecks." He got up slowly, taking his empty coffee cup with him.

"Thanks, Danny. And thanks for letting me come into surgery and follow this case through its entirety."

As Danny suspected when he entered through the curtains, Tara and Floyd looked more unnerved than he'd ever seen them before and he totally understood why. This would be the most invasive procedure yet to do on their son. Implanting the electrodes didn't compare to taking out brain tissue. However, Danny thought, the most potentially fatal experience David had encountered was still the secondary impact. He walked over to the empty side of the room alongside the stretcher.

"Dr. Tilson, I can't wait to get this over with," David said, staring at the IV in his hand. "I'm not scared one bit."

"That's because of what that doctor just put in your IV," Danny said and smiled.

"Dr. Tilson, how long is this going to take?" Tara stuttered out every word. She gripped her son's hand like that of a steering wheel in a storm.

"Now, Tara," Floyd said, "we've been through all this before. Let's not bother him. It's going to take as long as it takes." He took his hand off his wife and looked at Danny. "So … how long, Doc?"

"Let's say between two and four hours. Honestly, I don't expect any complications and I'll send a nurse out to give you an update. My work will be tedious and that's the reason why I'll take my time."

"Okay, thank you. Tara, let's go now and leave David to everyone's care."

Tara stayed near her son. "I'm going to say a prayer the whole time you're back there," she said. "We love you." She gave him a kiss on the cheek, finally let go of his hand, and stepped away.

"If it's okay with you," Danny said, "I'll say a little prayer while I'm scrubbing. He'll be in good hands no matter how you look at it."

"That's fine," she said, her eyes moistening. "That's very fine indeed."

Methodically, Danny scrubbed at the sink, said a few religious words like he'd promised Tara and pushed open the door with his back. David was asleep already and, as Vance stood against the wall, Danny gowned and gloved. All the same steps he had taken with David's last surgery were repeated: a bactericidal scrub on a shaved and pin-fixated head, skin incision, removal of skull bone, and clamping back the area for exposure.

He stood up straight to pause and glanced at the instrument table as well as the scrub tech. He frowned under his mask at some of the tools of his profession: a scalpel, a scissors, a mess of hemostats, clamps and sponges. Outcomes have little to do with these instruments, he thought. They have to do with the person wielding them. No different than Mary's art work; paintbrushes didn't matter, but she and her talent did. He smiled under his mask, acknowledging the pride he felt for his sister.

Watching from the side, Vance had stepped a bit closer. After some time, Danny grinned to see that David's brain tissue had a healthy, vibrant appearance. He worked on removing the former equipment he had placed – the electrodes, the antenna and the RF chip. A little bit of blood oozed from the site which made him intermittently use a small suction catheter.

"We agreed on approximately this much," Danny finally said to Vance, reconfirming their previous discussions about the length and width of the area to now be removed. He motioned with his thumb and index finger an area about a centimeter square.

"That's correct," Vance said.

"And a depth of half a centimeter."

"Correct again," Vance said.

Even to hear this reassurance from another researcher's opinion, Danny hesitated a moment then gave an order to himself. He must take out as few brain cells as possible so as to not disturb other mental facilities. But equally as important was to cut out the cells responsible for David's seizures.

"Okay," he said. He extended his hand to the scrub tech. "Scalpel, please."

Chapter 29

Three days later, Danny made rounds with growing optimism for David who had sailed through surgery and recovery. And although it was still early, the young man showed no signs of seizure activity.

His last patient to see, Danny pushed open David's door and also found his parents and Annabel inside. "Now I know where to find my daughter on this lovely morning," he said.

"We all can't wait to see if you discharge David," she responded.

All eyes focused on him. David sat on the recliner and the other three, all in sneakers, were ready to spring out the door.

"Let me take a look at him while you all wait outside," Danny said.

When they begrudgingly left, he examined the youth and then sat on the end of the bed.

David looked worried. "So what do you think, Dr. Tilson?"

"Right now, I couldn't be more pleased. You're going home."

David rose and pumped his fist. "Yessss."

"But here are my strict orders. The same conditions of no driving, no sports, and no extra physical activity apply. Walking is fine. If you have a seizure, come in before the appointment I'm giving you in a week. This is a wait and see game to find out if we have indeed cured your epilepsy from your secondary impact."

When Danny opened the door, the rest of them practically fell in.

"I'm coming with you two to court," Casey said. "As a matter of fact, I can drive." He stood in Danny and Sara's big room as Sara packed a handbag and Danny straightened his tie in a mirror.

"That's fine," Sara said. "And thank you."

"It's alright," Casey said, "And I still haven't told Mary a thing so as to not upset her. I told her I'm just going with you to your attorney's office."

"Which is partially true," Sara said, "And I agree she doesn't need the stress. She loves Julia as much as the rest of us."

Danny poked his head out the back door and said good-bye to Annabel, Nancy, Julia and Dakota; then they left in Casey's car. He could think of more pleasant things to do besides going to a custody trial regarding his own daughter and he frowned with displeasure.

Sara sat in the front passenger seat and Casey intermittently watched his best friend in the rearview mirror. With nervous apprehension, Danny had remained silent and stared out the window looking at nothing in particular.

"You haven't given us an update lately about David," Casey said trying to take Danny's mind off what would transpire at the courthouse.

"Danny," Sara said, "Casey asked you something."

"Oh, sorry," he mumbled and Casey repeated the question.

A faint smile crossed Danny's face. "I've seen him already for two follow-up visits. So far, not one seizure or even a suspicious twitch."

"That's remarkable," Sara said, "but how is he otherwise? You said that by removing brain cells, a patient could lose important functions because each part of the brain serves a different purpose."

"Yes," Danny said as Casey peered again into the mirror. "Even though he tells me nothing has changed, I sent him for testing … like a before and after comparison. The epileptogenic cells I removed have not made a difference in his functioning. He's had no motor deficits. Other functions such as long term memory, language recognition and the formation of new memories are also the same."

"We're thrilled for him," Casey said. "And this is a huge breakthrough."

"I believe so," Danny said. "I'm in the process of writing a paper with Vance. It will be submitted to the American Association of Neurological Surgeons, the American Neurological Association, and other major publications."

Casey parked in a parking garage and they all piled out of the car. Now there was another important aspect of Danny's life to take care of.

"Perhaps the judge is eating lunch in his chambers," Mark Cunningham said to Danny, trying to make a joke. Even though he'd spread paperwork at their table, his briefcase still bulged on the chair beside him. He squeezed his cell phone into a side pocket and nervously eyed his watch.

They'd all been waiting in the courtroom for fifteen minutes which gave Danny more time to regain his anxiety. He stretched his shirt collar off his neck and then tapped his shoe on the tile floor underneath the wooden table. Glancing behind him, he gave Sara and Casey a quick glance. They sat close together; Sara professionally dressed in a cream jacket over a blouse and Casey in a brown sports coat and white shirt. Their presence did more for slowing his heart rate than tapping his foot.

Phil Beckett and Rachel sat at their own table and kept up a running dialogue, their jovial demeanor worrying Danny even more.

Right after the court stenographer sat, the bailiff announced Judge Munoz. A husky older man, he gathered his robe in front, sat down and focused on the documents he'd brought in. "Rachel Hendersen vs. Daniel Tilson," he said, glancing forward, "regarding custody of your child, Julia. Are we to commence or have the parties come to terms with a suitable arrangement for said minor child?"

"My client believes there are new concerns that warrant this trial, Your Honor," said Phil. "And she believes Mr. Tilson would never agree to what's in the best interest of Julia."

Looking at their table, Danny scowled; Mark slid his hand a few inches and tapped his client's forearm.

"Okay, then," the judge said. "I have digested all the previous court documents and motions in this ongoing case and am aware of the perilous history of this child with your client, Mr. Beckett."

"Your Honor, all …."

"I'm not finished, Mr. Beckett. To Ms. Hendersen's credit, she has righted the situation regarding her daughter's abuse and it looks like visitation between both parties has proceeded along smoothly since that time. Additionally, there have been no more incidents." He leaned back in his chair and breathed deeply.

"That is correct, but there's a problem," Phil responded and then paused for dramatic effect. "Julia does not want to be with her father at all."

Danny felt his hands tremble. Was this as true? That one emphatic sentence cast him as some ogre or an unfit parent and he felt perspiration collect under his shirt. Looking over at the other table, Rachel appeared as relaxed as if she'd walked out of a massage parlor and her bespeaking eyes focused on the judge. Quite suddenly, Danny realized she'd probably been planning this trial for a long time.

"Mr. Beckett," the judge said. "You can't expect me to talk to this child in chambers about this matter. I won't do it. She is too young and it could leave a lasting scar."

Danny felt a bit relieved. At least this judge had common sense.

"I agree, Your Honor," Phil said, "and we would never suggest that. If the court would allow, I have subpoenaed a therapist who has spent time with Julia. She is a professional in her field and can share her findings with the court."

Danny's pulse quickened; he inconspicuously picked up his pen and wrote a note to Mark. *If Julia was seeing a therapist, I had no knowledge of it.*

Mark read it and scribbled below. *Exactly. That's the way Rachel wanted it.*

As Danny stared at those words, he realized Mark understood Rachel sometimes better than he did.

"Okay," the judge said. "We are getting ahead of ourselves. But since I am the speed-reader that I am and have the dynamics of these parties understood, then let's bring in the therapist. I take it from my papers, it's a Miss Kelly?"

"Yes, Your Honor," Phil said.

Several pews behind Danny, Sara grabbed Casey's forearm and squeezed. Leaning into him, she whispered. "They are being railroaded."

Casey nodded and turned around as a bailiff was escorting a young woman through the door. As her heels clicked up the aisle, Danny also turned and looked; the woman had a slender figure and walked with a feminine sway, her hair fell straight as a ruler onto the top of a chic pantsuit

After the lady settled into the chair next to the judge's bench and was sworn in, Phil Beckett strode up to her. "Please state your name, occupation, and place of work for the record," he said.

"Miriam Kelly. I am a family therapist who studied and trained at East Tennessee State University. I have been practicing for eight years at The Family Therapy Group here in Nashville." She spoke distinctly and with only a trace of a southern accent. Danny figured she had testified more than once because of her work.

"Okay, excellent," Phil said. "When did Ms. Hendersen bring Julia in?"

"It was months ago, sir. I'm not sure of the date. It should be on my record note which you asked for and I supplied."

"And only Ms. Hendersen brought her daughter in? Mr. Tilson has never shown up with his daughter at The Family Therapy Group, correct?"

"That is correct."

"And how much time did you spend with Rachel Hendersen?"

"Not much at all. We had the usual introductory remarks, she told me what she does and she explained her concern for her daughter and then left me alone with Julia. Almost the entire visit I spent getting to know and talking with Julia."

"So you couldn't have formed some kind of an attachment or empathy with my client? And you're sure you had no other personal conversations?"

"She did mention she was doing volunteer work in a children's hospital. Other than that, it was the briefest of encounters."

"Okay, thank you for that. I probed just to make sure you didn't become partial to the mother who is bringing this issue to court."

"Actually, sir, I don't know what the issue is. I only know of what transpired at that visit."

"Then, unless I need to ask you a specific question, why don't you tell the court what little Julia said to you behind closed doors that day?"

"Well … where to begin? She was very free with sharing her thoughts about her situation going back and forth between both parents and what occurred at both places. I learned that she spent lots of alone time with her mother but at the Tilson residence she described a more chaotic household. People coming and going and a large, rambunctious dog. Well, actually, the dog was supposed to really be her mother's."

She stopped briefly and licked her lips. "Go on," Phil said.

"She said that her mother loved her more and that her father loved some lady more than her. I don't know if she was referring to a wife. She also said she didn't want to live with the father at all. What she wants is to be in her mother's apartment or house or wherever she lives and that she loves her mother the most. I heard it over and over, 'I want to live with Mommy.'"

"Wow," Phil said. "How often do you see this kind of determination in a child this young?"

"I've never seen this kind of 'determination,' as you call it. This little girl is sure about what she wants and it's apparent she's not enjoying the present situation."

Since the judge was hanging on every word, Mark tapped Danny to get his attention. When Danny looked at him, Mark shook his head and Danny's horror at the testimony caused his heart to thunder in his chest.

Thinking that all the damage had been done and there was nothing that could make it worse, Mark decided to ask Miriam Kelly a thing or two as well before she left the stand.

"Miss Kelly," he said," you commented yourself that, in all your years of being a therapist, you have not come across a young child as determined as Julia to live with one parent versus the other. And all evidence that we have is that Dr. Tilson is an outstanding family man and surgeon and his character is not up for debate. Didn't you stop to consider that her strong, adamant desires *are* abnormal and wonder where do they come from?"

"Children can latch onto an idea from a pleasurable experience and make it like a fantasy that grows and grows. Somehow Julia loves and trusts her mother so much more."

Danny wasn't a therapist but he thought that Miriam Kelly needed to be on a couch herself to understand her profession better.

"You still aren't answering my specific question," Mark said.

Kelly gave a shrug of her shoulders and was dismissed from the room. After more reiteration of prior custody history, the judge made it clear their time in court was finished.

"Mr. Beckett and Mr. Cunningham, I will rule on this situation or change in a very prompt manner. I see the petitioner wants some monetary changes if she is given custody and she also wants Dr. Tilson to pay her legal bills. I will give you my answers soon."

Rachel pushed her elbow into Phil. "Don't forget that one last thing," she whispered.

"Your Honor," Phil said. "We would appreciate a timely ruling. My client will be leaving Nashville for a job relocation and it's obviously in Julia's best interest if she goes with her."

"You didn't tell me about that," the judge said and looked carefully at Rachel. "Not that it changes anything," he added.

Danny tossed and turned for a long time. Eventually he halted rocking the bed like he was in a canoe but how could he sleep when his mind raced like a wound-up clock? The day's events in the courtroom weighed on him too heavily and the therapist's words played in his head like a stuck record, that Julia had said multiple times "I want to live with Mommy."

He stared up at the ceiling, faint moonshine seeping through the blinds and the light dinner he'd had seemed lodged in his throat. Julia had become a beacon of light in his life and he could not bear to think about losing her.

"Are you still awake?" Sara asked while turning towards him.

"I can't sleep … at all."

"Your dad used to say sleep is like a cat. Ignore it and it will come."

"Good old Dad. Glad he's not here right now to know what's going on with my daughter."

"Good night, Danny."

"Good night, Sara. Thanks for coming with me today. I love you."

Chapter 30

As Danny waited to see his first patient, he read over the medical paper he and Vance had completed. It had just come back from the medical editor and the upgrade made a smooth difference.

His nurse walked in and he handed it to her. "Ask them at the front desk to get this in the mail today," he said. "They already have the cover letter."

As Cheryl reached for it, Jeffrey and Matthew came in and Bruce tagged behind them.

"Nice to see you, Bruce," Danny said. "The few times you've been here recently, we've missed each other."

"Your staff booked me a half day today as your schedules are booked solid."

"I'm certainly glad they oversee all of that," Danny said. "I realize we run smoothly because of them." He smiled at Cheryl who still stood there with the medical paper.

Matthew's eyes darted back and forth from Danny to Jeffrey. His long brown hair rested on the nape of his neck and he shifted his weight from one foot to the other like he was at a marathon's starting line. Jeffrey's hand rested near his chiseled facial features while he did a poor job of suppressing a grin.

"What?" Danny asked. "I give up … what are you all standing there for?"

"The three of us have nominated you," Jeffrey said.

"Nominated me for what?"

"The Tennessee Medical Society's Physician of the Year."

"Why did you go and do that?"

"Humility is one of your strong points," Bruce chimed in. "The way you have handled milestone cases in the last few years and your contribution to medicine in Tennessee and elsewhere makes you an excellent candidate."

"We think that for you," Matthew said, "it should be more than 'Physician of the Year.' It should be an award for the physician of the decade. There's nothing like that, so we've only put your name in for this year."

Danny shook his head and stood up. "There are plenty of doctors more deserving than I am. The three of you are certifiably crazy."

"Then don't worry about it," Jeffrey said, flicking his one long earring. "Just because we've put in a proposal, doesn't mean you're going to get it."

He left to go see patients, Bruce followed him, and Matthew tipped his head before rushing over to the hospital for surgeries.

"What?" Danny asked Cheryl. "Did you know what they were doing?"

"I just work here," she said, feigning ignorance. She left on her errand and, with a bemused grin, Danny enjoyed his Norman Rockwell print for just a moment before seeing his first patient of the day.

Rachel and Kevin stood side by side. She had his instruments ready for the next case while an orderly went to get their next patient. Between cases, they had both inherited Robert's obsession with crossword puzzles. Rachel brought them in every day; she'd even bought a book full of them. The best reason to do them, she knew, was to spend time together and enamor him more and more. And besides the sex and the dates, it was working.

She untied her scrubs, pulled the strings tighter, and made a bow.

"If we were at your place, I could have tightened those for you," he whispered.

She pinched his side. "Tightened them? I hope not. Loosening them and slipping them off me - one leg at a time - would be more like it." Leaning over the counter on her elbow, she pursed her lips at him.

"So leave them on and I'll come over after work and do just that."

"Kevin Mcbride, you're a very accommodating man. I'm so glad I met you." And I didn't think you'd be this easy, she thought.

"I'm lucky for the timing, too," he said. "And I can't believe the coincidence that we'll both be heading west soon."

"Yes. And who knows?"

"Who knows what?"

"Well, we should look each other up," she said, tilting her head down as if she was blushing. "But never mind." She straightened and peered closely at the puzzle, pencil in hand. "I can't figure this one out at all. What on earth is another word for 'and'?"

"What does it say?"

"It says 'a word used for the word and.'"

"That's crazy. That has to be the most used word in the English dictionary and I can't recall ever seeing a substitute."

They heard the metal noise of a stretcher entering the adjoining OR and the chitchat between the patient, the orderly, and the anesthesiologist. Kevin went outside first while Rachel opened a drawer and pulled out her handbag. After rummaging around, she pulled out a dictionary and even a thesaurus. She had no luck with the latter but liked what she found in the Merriam-Webster. She shoved them back in her bag and penciled in a nine-letter word which fit perfectly.

Kevin stepped back in after a short discussion with the patient as Rachel began to walk out to confirm the patient's name, operative procedure, and to assist the anesthesiologist.

"That was a tough one," she said.

"You figured it out?"

She nodded. "Ampersand."

He furrowed his brow. "Never heard of it. And by the way, we should do more."

"Do more of what?"

"Do more than just look each other up when we move out west."

Casey pulled his car into the garage after working an early shift and went to the mailbox as he contemplated going to the gym. It was stuffed as no one had taken the trouble to check it. He grabbed the pile and thumbed through it as he went in the house, seeing a large envelope for Danny from Mark Cunningham.

Swallowing hard, Casey contemplated calling Danny. If he did, his friend would know that the final determination of Julia's custody would be awaiting him when he got home. He couldn't judge what news the packet contained for, unlike his friend, he had less of a feel for family court decisions than Danny did. However, as an observer in the courtroom weeks before, he thought the situation looked grave.

He paced the kitchen floor and finally decided to call. Knowing ahead of time, Casey thought perhaps the call would soften Danny's blow if it turned out to be bad news.

After a few minutes, Cheryl put Danny on the phone.

"Danny, it's Casey. I just want to give you a heads up that there's a large envelope for you from Mark Cunningham." He stopped pacing. "You there?"

"Uh … yeah," Danny said. "Thanks. Thanks for letting me know. See ya later."

Casey wondered if he had made the right decision but then brushed the uncertainty aside. What was in the envelope is what mattered.

With a heavy heart, Danny opened the car door and started the ignition. He drove slowly at first, headed for home, but found himself circling blocks in the thick downtown area. Not only were the streets thick with 6:00 p.m. traffic but they were busy because of the early evening tourists and the bars, restaurants, and country music venues filling up. The earlier crowd confiscated the best seats for viewing live bands.

Danny veered his Lexus into the parking garage, walked to the street and began dodging pedestrians, especially the ones holding hands and blocking other people from passing. The river path was several blocks down and he fooled himself into thinking he would go over there to take a stroll.

Several establishments he passed had catchy sculptures in front of their doors; one even had a good Elvis impersonation and a man took a picture of his girlfriend giving the statue a kiss.

Danny kept going. On the corner of the next street he stopped and looked past the hired man at the door. The lights were dim inside but he could see a stage with musicians, tables for eating and a large room in the front with a circular bar. The man nodded at him and stepped to the side. Danny certainly qualified as over eighteen and didn't look to be a troublemaker.

He walked into the room - the floor, the bar and the ceiling all made out of wood – and pulled up a stool and sat in front of the bartender. Past the room which was half-full of people eating from baskets of food, a country band tried to excite the early crowd with quick guitar strumming and lyrics about kissing a farm girl in the back of a pick-up truck.

The bartender put a napkin on the counter in front of Danny. "What'll it be?" he asked.

"How about a Tennessee-crafted beer?"

"A Calfkiller Brewery beer is what you want. Their classic," the thirty-something bartender said.

Danny sipped the drink, thinking it didn't matter if he stopped off here because the paperwork he had to open at home wasn't going anywhere. And what difference did it make if he ripped it open anyway? He hadn't received a phone call from Cunningham announcing some kind of victory for Julia to continue with the present arrangement.

After the beer went down like a liquid slider, the attentive bartender placed another one down and also slid a bowl of seasoned popcorn over to him.

Danny knew this was it; the final straw. By some miracle, he'd had more time with Julia than he'd ever dreamt possible and had come to love her like his other girls. Oh, how he loved her; her beautiful eyes, her zesty spirit, her fast little-girl steps. She didn't even qualify as a toddler anymore.

The man behind the bar raised his eyebrows at him. "Like the choice? Want to try a different flavor?"

"Tell you what," Danny said. "I'll continue to support our own state. I'll take a Tennessee whiskey."

"Coming right up," he said. In a few minutes, he placed down another new glass. "Here's a Jack for 'ya."

As the bar and the restaurant area began filling to capacity, Danny held onto saving his spot at the bar like a kid hoarding his seat in the back of the classroom away from the teacher. Meanwhile, the lyrics up front had changed to a country dude stripping his clothes off on a riverbank with the sheriff's daughter.

Swirling around the whiskey, Danny didn't know how many he'd had; all he knew and cared about at the moment was Julia. The situation wouldn't be this way if it weren't for the poor girl's necromancer of a mother. But he blew off Rachel in his mind. She wasn't even worthy of his thoughts. Julia was. His precious Julia. How could he bear to lose her? God, you're being mean, he thought.

I already lost Melissa and Sara had a miscarriage. Please, not another one, even if it's by a different way.

He didn't stop drinking and the bartender wasn't counting either. In another two hours, after coming out of the men's restroom, he sat on the bench in the hallway and dialed Casey's number.

"Danny, where are you? I know you're not on call and office hours are way over."

"Casey, can … can you come get me? I can't drive."

Chapter 31

By the time Casey pulled into the garage at home, he had decided what he would do with Danny. Mary didn't know about her brother's night of excess drinking and would be sleeping. Sara was aware of the details, but not the girls. Casey wanted it to stay that way and told Sara he'd keep Danny upstairs and put him to bed on their couch.

Using all his upper body strength, Casey wrapped a grip around Danny's chest and maneuvered him out of the front passenger seat. He held up his friend and supported his every stumbling step into his part of the house. When they got in front of the couch, Casey lowered him, took his shoes off and fluffed a pillow on one end. Danny went supine without much help as Casey straightened out his legs.

"Bad, isn't it?" Danny mumbled.

Casey sat on the edge of the table. "What, the judge's decision?"

"Yeah."

"Do you want me to open it and read it?"

"Yeah."

Casey went to the counter, ripped open the envelope, and read Mark's cover letter. He skimmed over the thick court document and scowled. From the custody decision to the financial aspects of hefty child support to paying Rachel's legal bills, it was all really bad news and he muttered an expletive against Rachel.

Back at the couch, he sat down again and leaned over to Danny. "You're right, buddy. But get some sleep."

Danny's face crumpled as he closed his eyes, hoping to sink further into an alcoholic stupor where he didn't have to think about it.

Danny put on a new white lab coat with his name embroidered in a different color. The thick red thread was a lot cleaner and readable than the medium blue that the group had been using. He had a brighter outlook lately after he'd finally dealt with and accepted the court's ruling. And he was glad he headed his group and was making good business decisions, especially since Julia would be leaving his household to live out-of-town with her mother.

Cheryl pulled at her ponytail and motioned Danny into an examining room.

"It's been weeks," Danny said to David and his mother when he walked in. The youth looked summery wearing cargo shorts and a navy T-shirt with a sport's logo. And, for the first time during their visits, Tara greeted him with a large, genuine smile.

Danny shook David's hand and patted Tara on the shoulder; Cheryl stayed by the door. "Fill me in," Danny said. He laughed and added, "By now, you know the routine."

The whole time David carried on about still not having any seizures, Danny could feel his own tranquil heartbeat and felt assured that the young man's troubles from his head traumas were over.

David finished his long update and added, "And by next year, Dr. Tilson, I'm going to be playing a little recreational basketball again with friends ... thanks to you."

"You are not going to be afraid to go back out on the court?"

"No, I don't think so. But I sure wish it was the norm for players to wear some kind of a light helmet. Some device that doesn't look dorky but gives some protection."

"Yes," Danny said, "some protection would be better than none."

When the appointment ended, Tara gave Danny a big hug. "We can't thank you enough," she said.

"No problem," Danny beamed.

"And tell Annabel I said hello," David said with a smile.

Cheryl encouraged Danny to go straight to the kitchen when they were finished. Inside, Matthew swung his foot over his knee and Jeffrey pressed a letter into Danny's hand.

"Hurry up and open it," Jeffrey said. "We're dying to know."

Danny looked suspiciously at them and then glanced at the return address from the Tennessee Medical Society. He supposed it had something to do with their nominating him for that award they were so keen on him receiving. The envelope was thin, probably indicating they sent him their regrets, that another doctor deserved the award.

Peeling open the envelope, he pulled out the paper.

Dear Dr. Tilson,

We are pleased to announce that you have been selected The Physician of the Year. This award embodies excellence in medicine and your accomplishments in the field of medicine and neurosurgery are extraordinary. With your history, you have not only served Tennessee, the United States and the world with outstanding investigative work, research, and patient care this year, but several years in a row.

He stopped reading and handed Jeffrey the letter. "Are you happy now?" he asked.

Then he chuckled, gave them both an emotional 'thanks,' and said, "I guess we'll all be going to a black-tie event."

The day he dreaded had arrived. With Dakota by his side, Danny went into Julia's room and helped her get dressed into purple shorts and a dinosaur T-shirt. He gave her a hug knowing it might be the last time doing so while she was this young and while she was in his house. With a small gesture, she returned the hug, turned and darted out the room. She ignored Dakota who followed her like the faithful companion he was and Danny held back breaking into tears.

He opened the back door and walked out into a foggy Saturday morning where Dakota relieved himself, Danny stretched, and Julia picked flower petals off a bush. Soon Rachel would be over to take Julia and, at this point, he felt he had exhausted all possible parting words with his daughter. How many more times could he tell her he loved her and how many more times could he tell her he'd miss her? Besides, he thought, she is so little ... she won't remember him telling her anyway.

The next hour dragged on like a funeral procession as Sara, Annabel and Nancy watched Danny check and recheck Julia's duffel bag which would accompany her. Twice he picked her up and held her in his lap only to have her squirm and jump down. Once Dakota came over and sniffed her pink and white tennis sneakers and she pleasantly yelled out "Da-Ka."

A knock came from the upstairs door, then Casey yelled down. "Danny, Rachel's outside."

"We're coming," Sara said.

With long faces, Annabel and Nancy went up; Sara picked up the bag and followed them. Danny picked up his daughter for the last time. "Come on, Dakota," he said.

They proceeded up the steps and, at the top, Mary held a soggy tissue in her hand. They had shielded her from the disappointing custody news for quite some time but there had been no way to keep it secret the last two weeks.

Annabel took Julia from Danny's arms. "Bye, little sister. I hope I see you soon." Nancy stood close and gave Julia a kiss on her cheek. "Me, too. We love you," she said.

Sara extended her arms, took Julia, and squeezed her like a stuffed animal. "You be a good girl. Remember us because we're going to remember you every day." Mary hung onto her sister-in-law's arm and wrapped her free arm around both of them, kissing Julia's hand.

"Julia, you're getting to be a big girl," Sara said with a more upbeat tone. "I can hardly hold you anymore," She passed her to Casey.

With one arm, Casey held her and cast a glance at Danny. Both men nodded and started to the front door. Everyone followed but, when they got to the front step, the women stopped right there.

In the driveway was Rachel's little Mazda Miata and behind her was a four-door sedan hooked to a U-Haul. The driver's door of the second vehicle was open and a casually-dressed man was inspecting his back tire.

Rachel wore a short-sleeve blouse and loose cotton shorts; with a pair of light sun glasses, she looked ready to star in a road trip movie. Meeting Danny and Casey halfway, she held out her arms for her daughter.

"Bye, sweetheart," Casey said, putting Julia down. He gave Rachel a hard scowl, turned around and joined his wife. Dakota stayed next to Danny but stopped wagging his tail.

Danny narrowed his eyes at the man who approached and held out his hand. "Nice to see you again, Dr. Tilson," the man said.

"I'm sorry, I forgot your name," Danny said.

"Kevin Mcbride. We met at the art exhibit."

"Oh, yes, the urology doctor." Danny felt at a loss. He had questions for him and Rachel as well, but in essence, they were none of his business.

"Well, I know Rachel wants to get on the road," he said. "We have planned a long drive every day. Your daughter is a doll and I'll help out with her, too." He shook Danny's hand. "Bye," he added and went back to his car.

From Kevin's back window, a dog stuck its head out and barked. Dakota went over and sniffed his nose up towards the beagle while Julia shouted out, "Snoopy!"

"Just for your information," Rachel said, "we're going to California. Kevin is starting a practice there and I have a few interviews."

The last thing Danny wanted was to be ensnared into an argument with her in front of his daughter. He went over to Julia standing below Snoopy, crouched down, and gave her one more kiss. "I love you," he said for the hundredth time, holding onto his sadness and any tears like a steaming hot dish with a potholder.

When he got up and paused, he said, "So, are you two together or is he just helping you out?"

"Together." She took Julia's hand and settled her into the front passenger seat, all buckled up. When she came around to her side, she spoke to Kevin. "I'm ready, you can pull out."

Kevin gave her a nod, waved at Danny, and cranked on his engine. Rachel opened her door.

"Who knows," she said to Danny, "He may be worth enough to marry."

She pulled out but didn't wave as he stood there with a blank expression. It was the first time she'd ever let him in on her scheming thoughts. Poor guy, he thought. Kevin Mcbride would just have to learn the hard way like he did. But, God, I'm going to miss Julia.

Chapter 32

The days had grown shorter and the leaves had turned a myriad of colors. High school and college had started again and the date for the Tennessee Medical Society's formal dinner banquet had finally arrived.

Danny showered and threw on some clothes. He didn't want to change into his tuxedo until the last minute so he sat in their big room reading newspaper headlines.

A bedroom door opened and Annabel came prancing out wearing a sophisticated long-sleeved dress; a pearl necklace and earrings completed the outfit and her hair shined.

"You look fabulous," Danny said.

"Thanks, Dad," she said, sitting next to him. "And thanks for inviting me."

"How could I not?"

"Well, I gave you a hard time in the beginning about David and his injury and the fact that he was going to have to be monitored for weeks on end in the ICU. That wasn't your fault. I'm sorry I was nasty. And it's taken a long time for me to tell you that."

"You've alluded to this before and I appreciate you saying so. You got me thinking and, if it weren't for you, I don't know if I would have brainstormed the current seizure technology and discovered a new method."

"Really?"

"Really. And your thinking outside the box is exactly what is needed in the future of medicine and medical research." He patted her leg and smiled as Nancy joined them.

"You're looking nice," Danny said to his younger daughter and she turned around showing off the wavy folds of her skirt.

"So, Dad," Nancy said, "do they just pick a doctor each year to have this fancy event?"

"They do, but it's more than that. The tickets per person are very expensive to attend. Minus the expenses, all the money goes to a fund. The doctor being honored each year gets to pick their cause or charity which will be the recipient of that fund."

"Which is you," Nancy said. "That's pretty cool."

"So who are you going to delegate the proceeds to?" Annabel asked.

"Different aspects of sport's injuries. There will be money for athletes who can't afford their entire medical bills and money for continuing research to help with treatment improvements."

"That's terrific, Dad. I bet the athletic department of my college will be happy to know that."

"I believe so." Danny checked his watch and jumped up. "I better get tuxed up and tell your mother how gorgeous she looks."

"What is she wearing?" Nancy asked.

"I don't know. But it doesn't matter because she'll look beautiful no matter what."

Doctors, researchers, other medical personnel and guests spilled out of the downtown hotel's conference room holding drinks and eating hors d'oeuvres. Most of the professional medical people practiced in the Nashville area but others came from the rest of the state. A constant group of attendees gathered around Danny as well as the society's board members, and individuals eased in closer wanting an opportunity to meet Danny individually.

For over an hour, food trays of bite-sized cheeses, and seafood on crackers, and mushrooms stuffed with spinach held by men and women in uniform kept coming. The tip jars on the minibar counters were filling up as the bartenders worked to restock their margarita and whiskey sour mixes.

With pride, Danny introduced Sara and the girls whenever he could and they stayed as engrossed in conversation as he was. The time flew by quickly and the next twenty minutes was a struggle to get everyone to sit inside at their tables. For the entire Tilson family, it took the longest.

Their ceremonious table with the largest flower arrangement was closest to the podium and the longest table in the room. Place cards were set for the board members and Danny and his family; Bruce, Mathew, Jeffrey and their wives were seated at the table next to them.

Casey pulled out a chair for Mary. Looking elegant, his wife wore a floor-length turquoise dress and her red hair was swept up with a beaded hair pin.

"You not only look glamorous," Danny said, standing close to her, "but you also look like you're going to drop those babies any minute."

She laughed at her brother. "I can't wait."

When the three-course dinner began, the chandelier lights brightened and, by the time dessert was served, someone had toned them done to a soft hue. Danny realized as he stirred his coffee why the event was extra-special. He had his family all around him.

The president of the society tapped the microphone at the podium. "Good evening, ladies and gentlemen," he began. "Thank you all for being here." He gave more introductory remarks but then turned his attention to the purpose of the evening.

"I realized how difficult it was going to be for me tonight to present this award to a man whose medical accomplishments and contributions are so many. Dr. Danny Tilson, a Nashville neurosurgeon, is this year's winner of the Physician of the Year and the pamphlets on your tables include his remarkable bio.

First, as you know, each year the recipient chooses his or her own philanthropic cause and the monies we collect go towards that charity. Dr. Tilson has chosen to contribute to the furtherance of medical treatments for sport's injuries as well as to treat athletes in need.

"This year, our recipient's innovative development to monitor seizures with a wireless system has accomplished in that area of neurology and neurosurgery what broadband did to dial-up internet connections. In addition to this new technology, more of a discussion has ensued regarding head injuries. The concussions which happen to youths, college students and others are often preventable, and the host of sports activities involved can – hopefully - all be made safer. Just think, there was a time in the past when it wasn't cool to wear a bike helmet. Now it's frowned upon if a biker doesn't wear one. And in Danny's patient's case this year, a secondary impact occurred. As we know, that is extremely dangerous."

The man sipped from a water glass and looked back at the audience. "I like to make my time at the podium brief but I'd like to mention Danny's other work in the last few years. You can read more about it, but he was responsible for the discovery of abnormal brain circulation in patients last year along with the discovery, research and treatment of a pandemic two years ago. And one of his surgeries regarding a brain parasite was brilliantly skillful."

Danny thought he couldn't handle any more praise. He did his job just like all the other doctors there. But when he thought about it, he remembered previous years' honorees and he had thought they were deserving of the accolades. He reached out his hand to Sara and squeezed; Casey, filling out his tux like one of the James Bond characters, sat next to Mary and gave him a nod.

When Danny turned his attention back to the speaker, he was asked to come up for his award and to say a few words. He walked across the empty dancing area, went to the podium and was handed a statue of a doctor holding a caduceus.

"Thank you," he said. "I'm honored and tongue-tied to hear these remarks. I'm not sure if I'm the doctor who has done all those things. Sometimes in medicine, we're doing more than we think we are. And I think that's important. To keep up the learning, to keep up the inquisitiveness, to keep taking care of patients the best we know how.

"So that I don't have to bore some of you tonight, I've brought a sample of my device and anyone who would like to learn more details can take a dance break later and get a little demo."

Danny continued for a short time while his family practically had tears, their pride spilling over. Casey scooted his chair closer to Mary and she whispered to him. "Confident, direct, and striking, isn't he?"

He looked into her eyes and bobbed his head up and down.

When Danny finished and came off the stand, the band soon started and he took turns dancing with the four most important women in his life.

Casey and Toni held a hot cup of coffee outside the ER doors waiting for their 3-11 shift to end. With only one more hour to go, they bided their time hoping they could drain their drinks in the crisp nighttime air and not make another call. Winter hadn't officially started but it was cold enough that they both wore leather jackets.

Toni finished her coffee first and pulled out a cigarette pack. She stepped off the curb to light one and looked up. "You know much about astronomy?" she asked.

"Probably not any more than you," he said.

"When I was a girl and we'd vacation up north, I thought those northern folks had better stars than we did. Hell, they're all the same."

"That's for sure," Casey said. "They better be. Humans have been following them for centuries. Ever read Kon-Tiki?"

"Nah. I could barely get through books I had to read in school."

"Studying is different than reading books for pleasure," he said and stared up at the night sky. He wondered if there was any merit to astrology and he thanked the stars that Mary was nearing the end of her third trimester as the babies should be mature enough to have adequate birth weights by now.

His partner turned around and stood back beside him, blowing smoke off to the side. "Every day you're a bit more pensive," she said. "Don't worry. Mother Nature'll take care of things."

From inside his jacket, Casey's cell phone rang. He pulled it out and answered. "Mary, it's late for you to call. Everything okay?"

"It's time. Sara's driving me to the hospital."

His eyes bulged and his one-handed coffee fell to the ground.

"Okay, okay. Hold on. Drive safely. Your water's broke? Wait for me. You there?" The words came out in one long stream and then he accidentally hit 'end.'

"I hung up on her!" he blurted.

Toni eyed her partner and then her cigarette. "I think I'm driving you to the suburban hospital."

"Yeah, yeah."

Toni snapped the butt off her fingertips. She didn't have to hustle him into the ambulance. He was already there, trying to call Mary back.

"Shit, I forgot her number," he said.

"Just hit redial," Toni said.

He did but there was no answer.

"And put on your seat belt," she said.

He strapped in and ran his hand over his head. "But I'm a faster driver than you."

"You ain't tonight," she said.

She pressed the accelerator and the ambulance rushed down the boulevard. Catching most of the lights in a synchronous fashion, she slipped through a handful of yellow lights and avoided putting on their siren. Casey squirmed in his seat and fidgeted with his phone.

Ten minutes later, Toni pulled the ambulance to the front door of the suburban hospital's ER. Casey threw open the door and lurched to get out.

"Unbuckle your seat belt first," Toni said.

He pulled the buckle and then swung away the strap.

"Now get out of here," she said, "and go become a father."

Casey stopped at the front desk where a volunteer told him where to go. He ran up to labor and delivery, knocked on the door, and entered. The female obstetrician sat on a stool at the end of Mary's bed; Sara was holding Mary's hand.

"Are you okay?" Casey almost yelped.

"No, I'm not okay," she said between breathing and pushing.

"It's not going to last long," Casey said. "I promise."

"Easy for you to say," she squealed.

"Sara," Casey said with a frown, "I haven't called Danny yet."

"I did. And he's on his way. Now, coach, you take over and good luck." She gave Mary's hand a squeeze and left the room.

When Danny arrived, he paced the hallway like the day his own daughters were born while Sara sat on a chair watching him. She rubbed her hands and rotated a ring around her finger with enough nervous energy for the both of them.

A half hour after the pediatrician had run into the room, the door finally opened. The obstetrician poked her head out. "Your presence is requested," she smiled.

Danny hurried in with Sara following. Mary lay in the bed with a baby in her arms and Casey stood holding one as well, swiping a tear from his eyes.

"Just another minute," the pediatrician said. "We're taking them away for their more definitive physical. But, so far, they're looking great. Apgars 8 and 9 and 7 and 8."

Looking through tears, Mary signaled to her brother. "Take this beautiful bundle," she said.

Danny leaned forward and cuddled the baby in his arms. "Boys or girls?" he asked.

"And what are their names?" Sara asked, peering at the baby Danny held.

"This one's Tommy," Casey said.

"And the baby you're holding is Melissa," Mary said.

"I'm almost speechless," Danny said. "They're fantastic and so are their names."

"We're going to have a blast raising these identical twins," Mary said. "All of us."

"We'll be helping, sis," Danny said. "But Melissa and Tommy aren't identical twins. They're fraternal twins because boy-girl twins are always formed from two separate eggs that are fertilized by two separate sperm."

"Huh?" she said.

They can't be identical," Danny said, "because those types of twins – monozygotic - are always formed from a single zygote that contains either male XY or female XX chromosomes." He rocked the baby in his arms and then handed her to Sara.

Mary watched the family's enjoyment and the passing of her babies from one to another. She nodded her understanding of Danny's explanation. "I'm glad my brother is a doctor," she said.

"So am I," Casey said, while stroking Tommy's face. "So am I."

-END-

From the Author

Barbara Ebel is an author and a physician. Since she practiced anesthesia, she brings credibility to the medical background of her plots. She currently lives with her husband and pets in a wildlife corridor in Tennessee but has lived up and down the East Coast.

Twitter: @BarbaraEbel
Facebook Author/Reader Group: Medical Suspense Café:
Visit or contact the author at her website:
http://barbaraebelmd.com

The following books are also written by Barbara Ebel and are available as paperbacks and as eBooks:

If you enjoyed Dr. Danny's daughter, Annabel, in Secondary Impact, be sure to check out …

The Dr. Annabel Tilson Series: (Individual paperbacks and ebooks):

DEAD STILL: A Medical Thriller (Dr. Annabel Tilson Novels Book 1)

DEADLY DELUSIONS: A Medical Thriller (Dr. Annabel Tilson Novels Book 2)

DESPERATE TO DIE: A Medical Thriller (Dr. Annabel Tilson Novels Book 3)

DEATH GRIP: A Medical Thriller (Dr. Annabel Tilson Novels Book 4)

DOWNRIGHT DEAD: A Medical Thriller (Dr. Annabel Tilson Novels Book 5)

DANGEROUS DOCTOR: A Medical Thriller (Dr. Annabel Tilson Novels Book 6)

The Outlander Physician Series:

Corruption in the O.R.: A Medical Thriller (The Outlander Physician Series Book 1)

Wretched Results: A Medical Thriller (The Outlander Physician Series: Book 2)

Stand-alone Medical Fiction:

Outcome, A Novel

Her Flawless Disguise

The Dr. Danny Tilson Series: (Individual paperbacks and ebooks):

Operation Neurosurgeon: You never know… who's in the OR (A Dr. Danny Tilson Novel: Book 1).

Silent Fear: a Medical Mystery (A Dr. Danny Tilson Novel: Book 2). Also an Audiobook.

Collateral Circulation: a Medical Mystery (A Dr. Danny Tilson Novel: Book 3). Also an Audiobook.

Secondary Impact (A Dr. Danny Tilson Novel: Book 4).

Also written and illustrated by Barbara Ebel (a children's book series about her loveable therapy dog):

Chester the Chesapeake Book One
Chester the Chesapeake Book Two: Summertime
Chester the Chesapeake Book Three: Wintertime
Chester the Chesapeake Book Four: My Brother Buck
Chester the Chesapeake Book Five: The Three Dogs of Christmas

The Chester the Chesapeake Trilogy (The Chester the Chesapeake Series); eBook only

Visit Chester at his website:
http://dogbooksforchildren.weebly.com

Excerpt from Dead Still:

Dead Still
A Dr. Annabel Tilson Novel: Book 1
by Barbara Ebel
(copyright 2016)

Chapter 1

She had started the surgery rotation the day before so Annabel Tilson barely knew her patients from the list of names that had been shoved into her hands. As a third-year medical student, the day had been hectic; therefore, a short introduction to them and a quick listen to their chests with her first shiny Littmann stethoscope had sufficed. But this morning as she squeezed in close to the bed and looked down at a dead corpse, she remembered the sixty-five-year-old woman, Mrs. Hardy, with clarity from visiting her in her room and watching her surgery in awe.

During the first surgery that Annabel had witnessed on her clinical rotation, the chief resident performed a minimally-invasive gallbladder removal - or laparoscopic cholecystectomy - causing the long mechanical instruments to protrude from her patient's belly like the squirming arms of a squid. No one indicated at the time or postoperatively that anything had been complicated about the case, so why was her patient dead? She admonished herself for missing the resuscitative attempt before she'd walked into the room; medical supplies, carts, and equipment were scattered about the bed and floor but personnel paid no attention as they began exiting through the doorway.

"Most likely a heart attack," Marlin Mack said, waving an EKG and signaling her to follow him out of the room. Excluding the chief resident, he was one of the two residents on the team, an unkempt-looking fellow with a ridiculous mustache for his age and a lab coat that needed ironing.

Annabel lagged, taking a last impressionable stare at the deceased woman: mucus smudged her cheeks, urine soaked the bed, and the smell of bowels having opened up was pervasive. A nurse moved the patient's stocky legs closer together and covered them with a sheet, hiding the unnatural way they seemed to lay. Someone else jammed a pillow under her head before housekeeping came in and started removing the black bags from the trash cans.

As she peeled her eyes away, Annabel tried to shake off her conflicting thoughts of sadness, unsettled nerves, and nausea before rushing out like a puppy after the resident. This was her second day out from the two first years of course work during medical school and the second day on clinical rotation in hospitals. She shuddered. Already this was emotionally difficult.

Outside, Dr. Mack waved her over to a desk in a small cubbyhole. "You're going to deal with life and death," he said. "It's not all a bed of roses. Do you know that blood pools at the bottom of a dead body, whatever area is most gravity dependent?"

Was that something she needed or wanted to know? She didn't see the relevance of him telling her that and she shook her head.

"Furthermore, since there's no more circulation and no more heat, the muscles harden, thrusting a corpse into rigor mortis which sets in after about four hours. Then you better do something with it because if it's left for a day it'll start to bloat and blacken. And I won't even mention the smell."

Annabel gulped. She was beginning to regret that she'd been assigned to surgery right off the bat. Were all the residents as blatant and cold as he was?

Marlin glanced her way. "Oh, sorry. My dad owns a funeral home. It's natural for me to know about cadavers. Anyway, now comes the second part. I have to go talk to the deceased's sister. The patient wasn't married, no kids, not much of anybody in her life it seems." He got up and brushed past her.

"What's the matter, Annabel? You look like you've seen a ghost." The other female medical student on her team, Ginny Young, sat on the edge of the main desk's counter and gave Annabel a warm smile. She was thirty years old compared to Annabel's twenty-three and had sought admission to medical school after reconsideration of her first career in biological research.

Annabel leaned over. "Mrs. Hardy, one of my few patients passed away," she said in a low voice so no one overheard her. "She went from being a living, breathing person with whatever past and with whatever ties to family and friends, to not leaving the hospital. Dr. Mack makes it sound like she's a lifeless disposable sack of flesh."

"Sorry to hear about your patient," she agreed. "That's too soon after we just started. She frowned and, in a few minutes, settled her eyes on Marlin Mack as he walked towards them.

"Good morning, Dr. Young," he said. "Annabel's gone and lost her first patient before official rounds with our attending doctor. Anyway, the sibling of the deceased doesn't want to see her sister but wants to wait until she's beautified by the funeral home. She's pretty much in shock."

While Marlin grabbed the patient's chart, Annabel and Ginny stole a glance.

"Come on, don't just stand there," Marlin said. "Let's assemble the team in the office and be ready for Dr. Burk."

They filed out and, as they passed the dead patient's room, stopped so Marlin could talk to the transporters waiting in the hallway. A nurse in the room put a blouse on Mrs. Hardy, holding her forearms with a tennis-racquet grip; the body fell quickly back on the mattress when she let go.

Two male transporters filed into the room while Annabel dawdled in the hallway. They lifted the dead woman and her head, arms, and legs fell away as they put her in a big black bag. Annabel closed her eyes for a moment. In the last few years, her physician father had been a role model with his religious overtones. She thought of him and then gave a little blessing for her patient to rest in peace.

Made in the USA
Monee, IL
14 April 2023